Also by J. A. Hennrikus

The Theater Cop Mysteries

(by J. A. Hennrikus for Midnight Ink)

A Christmas Peril (2017)

The Clock Shop Mystery Series

(by Julianne Holmes for Berkley Prime Crime)

Chime and Punishment (2017)

Clock and Dagger (2016)

Just Killing Time (2015)

The Garden Squad Series

(by Julia Henry for Kensington)

Pruning the Dead (2019)

WITH A KISS
I Die

WITH A KISS *I Die*

J. A. HENNRIKUS

First Edition
First Printing, 2019

Book format by Ted Riley
Cover design by Kevin R. Brown
Cover illustration by Bill Bruning/Deborah Wolfe Ltd.

Midnight Ink, an imprint of Llewellyn Worldwide Ltd.

This is a work of fiction. Names, characters, places, and incidents are either the product of the author's imagination or are used fictitiously, and any resemblance to actual persons living or dead, business establishments, events, or locales is entirely coincidental.

Library of Congress Cataloging-in-Publication Data
Names: Hennrikus, J. A., author.
Title: With a kiss I die / J.A. Hennrikus.
Description: First Edition. | Woodbury, Minnesota : Midnight Ink, [2019] | Series: A theater cop mystery.
Identifiers: LCCN 2018053963 (print) | LCCN 2018056394 (ebook) | ISBN 9780738755861 (ebook) | ISBN 9780738754697 (alk. paper)
Subjects: LCSH: Murder—Investigation—Fiction. | Women detectives—Fiction. | GSAFD: Mystery fiction.
Classification: LCC PS3608.E56454 (ebook) | LCC PS3608.E56454 W58 2019 (print) | DDC 813/.6—dc23
LC record available at https://lccn.loc.gov/2018053963

Midnight Ink
Llewellyn Worldwide Ltd.
2143 Wooddale Drive
Woodbury, MN 55125-2989
www.midnightinkbooks.com

Printed in the United States of America

To the StageSource community, and in memory
of Jack Welch. The arts matter, and these folks prove that
with the work they do to support the New England
theater community in dozens of different ways.

One

What happens when your late father's best friend owns a restaurant/bar, and you hate to cook? Especially when the bar has Wi-Fi, more heat than your office, and someone to talk to? You gain weight. Gene had called me that morning and asked me to come to the Beef & Ale to help him move some tables around. We both knew he was making an excuse to see me, but I'd come in bright and early with my laptop, elastic-waist pants, and an empty stomach, more than happy to play along. I didn't have the corner on the loneliness market during the bleak midwinter of a Trevorton February.

Gene O'Donnell put another plate of fries in front of me. "Truffle fries," he said. "Hear they're all the rage." It was barely ten o'clock in the morning, but Gene was already experimenting in the kitchen. Though he didn't open until the evening in the winter, he fed his regulars, of which I was one. With a last name like Sullivan, eating potatoes for every meal was part of my DNA, so it was never too early for fries.

"Does a great seasoning go out of style?" I asked. Truffle fries had been all the rage for a few years, hadn't they? Gene had never been one to glom on to fads, so he was probably waiting until he could trust that truffle salt had grabbed hold. "I love them. Let me give yours a try." I blew on one and took a small bite. I ate the rest of the fry quickly, risking the burn. Yum.

"What do you think?" he asked.

"Too good. Much too good," I said. At this rate, with Gene's cooking and the beer he served, I was going to gain twenty pounds before spring. Maybe I should start walking to and from the bar to burn off some calories? It was what, five miles? No sidewalks? Dead of winter? Nah. I ate another fry.

It had been a while since all the brouhaha of December and the closing of our production of *A Christmas Carol*. For most of January, I'd looked forward to and enjoyed peace and quiet. But now, halfway through February, I was bored. Sure, there was work to do, but none of it was as exciting as being in the middle of the theater season. Still, if I could get these grants done, the summer season would be more than exciting. It would be a game-changer for the company. I sighed loudly and went back to my computer screen.

"I've been staring at this screen so long my eyes are crossing," I said.

"What're ya doing there, Sully?" Gene asked. He was behind the bar, lining up empty ketchup bottles to be refilled. It was Monday, deep-cleaning day at the Beef & Ale.

"Trying to get this grant done for the Century Foundation."

"Century Foundation? Anything to do with those Century Projects?" he asked.

"Yup. Both are part of the Cunningham Corporation. The Foundation is the Century Project's charitable arm. They donate big money for nonprofit construction projects. I'm trying to get a grant so we can finally build that new production center for the theater we've been talking about for years."

"Production center?"

"We want to build it next to our outdoor amphitheater. The lot was donated to us a few years back. In order for the Cliffside Theater Company to move up to another level, we need to expand and update. As a summer theater, we do a lot outside, and in the high school during the winter. But we'd love to expand our season, and having our own production center would allow us to divert the money we spend on rent to other needs."

"That sounds terrific. Seems to make sense, so long as you can afford it."

"Exactly. It's only been a dream for the past few years. But now, with this grant and some other funding we're working on? This dream may come true as soon as this summer."

"So that's what the grant is for?" Gene squinted at the ketchup bottles arrayed in front of him.

"Yes, making the case. Of course, the challenge is to put all of this into five thousand characters or less, but I'm giving it my best shot."

Ketchup refilling was quite an art the way Gene did it: never forcing, adding a bit to each bottle, waiting for gravity to help pull the tomato magic down. He used high-end ketchup and treated it like liquid gold. He had packets of the commercial stuff for folks with pedestrian tastes, but those of us in the know always asked for house ketchup in our to-go containers. I, myself, was not normally a ketchup girl with my fries, but I did enjoy the house ketchup on occasion.

"You working on the grant by yourself?" Gene asked. "Why isn't Dimitri helping you?"

Dimitri Traietti, the artistic director of the Cliffside, was the first person I'd talked to when the grant opportunity came up. He'd already helped me with the case needs for the project, but at this point it was all about editing and budgets—not his strengths.

"Eric Whitehall is helping me with some of the numbers," I said.

"Eric's a good number guy. He helped me figure out how to refinance this place and do some of the upgrades the town was requiring," Gene said. "Couldn't have pulled it off without him."

"I didn't know that," I said, blowing gently on another fry. I wondered when this had happened.

"He's helped out a lot of folks in town. Probably to help offset some of his father's ill deeds. Balance the Whitehall karma. Not to speak ill of the dead, mind you."

"Not to speak ill of the dead," I agreed. Peter Whitehall had died—been killed—last December. His best legacies, his three children, were doing their best to get the family business back on track. Eric and I had been spending a lot of time together these past two months, and not just working on grants. Eric was my second cousin, but our relationship was more than that. He was probably my best friend in Trevorton.

"Dimitri's down in Boston at the Bay Repertory Theater, directing their *Romeo and Juliet*," I told Gene, changing the subject. "Their director left unexpectedly a couple of weeks ago. Babs Allyn—"

"Babs Allyn? Is that a real name? Sounds like a '40s movie star, doesn't it?"

I stared at Gene for a second before responding. He reminded me of my father, making conversation connections where there were none. "Short for Barbara, I'd imagine. Maybe her folks were inspired by noir novels. She runs Bay Rep. I've met her a couple of times at different conferences. Anyway, she saw Dimitri's production of R&J, and called and asked if he'd step in since he already knew the play."

"That's pretty exciting for Dimitri, isn't it?"

"It is," I said. "Thing is, he has to live with the decisions the other director made about sets, lights, props, and costumes. That might be tough. But it's a great opportunity for Dimitri to make Boston connections. Not enough people come up to Trevorton to see his work, and it deserves to be seen."

"Not that you're prejudiced or anything," Gene said.

"Me? Not at all," I smiled. "Hey, I'll be hanging out here for a while longer—that okay with you? I'm going to text Eric and let him know I'm here."

"Make yourself at home, Sully. I'll throw a burger on the grill for Eric. With Mrs. Bridges gone on vacation he probably isn't eating too well these days."

"I think he's living on wine, crackers, and cheese. Not that there's anything wrong with that," I said. That was my usual dinner when I was on my own.

"I'll get a salad together too," Gene said. "Can't have Eric wasting away. Assume you'll have a burger too?"

"I'd hate for Eric to eat alone."

"You're a good woman, Sully Sullivan. Always thinking of others." Gene walked back into the kitchen area. I heard him open and close the refrigerator and start to sing to himself.

New England winters are tough. If you work from home, getting out of the house is a chore that most folks skip. It takes too much effort to dig the car out, layer the clothes, put on the boots, warm up the car, chip the ice off the windshield, get the snow off the top of the car, and drive into town. But after a few days being housebound one thing is certain: unless you force yourself out of the house, you start to go stir crazy. My tolerance for being housebound was lower than I'd expected; definitely lower than it used to be. Trevorton and the Cliffside Theater Company had changed me. For the better, I thought. But now loneliness was part of the package. I missed talking to theater people. I missed their perspective on life, their energy, being able to problem-solve together.

Because Gene and I were the only people in the Beef & Ale, the Wi-Fi signal was strong. I kept looking at the online storage that Eric, in his role as my board treasurer, was trying to get me to use. The ex-cop in me didn't trust files I couldn't touch, but Eric was right. We needed to keep records where folks could access them easily. That didn't stop me from storing my own copies on my computer and printing things out. Old habits die hard.

I went behind the bar and poured seltzer water into my glass. Gene's burgers always tasted better with a local brew, but I really had to focus on this grant. I was hoping that Eric would be able to give me some advice about how to better present our finances. The theater was in good shape, but we didn't have huge cash reserves. The Whitehalls were experts at making numbers look the way they needed to look in order for people to react the way you wanted them to react.

For a long time, I'd tried to do every part of my general manager job on my own, which had mostly worked out. But I'd come to realize that asking for help also lets folks know they can ask you for help. I'd gotten Eric out of a jam in the aftermath of his father's murder, and I knew he was anxious to repay the debt. Not that there was really a debt. We were too close for that. But still, I knew he could help me get through this financial morass.

It wasn't all altruistic, though. Our accountant at the Cliffside had sat down with Dimitri and me and talked about the finances for the theater. They were good. Better than they had been in years. We had a strong surplus. But that meant we needed to pay more attention to what we were doing moving forward. Now that we could actually do improvements instead of patching things and holding our breath, hoping they'd last through the summer, we needed to be more intentional about raising money. Funny how I never understood this until I started running a theater, but you can't raise money unless you have money. And now the Cliffside had money.

Running a summer theater, I'd discovered, was very interesting. I looked forward to the summer people coming back to town as much as I look forward to them leaving by the end of August. But still, having visitors come specifically for our theater company? That would be a turning point.

I heard a rap at the door of the Beef & Ale and walked over to peer through the window shade. Eric was stomping on the front mat, either keeping warm or getting the salt off his shoes. Given his good manners, he was probably desalting. I smiled as I turned the lock and opened the door to let him in, closing and relocking it behind him. I gave him a big hug.

"Something smells good," he said, taking his coat off and throwing it over one of the barstools.

"Gene's making you a burger and a salad."

"And fries?"

"Oh yeah, fries. He's testing out new combinations on us."

"Combinations?"

"You know, like hot chili sauce with Cajun fries. Spicy fries with Gorgonzola sauce. He's even talking about cinnamon sugar fries with frosting dip."

"That should sound disgusting, but it sounds sort of delicious."

"That's because it's February," Gene said, coming back into the room with two plates of food. "In February, greasy sugar is a necessity. Have a seat, the both of you. What can I get you to drink, Eric?"

∞

"Wow, that was delicious," Eric said, pushing back from the table. "An extra hour in the gym for me tonight."

"Just one hour?" I asked. "How about an hour and a half and we have a brownie sundae?"

"I really shouldn't…"

"Come on, you know you want to. Besides, I need extra dairy these days. Vitamin D is a necessity."

"Why, when you put it that way, how can I say no?"

I walked over to the bar and took the brownie sundae from inside the ice chest, where Gene had left it after he'd made it. I brought it back to Eric along with two spoons, and then went and grabbed two cups of coffee. Gene was in the back, prepping for the evening. He looked up and gave me a smile. I lifted the coffee pot, and he shook his head then went back to chopping. He really did take good care of me. My dad would be so grateful. I came back to the table and asked Eric if he wanted sugar.

"No, black's just fine," Eric said. "So, I've got some notes on the budget you sent me. Thoughts on where else the Cliffside can go for funding if the Century Foundation doesn't come through."

He opened his bag and took out a manila folder. Opening the folder, he handed me a stack of clipped papers and took out his own copies. I took the binder clip off and looked at each of the pages carefully. More than notes. A complete budget, with different scenarios, for the production center.

"Wow," I said. "This is amazing. Thanks so much—"

"Well, isn't this what a board member is supposed to do? I'm used to sitting on foundation panels giving money away; I know what folks are looking for. I enjoy this kind of work, looking at budgets, seeing opportunities. This is a great project. Getting the Cliffside funding is good for the entire town, and a great investment. You'll see I put a couple of notes in for additional ways you might be able to frame this, to get some funding from other foundations too."

"What do you mean?" I slid the rest of the sundae toward Eric. The thought of adding more fundraising work for the overextended staff of the theater didn't sit well with me.

"Highlight the work you do, and look for funding options that fit it. Add more opportunities for students to work in the shop in the summer, for example. Make *A Christmas Carol* a votech project for the high school. Talk about the way the costume department might be able to help fix clothes for the thrift shop in town. You know, that sort of thing."

"Great idea," I said. "Getting some funding opens the doors for other funding. At least that's the hope. The good thing about the Century Foundation is that it's a big chunk of money all at once, without a lot of hoops to jump through. We've got that matching grant we can leverage, too, as long as we get some cash in by April 1st."

"You know, I've been thinking about that," Eric said, using a fry to get the rest of the ketchup off the plate. "Why don't we approach the Whitehall Foundation as one of the funders of the construction project, so that you hit the matching dollar amounts—?"

"Thank you so much, Eric. You know how much I appreciate that. But let's go to the Century Foundation first. If I can't pull this off, or get support from one of the other avenues, I'll definitely come back to you." I knew the Whitehall family business was going through some challenges. While I had no doubt that between Eric and his sister Emma, they would come through it, it had been a rough couple of months.

"Well, the grant looks good to me," Eric said. "But I've heard that the Century Foundation may be slowing down on grants a bit. Emma mentioned it in passing over the weekend."

I sighed. "Well, it's still worth a shot."

"Of course it is," Eric said. "Besides, I haven't heard anything official."

"Where is Emma, by the way? I haven't seen her for a while. Is she still in Boston?" I asked.

"She is. You know how we split our time between Trevorton and Boston? But I think she prefers Boston these days. Fewer memories."

"Understandable," I said. Emma had been hit by the events of last Christmas hardest of all.

"I'm glad that the apartments are getting used," Eric said.

"Apartments?"

"It's an old townhouse on Beacon Hill, been in the family for years. My father decided to do a rehab about twenty-five years ago, and give us each a pied-a-terre in the city. When he married Brooke he considered turning it back into a single family home, but she nixed that, thankfully for us."

"I knew your dad and Brooke owned a condo. I thought you would use that?"

"No, the townhouse is more our speed. We're using the condo for the business, but we'll probably sell it this spring. Anyway, Dad signed the townhouse over to us five years ago. Emma's on the top floor, my apartment's in the middle, and Amelia's on the first floor. Of course, it's become a bit of a theater frat house with Harry staying in my apartment. I think Emma's having fun hanging out with him."

"How could she not? Harry is great company. You should know that," I said, teasing. Eric just smiled. Harry Frederick was his partner, a wonderful actor, and one of my favorite people.

"I've done more work on my apartment than my sisters, but then again, I spend more time in Boston," Eric continued. "I really do love it there."

"I'm surprised you're not there right now, with Harry." Harry had been cast in *Romeo and Juliet* by the original director, so he'd been in Boston for a few weeks.

"I was planning on going down, but we don't like to leave Amelia alone these days."

"How she doing?" Amelia, the youngest of the Whitehall children, had always been seen by the family as a little frail. I didn't think of her as frail as much as living in her own world. Her father's death had pushed her to the brink. I thought she was doing better, but not well. None of them were really doing well. There was a lot to recover from. But I did think, or at least I hoped, that the entire family was on the mend.

"She's spending most of her time in the greenhouse, making sure Mrs. Bridges's plants live until she gets back from Ireland. It's been a great distraction for her. I think we're all a little too overprotective of her, Emma and me especially. But now Amelia's thinking about creating a foundation to help with the green space in Trevorton. You know, pay to keep up that little park in the harbor, help pay for the community gardens by the high school."

"What great projects," I said. "Are you sure she's up to running this new foundation?"

"We're keeping it small to begin with, and that should help. But Amelia's been thinking about it for a long time, and really wants to make it work. I think it may be the perfect solution—gives her something to do, keeps the demand low but the outcome high."

"Let me know what I can do to help," I said.

"Thanks, Sully. We may ask you to help us brainstorm an event to launch the project later this spring. I know you'll be busy getting the Cliffside season going—"

"We've got a few projects we're going to be launching just before the season starts. Maybe we can make them all happen at the same time somehow? Add a garden to the new production center? We'll figure something out," I said.

"Sounds great. Thanks again, Sully," Eric said. "So, do the budgets make sense to you?"

I looked back down at the sheets of paper he'd given me. They needed to make sense to me, and when better than when Eric was sitting there? I pointed at a blank box he'd highlighted in yellow. "What's that?"

"I didn't know what to put in for marketing," Eric said. "Didn't I hear that Hal Maxwell was pitching the Cliffside Theater Company for rebranding?"

"Yes, can you believe it? When I heard that Maxwell and Samuel was going to bid on our rebranding project, I thought it was a pity bid Hal put in because he knew us, and knew you guys. But Hal really seems to want the business. He's had meetings with Dimitri and the board, and a couple of meetings with me."

"Maxwell and Samuel is a great marketing firm…*was* a great firm," Eric said. "I think they've lost a step since Martin Samuel vanished." Martin Samuel, Hal's partner in the firm, had disappeared a year ago after a boating accident of some sort in the Caribbean. "Hal seems to be taking on more projects, but as much to keep himself busy as to keep the doors of the firm open," Eric finished.

"Did they ever confirm what happened to Martin?" I asked. "I thought his body was never found. Didn't he reach out to people at one point? I thought there was a rumor he'd run away with most of the company's assets?"

"Tons of gossip. A lot of rumors were flying around last, what was it, February? March? When it all happened. But not much since, at least none that I've heard. Hal's been working closely with the Cunninghams on the Century Projects, as their marketing firm, and that keeps him busy. Hey," Eric said, "does Hal know you're applying for the grant?"

"It was Hal's idea to apply," I said. I looked down at the pile of papers and then back up at my friend. "I don't suppose you could email these to me—"

"I'll do better than that. I'll share it in a folder online, and add more stuff to it as I think about it. Would that work?"

"It would. I can't wait until the new intern starts next month. She's a whiz at computers, and she'll help make sure our online files are up-to-date and accurate. Email me the link, and I'll call you if I can't figure it out."

"I'll send it to you within the hour," Eric said. He leaned down and gave me kiss on the cheek, leaving me to finish the French fries on my own. It was a tough job, but someone had to do it.

∞

"Thanks for letting me use your restaurant as my office, Gene," I said.

"No problem, sweetheart. I like having you around. You know that," Gene said.

My phone made a knocking sound, my latest text message alert. I was a terrible texter. Half the time I didn't even pay attention when my phone buzzed, rang, or beeped. But these days so many people used text as their primary way of getting hold of me that I had to pay attention, and I was hoping knocking sounds would wake me up. Texting was Dimitri's favorite way to have conversations these days. Whenever he texted me I could actually hear him speaking, with his loud dramatic tones and grand gestures. Other people used texts to tell me to call them, since I'd stopped answering my phone. I was becoming more and more of a hermit with every passing day.

I picked up the phone and adjusted my glasses so I could read clearly. It was from Connie, our stage manager extraordinaire.

Call me, Connie texted. She knew me too well.

I dialed her cell phone. "Have you heard from Dimitri?" Connie said by way of salutation.

"Hello to you too, my friend," I said. "I'm well, thank you. No, I haven't spoken to Dimitri since he went to Boston. Why, what's up?"

"Sorry, my manners are crap lately. Glad you're well, so am I. Now, to the situation at hand. I think Dimitri's having a rough time down in Boston," Connie said.

"A 'Dimitri being his overdramatic self' hard time, or a 'something really isn't going well' hard time?"

"Romeo quit this morning," she said.

"That *is* bad." I opened up a browser on my computer and googled "Romeo and Juliet" and "Bay Repertory Theater."

"That's not all. Apparently the set is a nightmare and they're stuck with it. Pierre what's-his-face wasn't just the director, he was the set designer and costume designer as well. His ideas are almost impossible to undo."

"I thought he left because of a family emergency—"

"Public spin. He was fired. Company revolt. Dimitri didn't go into details. Anyway, he's walked into a disaster."

When Dimitri first got the offer from Bay Repertory Theater, he'd called me and asked if he should take the job. I'd talked him into it, and now guilt nibbled at me. "Should we do something?" I asked. I figured Connie had some sort of game plan she would let me in on it. Or, as was often the case, she was prepping me for something she needed me to do.

"Where are you?" she asked.

"I'm at the Beef & Ale, working. And eating. Gene's doing miraculous things with French fries these days."

"I'll stop by before I leave. I could use one of Gene's burgers."

"Leave for where?" I asked, but she'd already hung up.

I picked up my phone to call Dimitri, and put it down again. Bay Rep wasn't my theater. What was happening in Boston was technically none of my business. But, Dimitri. Dimitri could drive me crazy, sure. But he was also my friend, and in a sense my business partner. I picked up my phone again and wrote him a text.

You okay, big guy? Text or call if you need to talk.

Gene was busy in the kitchen chopping up salads, frying bacon, slicing cheese, and doing everything else to prep for the dinner rush at the Beef & Ale. Of course, in February the dinner rush consisted of ten regulars who came in after work for a beer and maybe some wings. Gene made great wings—the traditional Buffalo chicken wings, which were good, but he also made wings that had some sort of ginger marinade, and he served them with a magic sauce he kept a secret. These were my Waterloo. I couldn't get enough of them. Neither could most of the people who lived in Trevorton.

I checked my email. True to his word, Eric had sent me a link to a file. I went online to make sure I could see the documents that were inside. I made a copy of the file and put it in a separate folder on my hard drive, adding a date. Eric wouldn't approve, but I needed a system I could trust.

I felt a dull pounding behind my eyes. Was it too early to have a beer? I was about to ask for Gene's opinion when my phone vibrated on the table. Another text. This one from Harry Frederick.

I'm going to call you in a minute, Harry texted. *Pick up the phone. We've got a situation.*

· Two ·

"Harry, how are you?"

"I'm okay, Sully. Unless you count watching while your career goes down in flames. Then, not so good."

"What are you talking about?" Though an actor, Harry was not a drama queen offstage. Usually.

"For the second time in as many months, I'm working on a production that is a disaster. Is it me? Did I do something wrong in a previous life?" Harry had played Bob Cratchit in our December production of *A Christmas Carol*. The road to opening night had been rocky. To put it mildly. The show itself was terrific when all was said and done. Harry had been excited about playing Lord Capulet in *Romeo and Juliet*, and I hated that he sounded so despondent.

"Whoa. What do you mean, 'disaster'? Even with Dimitri in charge?" I asked. Connie had warned me, of course, but hearing it from the front lines was surprising.

"It may be too late," Harry said glumly. "We've been trying to keep it in house, but the news will be out soon. They should have known Pierre would be a disaster from the first concept meeting, but I guess they hoped that his artistic vision would gel. But to wait until after the first rehearsal to fire him was nuts. I guess they finally started to understand that he really meant what he'd said about his concept for the show."

"Concept? What was he going to do to *Romeo and Juliet*?"

Harry sighed. "You know I'm a fan of shaking things up. Pierre was working with this whole concept that took over every aspect of the production, but it made no sense. Then, at that first read-through, he told everyone exactly how he wanted their roles to be played, including line readings right off the bat. He made it clear he wasn't open to questions. He started fighting with most of the actors, and a lot of the staff, the first week of rehearsal."

"Fight or argue?" I asked. Fights left no room for compromise. Arguments were part of the creative process. Dimitri and I argued all the time.

"Fight. And you know how a rep company is. They band together. They got his ass fired." Repertory companies used to be more common at theaters, but now they're fairly rare because keeping a company of actors on contract is so expensive.

"Dimitri isn't the first director I'd hire to try and negotiate peace with a rep company," I said quietly.

"Most of the Bay Rep company saw his production of *Romeo and Juliet* at the Cliffside, so they knew he got the play," Harry explained.

As I'd come to learn, Shakespeare's plays still held up not only because their familiarity is comforting to audiences, but because the plays themselves leave room for grand interpretation. You can delete scenes, get rid of characters, move things around, switch genders, combine characters. Really, anything is possible. Under a strong director who understands the text, rethinking Shakespeare can be very exciting. But under the guidance of someone who doesn't trust the play—who doesn't get the play—it can be a disaster.

Dimitri's *Romeo and Juliet* for the Cliffside was an example of the former. It was set in a war-torn country of no particular origin, in the near-distant future. We had a tank as one of the set pieces. It had taken us a couple of seasons, and a couple of *Christmas Carols*, to save up enough money for one *Romeo and Juliet*. I was dubious at the beginning, but I'd learned to trust Dimitri's vision and talent. And the production had been magnificent, one of Dimitri's finest. I'd been a bit worried about him trying to replicate the magic again, but I knew his familiarity with the text would enable him to jump right in, and would be his calling card with the Bay Rep.

"Dimitri does in fact get the play. I mean, there are layers and nuances. But honestly, what's to get in this situation?" I asked.

"Well, Dimitri gets the fact that Capulet wouldn't have the hots for his own daughter," Harry offered.

"Ew. Yuck."

"Pierre decided that Juliet's father would be her stepfather, and that her mother would be much older than Capulet. He had this whole 'love is insane and has no boundaries' concept that he was driving through the piece. 'No judgment,' he'd say. 'All emotions are pure.' Then he decided that everything would be white to help underscore the purity of love."

"White?" I asked.

"Sets, costumes, props. Glossy white. Looks like a stylized insane asylum. Feels like one too."

"Well, Dimitri can..." I paused because I understood how limited Dimitri's options were. This close to opening, chances were that the set and costumes were well underway. "Any design changes possible?"

"From what I understand, tweaks are possible, but not changes. Plus they've installed the stream already, and the stage deck has been covered with vinyl."

"Stream? Vinyl?"

"There's a lot of water in this production. Part of the purity theme. They created a stream in the middle of the set and levels all over the place, and traps. Could be kind of cool, but like I said, it's all white. Like, shiny laminate white. The laminate was on purpose, so the blood could be washed off easily—"

"Blood?"

"Blood. There's a lot of blood in that last scene, at least the way Pierre saw it. Dimitri's already nixed the blood. I think the white is freaking him out as much as anything else."

And freaking out the lighting designer, I thought. White on stage was tough enough to deal with in small measures. But the entire set?

"What do you mean by freaking out?" I asked. "Losing his temper?"

"He's scaring me. He's not yelling at all. You can tell he has respect for every artist in the room, and that's giving him a lot of credibility with the company. But he can't get his arms around the production. He's freaking out in the 'I'm going back to my room and not talking to anyone' way. I told him to give Connie a call. She's always been a great sounding board for him."

"I heard. She's coming by to fill me in—"

"They're calling me back into rehearsal. I'll call or text later with more updates. This would all be funny if it wasn't so awful." Harry ended the call.

∞

I was opening my computer, looking at the files, making triple copies of each one just in case my great fear of doing something wrong came to pass and I lost all records of the Cliffside Theater Company. I tried to concentrate, but I couldn't.

If you'd told me six years ago that I would care as much about saving a production of *Romeo and Juliet* as I did about arresting a bad guy, I would've thought you'd lost your mind. But it really wasn't the show as much as it was the people involved with the show. Dimitri could make me lose my temper, question my leadership skills, and drive me to the brink. But he was also enormously talented, very kind, and incredibly passionate. He was also very charming, which didn't hurt. I was feeling protective of him, and wondered what I could do to help.

I'd gotten up to go behind the bar and get a cup of coffee when Connie arrived. I went over to let her in, and then went back to the bar. I lifted the pot toward her.

"Yes, please. Is it fresh? Who am I kidding? I'll drink anything with caffeine at this point," Connie said. She put her knapsack down on a chair and started to take her layers off. This took a while. Connie didn't have a car these days and walked everywhere. Trevorton wasn't big, and in the summer walking was a terrific way to get exercise. But in the winter, it was another story. Not for the first time, I wished I could give Connie full-time work between the end of *A Christmas Carol* and the opening of our summer season. Part of my budgeting had been trying to figure out how I could bring her on a month earlier in the spring. If we got the Century Foundation grant we were going for, it would go a long way to help.

"Are you hungry, Connie?" I asked. "Gene's back in the kitchen getting ready for opening, but he's been having me test out new French fry concoctions. I'm sure he'd love your opinion."

"French fry concoctions? Any good?"

"Fabulous, I'm afraid to say." And as if by magic, Gene handed three plates of fries through the kitchen opening. He also handed me a cheeseburger with avocados and salsa, Connie's favorite.

"Connie darlin'," Gene said, "let me know what you think of those cinnamon French fries. Sully seems quite taken with them but I'm not sure I trust her judgment."

"Hey now," I said, "just because I'm addicted to grease and sugar does not mean I'm a pushover for anything in that food group."

"Anything you say, Sully," Gene said. "If you ladies want anything else, just let me know. We've got another hour or so before we open. I may need some help behind the bar tonight. Connie, if you're free—"

"Not tonight, sorry, Gene," Connie said. "I can help you set up, though."

"Good enough, then," Gene said. "I'll take what I can get. Your fault there's so much to do. You've got me on a cleaning jag."

I walked the plates over to the table Connie and I were sharing. She pulled another table over so we'd have more room to work. Then she went back to her phone, fingers flying.

"Who are you texting?" I asked.

"Not texting, tweeting," she said. "I'm letting folks know about the testing of French fries. Suggesting we think about beer pairings. It may get a few folks to drop by."

"You're quite the pair, aren't you?" I asked. I noticed Connie blush. Since Gene had been a friend of my father's, I always thought of him as my father's age. But truth to tell, he was probably a generation younger than my dad. Connie was about ten years older than I was, with her youngest finally away at college. So maybe there was more going on between them than Gene just giving Connie a part-time job to help her make ends meet. He had been a widower for ten years, and nothing would make me happier than to see him with somebody. Same went for Connie, though I had to admit I'd always pictured her as alone. I thought of her as so dedicated to her work and her kids that there wasn't room for anything else. Obviously I was projecting. Just because I'd decided to fly solo that winter didn't mean that everyone else needed to make the same decision.

I looked over at Connie as she took a bite of her cheeseburger and closed her eyes.

"Gene makes the best burgers," she said.

"I agree. I could live on them."

"You sort of do, don't you?" Connie smiled. "You're here every day, practically."

"I am," I said. "You know how Gene takes care of me. Being with him reminds me of my dad, and I like that feeling. I don't know how I would've made it without him."

"I appreciated him offering me some work after *A Christmas Carol* closed," Connie said. "When the car broke down last month, I wasn't able to come in as much. But he's kept an open-door policy, which I really appreciate. He's a nice guy."

"Just a nice guy?" I asked. The color rose on her cheeks again and she smiled a half smile.

"None of your business," she said. "So listen, have you heard from Dimitri?"

"Not directly, but Harry called a little while ago. He's worried about Dimitri. He's also worried about himself. It sounds a little tricky down in Boston."

"Tricky is one word for it," Connie said, taking a bite of a regular fry. I pushed the cinnamon fries toward her and gestured toward the frosting dipping sauce. She looked dubious but picked one up and dipped it into the frosting. "Wow, that's good," she said, picking up another fry. "The production sounds like a nightmare to me. Dimitri asked me to come down. The Bay Rep has a resident stage manager, so they don't need me for that. Dimitri said he'd try to figure out another official job for me."

"Besides his minder?"

Connie laughed. "I always enjoy the challenge. I'm taking a bus at five o'clock."

"Where are you going to stay?"

"With him, for now. The company rents some apartments for out-of-town artists and Dimitri got a two-bedroom. He wants to get me on the Bay Rep's payroll. He's talking to ... Bat?"

"Babs," I corrected her. "Short for Barbara. It doesn't really suit her as a nickname. She's a little more no-nonsense than a 'Babs' sounds. You've met her, I think. She's married to Hal Maxwell."

"Hal Maxwell, the advertising guy from Boston?"

"That's the one," I said. Of course, "advertising guy" was an understatement.

"Do you know Babs?" Connie asked.

"You know how small our world is. I've met her a few times. How are she and Dimitri getting along?"

"Okay I guess," Connie said. "The only complaint he has is that she keeps telling them there's no budget for changes. But he says you've helped him get used to that over the years."

"From what Harry said, it sounds like this is trickier than just throwing money at the problem."

"In order to save this production, Dimitri feels like he's got to make some bold moves. He promises he can do them on a shoestring. He just needs to bring in his own people to help."

"Tell you what, Connie. Let me give Babs a call. Sounds like this is a managerial nightmare. Who knows, maybe she needs a sounding board too. No promises, but I'll see what I can do."

"Thanks, Sully. That's all any of us can ask," Connie said, finishing up the fries. She stacked up the dishes and stood up.

"You don't happen to have Babs's number—"

Connie took her phone out of her pocket, her fingers flying over the screen. "Just texted it to you."

"You're always prepared, aren't you?"

"Stage managers. It's in our blood. Always be prepared." Connie picked up the plates and walked back toward the kitchen. I opened the text and hit the number.

∞

Babs picked up the phone on the second ring. I'll admit I was surprised. I never picked up calls from unfamiliar numbers. Every time I thought better of myself and decided to pick up an unknown number, I got bitten—relegated to the charms of a political campaign or a computer voice who wanted my input, my money, or both. No, better to let voicemail pick up and then call folks back. Maybe running a larger theater in Boston didn't afford you the luxury of screening calls.

"Babs Allyn," she said. I did the same thing, answering the phone with my name rather than a "hello?" Manners were morphing in this new century, mostly not for the better.

"Babs, it's Sully Sullivan. From the Cliffside—"

"Sully, how great it is to hear from you. You saved me going through my desk desperately looking for your business card. I wanted to get in touch with you about our production of *Romeo and Juliet*. Have you spoken to Dimitri lately?"

"I haven't spoken to Dimitri," I said, waiting for her to go on. This was her theater, her story to tell. I certainly knew how I'd feel if someone tried to tell my story. Besides, I didn't want to let Babs know that Harry was telling tales out of school.

"Well, I'd be surprised if Dimitri doesn't call you tonight. He stepped into quite a mess, none of it his making, and his frustration is mounting—"

"Dimitri is enormously talented. He can be given to drama sometimes—"

"Given what's going on, he really isn't being that dramatic. He's asked whether Connie . . . ?"

"Connie Reed. Resident stage manager at the Cliffside."

"Right, right. He's invited her down. He wanted to bring her on as stage manager, but that would be tricky. Our stage manager is a member of the company and has a season contract."

"Connie's terrific. Very talented."

"I'm sure she is. I'm going to suggest to Dimitri that Connie be his assistant director, which will get her on payroll but will keep the peace in the company. It'll also give her more agency than if she came on as his assistant."

"Isn't there an assistant director already?" I asked. The Bay Rep had a strong mentorship program, and they always had assistant directors.

"A woman named Marcia Bartusiak—"

"Marcia interned with us last summer. I think I may have written her a recommendation for your program. She's wonderful, knows Dimitri well . . ."

"She's excited about Dimitri coming on board and decided to stay to work with him on the show. It's been helpful for him, since she's been here all season."

"She knows Connie too. They'll both be good for Dimitri."

"And there's enough work for both of them, trust me. We have to do some recasting today. Dimitri suggested calling someone named Stewart Tracy. He said he's worked at the Cliffside?"

"Several times." Stewart Tracy was a very talented, very handsome, very charismatic actor who I knew very well. Very, very well. "He's a terrific actor, and more than capable of stepping in late in the process. He saved our bacon in December with *A Christmas Carol*. I don't know if we could've pulled that show off without him."

"I'd love to hear more about that whole situation," Babs said. "I didn't know you used to be a cop until I read it in the paper after everything—after it was all over."

"Well, I don't need my cop skills very often in this job."

"I may need some of them, but not for *Romeo and Juliet*. Yet. Listen, I don't suppose you'd be willing to come down too, just to stay for a couple of days and help settle things down?"

"Come to Boston? I guess I could. My work right now is mostly on computers and in the cloud, as they say."

"The cloud is both a blessing and a curse. I don't trust it completely, do you?"

"I don't, and neither does my accountant. He has me backing up everything in three places, including on memory sticks I bring home once a week in case something happens at the office and/or to our online backup system."

"Oh, that's a good idea. I'm going to steal it. After this show opens. So, what do you say about a road trip?

"It might be fun to be around a rehearsal again. I can probably crash with Harry."

"Harry Frederick? That would be great. It would save us some money we can put somewhere else."

"I know that game," I said. "Take from one pot to add to another."

"That's how I run the business. As long as the bottom line stays the same and we meet our ticket goals, it's all good. On this show, those two scenarios are a challenge, but I'm trying."

"I've been there, more than once. I was worried sick about *A Christmas Carol*, but it ended up making a decent amount with some creative scheduling of additional performances."

"I can't wait to hear the stories about that. Also, honestly, while you're here, I'd love to see if you could help me sort through another mess that's risen up lately. Personal, not professional. I need some advice."

"I've always found talking things through helps a lot. Happy to be a sounding board. In fact, I just had a board member talk me through a budget for a grant I'm working on for the Century Foundation that's due in a couple of weeks—"

"Jerry and Mimi Cunningham's foundation? I know them well. Too well. That's another story. Actually, they're hosting a reception I have to go to tomorrow. Command performance by my husband. Maybe Hal could get you on the list. Will you be in town by then? It always helps to pre-game things a bit with them, chat up your proposal. I don't want to rush you, of course. But I do need to learn some of your Dimitri techniques ASAP."

I laughed. "No real techniques, but I'm happy to teach you what works for me. Tell you what—I'll drive Connie down this afternoon," I said. Connie had come back to the table and put down two cups of coffee. I lifted my mug up as if toasting her. "Look forward to seeing you tomorrow, Babs." I ended the call and double checked to make sure the line was clear.

"Whoa, you're a magician. Was it hard to talk her into that?" Connie asked.

"That's the odd part. It wasn't hard at all." I texted Harry, asking if I could stay with him for a few days.

For sure, Harry texted back. *There are keys in the bottom of the urn on the front step just for cases like this. Go to second floor, find your guest room on the right!*

Be there tonight, I texted back.

He sent a smiley face emoji and a martini glass emoji in response.

I got a twinge in my gut, the kind of twinge I used to have back when I was a cop. The kind of twinge that told me there was more to the story, more to the situation than first appeared. I'd learned not to ignore my gut back then, but now? It was only a play. It wasn't life or death.

Or so I thought.

· Three ·

I was always a quick packer. It helped that I wore all black these days, and layers were my friend. Connie and I were on the road by five o'clock. We spent most of the drive to Boston going over my grant proposal for the Century Foundation. I knew what a production center should have—I'd included washers, dryers, steamers, and racks for the costume shop; tools, lumber storage, and a painting room for scenery. But when I'd talked with technicians and run things by Connie, the wish list had gotten more specific, and the opportunities for compromise got greater. The Cliffside wasn't looking to build a palace for production; we just needed a practical place to store, build, paint, administrate, and create. Connie had been instrumental in helping me focus while I was working on the narrative for the grant. We'd decided to include both a covered lanai to go over part of the audience and a rebuilt stage for the amphitheater. I was hoping that a grand vision of our facilities would make our proposal more enticing.

"So what happens if this funding doesn't come through? I suppose it could wait until next year," Connie said.

"No, I don't want to wait. It took too long to get the town council to approve the use of the land. Even if all we do is build the shell of the production center, with two floors for concessions and box office this summer, we need to get the barn raised this spring. I don't want folks to have time to change their minds. "

"Barn raised?"

"Dimitri and I have been calling it a barn raising. An architecturally appropriate barn, of course. Colonial clapboard painted white, black trim, red doors. Large opening on the side facing the theater for load-ins and load-outs. All very New England from the outside."

"And very concrete, strong, and open on the inside, from the looks of the drawings," Connie said, flipping through the documents.

"Very concrete. We've already poured the slab."

"Is that what that is? I saw it by the theater but couldn't imagine that construction had really started."

"We had the ground flattened at the end of the summer, as you know, so we could get a jump start this spring. There was that warm snap in October, and someone in town offered us his extra concrete from a project he was working on."

"Extra concrete? That was enough?"

"Do you know Ray Cooney?"

"Who doesn't? He's one of the town elders."

"He's a cranky old buzzard. He was also friends with my father. He wanted to make sure the town council couldn't pull a fast one after the first thaw, so I think he pretended the concrete was extra. Anyway, the first part of the project is done. They'll lay plumbing and electrics over the slab and box them in. This is going to be a functional building."

"It's so exciting," Connie said. I looked over at her as she studied the drawings. She'd started grinning from ear to ear. The project had been on the dream list for years, well before my time with the Cliffside. The happiness on her face made me even more determined to pull it off.

"The goal is to make the building as fire-safe, snow-proof, and rodent-deterring as we can make it," I began. "Solar panels on the roof to offset costs. Plus we're going to be benefiting from the new school that's being built. Getting extra concrete and other construction castoffs. The timing is tight, but by taking advantage of the construction goodwill and the fact that we aren't being picky, we'll save a fortune. Between you and me, Eric Whitehall is working on a bridge loan in case we need it. I'm hoping it won't come to that—the project hits all the criteria for the Century Foundation and also a few other grants we've applied for. We'll know where we stand by mid-March."

"Sounds great," Connie said. "Really great. We've been fantasizing about this for so long, I can't believe we're finally going to have a production space of our own."

She sounded so happy, I didn't dare burst her bubble. I was a wreck about the finances, but I kept moving forward. If not now, when? At least that was the plan. I had to take a leap of faith that it would all work out. Problem was, I was always lousy at jumping.

We got to Boston before we knew it and I set my phone GPS to the apartment where Dimitri was staying. I'd lived in Boston for years and knew my way around, but I'd come to depend on the traffic alerts and alternate routes the GPS told me about. There was a lot of construction going on these days, and many familiar paths were blocked.

After I dropped Connie off, I reset my phone to help me find my home for the next few days. I finally found a parking spot three blocks from the the Whitehall siblings' townhome and struggled toward it with my knapsack, suitcase, cat carrier, and Max's bag. Yes, I brought Max. I wasn't sure exactly how long I would be away and my ten-year-old cat didn't take well to being left alone for more than one night. Not that he ever had been. Since leaving the police force and moving back to Trevorton, I'd been home nights. Usually alone.

I stopped to take in the building where I was staying. It had the faded charm of old Yankee money: well maintained, beautifully detailed, and not ostentatious in the least. Still, the granite steps, wrought-iron railings, boot cleaner on the bottom step, and hitching post weren't add-ons but part of the original design. I hauled myself up the stairs, holding tight to the railings. And by hauled, I mean hauled. These were original steps, made for feet much shorter than mine and ideal for warmer weather when the granite didn't coat up with ice. I made it safely to the top and put my bag down. The keys were where Harry said they would be, and I let myself in after figuring out which key went in which lock.

The front entranceway must have been breathtaking in its original state, when this was a single family home. It was still impressive, with slate floors, a stunning mail table to the left of the door, and a curved stairway that led to the second floor. I walked up the stairs with Max in his carrier and my knapsack. I let myself into Eric's apartment and followed Harry's directions to the guest bedroom. The room was lovely. Two large windows looked out to the next building, but between floors since we were on the side of a hill. To the left of the entrance I opened a door and was thrilled to see that the guest room had its own decently sized bathroom. The bathroom was modern, with a spacious shower in addition to the claw-foot tub. Still, the fixtures were in keeping with the age of the building.

I went down and got the rest of my belongings, then set up Max's litter box in my bathroom and let him out of his carrier, facing inside the bathroom. He hissed once and then set out to explore, acknowledging by walking past me and flicking his tail that he'd seen the litter box.

I followed him, and together we walked into the kitchen. Max stopped and glared at me, so I pulled out his place mat and dishes and created his food space in the corner of the room, by a large cabinet that was freestanding along the wall.

With Max set, I put my coat on again and went back to my car. Eric had long-term parking in the Boston Common Garage, and he'd offered to let me use it. Parking was always a bear in the city and worse on Beacon Hill, so I was happy to avail myself of his generosity. Even if it meant climbing over snow piles and avoiding ice-covered bricks on my way back to the townhouse.

Once I'd found a space in the garage, I'd texted myself the location. I was forever forgetting where I parked, spending way too much time looking for my car. I made my way back to the apartment, maneuvering through the brick sidewalks of Beacon Hill. Years of abusing my knees was catching up to me, and I found myself having to pay more attention to where I stepped, and how. This neighborhood of Boston, one of its oldest, still held its Colonial charm, intentionally. Lovely, but not easy to traverse. Even the newer shops look like they'd been there for years.

I scoped out the neighborhood on my way back to the apartment, making mental notes of what the area offered. Since moving back to Trevorton I'd come to realize how important it is to support the small businesses of a town. Even in big small towns like Boston. Beacon Hill always surprised me, with the stores that were able to stay in business year after year. I doubted my small purchases would help much, but I knew they wouldn't hurt. I stopped by a wine and cheese store and filled up the shopping bag I'd brought with me. Trevorton had banned plastic bags as of January 1st, and carrying a shopping bag had become second nature. I indulged in three sorts of cheeses, a six-pack of local beer, and two bottles of wine. Hard salami and some crackers rounded out what I knew might likely end up being my meal for the night. Fairly typical fair for me except for when I went to the Beef & Ale and got taken care of by Gene.

I pulled myself up the granite staircase one more time, fumbled with the front door lock, and then stepped into the foyer again. I took a deep breath, wished I were staying on the first floor, and then slowly walked up the grand staircase. It had been a full, full day. I looked forward to my crackers and cheese dinner and then crawling into bed. I went to unlock Eric's apartment door, but it swung open on its own, giving me a jump scare.

"Sully!" Emma Whitehall stood in the doorway, the warm glow of the overhead light creating a halo around her red curly locks. She opened her arms wide and I stepped into them, giving her a one-armed hug.

"Sorry, I picked up dinner on my way here," I said, stepping back. I lifted up the bag and tried not to wince when the bottles clanked.

"Oh, darn," Emma said. "I was hoping you'd join me for dinner. I've got a sauce cooking in my crockpot and was about to put the pot on to boil for some pasta. Bread is in the oven. Nothing fancy; a salad will round it out. Maybe we can combine the meals?"

"Of course we can. My meal is more on the hors d'oeuvres side of life anyway. We can nosh on it while we get the pasta cooking. Should we eat here or in your apartment?" Climbing up to the third floor every single day must be a challenge. I knew my knees would object.

"I cook on the second floor and usually eat here too," Emma said. "Hope that's okay while you're here? I covet Eric's kitchen."

"Of course," I said. "I'm grateful for a place to stay." I looked around the kitchen again, spending more time appreciating the layout and finishes. I had to agree with Emma. It was lovely, and fit with the apartment, though it couldn't have been the original footprint. I doubted the late 1800s lent themselves to open floor plans, white-painted cabinets that went to the ceiling, an island with gray granite, an extra sink, and recessed lights.

Max stuck his head out of my bedroom and stretched his way toward us. He squished his eyes at me and walked over to Emma. She put her hand down and he rolled his head in her palm.

"Hello, you. What's your name?" Emma said.

"That's Max. I'd forgotten, you haven't met him, have you? Max, this is Emma. I hope you don't mind me bringing him."

"Not at all," Emma said. "I've been thinking about getting a cat. This will be a nice trial run." She walked into the kitchen area and took a large pot out of the cabinet under the peninsula that separated the kitchen from the rest of the apartment. She put it in the large farmer's sink and started to fill it with water. I put my bag on the table and started to unpack my bounty.

"I love those crackers," she said, motioning to the rosemary and walnut crisps I'd bought.

"You're the one who turned me on to them," I said. "Where would I find a plate?"

"Look in the corner cabinet there. That's where he puts serving plates."

I looked in the cabinet and was overwhelmed with choices. "He could open a restaurant with all of this," I said, reaching for the closest plate.

"You should see his glassware. Eric is a great entertainer. By the way, Harry texted. He's on his way home. I told him I'd have dinner ready. I still have to go up and get the sauce."

"Very domestic of you," I said.

"I know, right? I can still only cook three things well, but sauce is one of them. Happily, Harry loves pasta. We try to eat meals together when we can. Usually down here. I'm afraid my kitchen is more utilitarian. Standard stove, small sink. Apartment-size dishwasher. Eric's is made for serious cooking." She put the pot of water on the stove and turned it on, then tossed a handful of salt in and covered the pot. She took two wine glasses out of the cabinet and put them on the table.

"His place is much nicer for living in general," Emma continued. "I didn't see any point in renovating, since my apartment is just an overnight place when I came down for business. But Eric is making me rethink that. There's so much light with the walls down. I need to catch up with my baby brother in the having-fun part of life."

"I think Harry is good for Eric in that aspect."

"No doubt. Harry's a good guy. I'm grateful that we're getting to know each other better. By the way, I told Harry you could've stayed in Amelia's apartment on the first floor, but he wanted you to stay with him. That's still an option, though, if you prefer privacy."

"No, this is fine. I don't mind a roommate once in a while, and I love spending time with Harry. Plus, I'm a safe sounding board for him," I said. "It sounds like this show isn't going particularly well, so better he vents to me than carry it into the rehearsal room."

"I'm trying to be supportive, but I know he'll be glad you're here. Even when things are going well at the theater, it sounds like chaos to me. I know you can help him sort through what is really a problem and what is just—"

"Drama?" I said. In my five years working at the Cliffside I had, indeed, learned the difference between real drama and drama for drama's sake. The heightened reality of the theater world was both calming and challenging. It was a great relief from my previous life as a cop. Though theater wasn't life and death, there were stakes. I would never underestimate those stakes, or belittle them. People worked hard, collaboration was necessary, and cooperation was a must. When it didn't work, it was both heartbreaking and frustrating. And it did sound like this production of *Romeo and Juliet* was not, mildly put, going well.

Emma walked over to the sink and retrieved a cutting board that was leaning up against the refrigerator. I walked toward her and took it to put on the table. "How many kinds of cheese did you get?" she asked, handing me a knife.

"Three, plus some salami."

"Harry's got some cheese in the refrigerator too. I'm turning the water down so we can time dinner for when Harry gets here. I'll run up and get the sauce." Emma walked to the right of the room and through a door I'd assumed was a bathroom. Instead it led out to a back staircase.

I walked over to the refrigerator and opened it up, smiling when I saw what was illuminated. Harry and I were the same person. The content of our refrigerators was identical. We cooked maybe one meal a week and used it for leftovers for days. Other than that, there was cheese, pickles, various jellies, too many types of mustard to count, and assorted fruits and vegetables in varying degrees of decay. Harry had different tastes but the same plethora of condiments. If I ended up staying for longer than a few days, I would do us both a favor and go what my mother always referred to as "big grocery shopping." The kind of shopping that required a cart and guaranteed that the basics were back in stock. The kind of shopping that meant that healthy, home-cooked meals weren't out of reach. I found when I was cooking for someone else, I usually stepped it up a notch or two.

I took out some mustards and a few of his cheeses. I heard someone gently kicking the back door and I went over to open it. Emma came in, carrying a crockpot. I cleared a space and she put it down, plugging it back in. I went over and lifted the corner, allowing the glorious aroma of a bold red sauce to fill the apartment.

"Yum!" I said. My stomach growled.

Emma grabbed a corkscrew and was looking at both my bottles. I suspected she didn't totally approve of my bourgeois taste, but I knew the wines were good and in my price range.

"You won't hurt my feelings if you open up a bottle of your own wine," I said.

"I've got a couple upstairs. Let me bring them down," Emma said, moving back toward the door.

"Is that easier than going up the front stairs?" I asked.

"Much. We totally redid these stairs a couple years ago," she said. "We use them to move up and down between apartments. Also, just so you know, there's an entrance down the alley to the back staircase. That way you don't have to go up the granite stairs with big packages, suitcases, groceries. There's also a working dumbwaiter in the back hallway."

"Now you tell me," I said, rubbing my knees. "Good to know for the future. Though I would never put Max on a dumbwaiter." Max tilted his head at me as if to say "because you know better than that" and went back to exploring.

"We treat these apartments like a dormitory. The back door to each apartment is always unlocked, and we just let ourselves in. If the door is locked, it means you want some privacy. We almost never have meals alone. That's why it's only friends and close family who get to stay here. I'll be back down with wine and a loaf of bread. Do we need anything else?" I shook my head. "Great. Be right back."

I laid out some cheeses on the plate and was adding a roll of crackers down the center when Emma came back. She was carrying three bottles of wine and had a loaf of bread under one arm.

"Wow, are you expecting a big party?"

"No, no this isn't all for tonight," she said. "But with you here as a magnet for visitors, I figure we'll all be spending more time in this apartment. I might as well start stocking up."

"That way you know you'll have something you want to drink at hand," I teased. "I saw your brother earlier today, by the way. He was helping me get my ducks lined up for this Century Foundation grant. He's been such a great help. I don't know what I'd do without him. Or you for that matter."

"When's it due?"

"Next week, but I'd love to get it done while I'm here. I'm really close—at the proofreading stage. I was talking to Babs Allyn, and she mentioned that there's a reception of some sort tomorrow night the Cunninghams are hosting. She said she'd ask Hal to get me an invite."

"I can help you with that too," Emma said. She poured herself a glass of wine, saw that I didn't have one myself, handed it to me, and then poured another. She raised her glass in a silent toast and took a sip, closing her eyes in appreciation. I toasted back and took a sip. I understood why she'd taken a moment to savor the wine. It was good, really good. I took my phone out and took a picture of the label. Always good to remember a great bottle of wine. Even if I'd never be able to afford it.

"I'm surprised Babs offered to put a word in with the Cunninghams through Hal," Emma added. "I thought they were all on the outs these days. But I can't keep up."

"On the outs? What do you mean?" I asked, taking a piece of cheese and nibbling the corner of it.

"Well, I'm not one to gossip—"

"Whatever you say doesn't leave this room, promise." I mimed zipping my lips closed, locking them with a key, and tossing the key over my shoulder.

"Well, rumor has it that she and Hal are having marital problems."

"That's a shame," I said, remembering Babs's "command performance" remark. "They've been married for years, haven't they?"

Emma looked a little pained and took a sip of wine. "As I know all too well, public perceptions of marriages can be misleading. People thought Terry and I were the couple of the hour. They had no idea what was really going on. Of course, I didn't either."

I kicked myself for causing Emma to think about Terry Holmes and their failed marriage. This recent, terrible history was a chapter we both needed to get past. Fortunately, Emma changed the subject herself.

"A few years ago, maybe ten, Babs and Hal separated for a while, but the separation was short. They seemed good, really good, but they've all been through a lot since Martin disappeared last winter. I had my own troubles, so I didn't keep up on how everyone was doing. Looks like maybe their marriage suffered under the strain. There were rumors."

"That's tough," I said. "Has Hal's business suffered?"

"I think so. He still has a great staff, and long-term clients are sticking with him, but when your business partner disappears while you're sailing in the Caribbean, it does cast a shadow."

"You don't think that Hal had anything to do with it?"

"I can't believe he did. No, of course not. There were a half dozen people on the boat and everyone seemed to alibi each other. The Cunninghams were there too—did you know that?"

"Truthfully, no. I do remember reading a few articles in the paper last winter but I don't remember much follow-up. I thought I read that Martin had reached out?"

"Yeah, I think a couple of people got postcards, but no one has heard from him since, as far as I know. Hal hired a PR team to manage the situation, which kept it low key, considering it was a juicy story. Most people don't even mention poor Martin, even though the anniversary of his disappearance is coming up."

"You keep calling it disappearance. What exactly happened, do you know?"

"Harry and I were just talking about this, so the details are sort of fresh for me. Everyone said they went to bed, and when they got up in the morning, Martin was gone. So was a lifeboat. Is he dead? I don't know. Am I wrong to hope it was a disappearance…that Martin wanted to start over? No. But the fact that his daughter hasn't heard from him makes me doubt he's still alive. Martin was her only parent, and he doted on her. Babs and Hal have been taking care of her this past year. I've seen her at their house several times. They seemed fine, as fine as they could under the circumstances. Babs never indicated she was thinking about leaving Hal, which does make me doubt the marriage-in-trouble rumors. Honestly, people can be such gossips. As well you know."

"I sure do," I said, taking a sip of wine. Emma was the kind of person I'd loved to meet back when I was a cop. A collector of information who disdained gossip but participated in it when it served her. I smiled slightly. "So you think Babs would leave Hal? Not the other way around?

"Never the other way around. Hal was crazy, is crazy, about Babs. But I've heard she's been looking for a new place. Down in New York."

"In New York? I hadn't heard she was leaving Bay Rep."

"Just rumors," Emma said, cutting another piece of salami and popping it into her mouth. "Nothing's been confirmed. Tomorrow night at the reception may be a good opportunity to get more information."

"Well, keep me posted on what you find out," I said. "I'm going to see Babs tomorrow. Thanks for letting me know, so I don't step in it."

"You'll be fine," Emma said. "I've never met anyone who plays her cards so close to her vest as Babs Allyn. I've known her for years, but I couldn't tell you anything personal about her. I've been thinking about this lately, after everything that's happened. It's true of most of the people I know. We're all putting on a front. So I'm making a concerted effort to change, to be more open to letting folks in. Anyway, I'm glad you're here, Sully. Glad we can spend some quality time together."

I poured Emma some more wine and added more to my glass. "Me too," I said. We both let our silence sit for a minute. Emma and I had been close as children, but we'd only gotten to know each other as adults these past few months. I was looking forward to spending time with her.

"Now, about the Cunningham Corporation and their tentacles of business—" Emma said, slicing off another piece of cheese and popping it into her mouth.

"Yes?" I put my glass down.

"You know, the Whitehalls and the Cunninghams have been doing business together for a while. Investing in projects, that sort of thing. Ever since we brought Gus on board—you don't mind me talking about Gus, do you?"

Why would I mind Emma talking about Gus Knight, my ex-husband and biggest heartache? Gus hadn't been an in-house lawyer for the Whitehall Company for long, but I knew that he'd been working closely with Eric and Emma ever since their father was killed.

"Of course I don't mind," I said. "I still can't believe Gus left criminal law, though. He spent all those years in the DA's office and then opened his own defense practice. It's quite the leap to corporate law."

"He's been a godsend, let me tell you. Immersing himself in some of our more recent business dealings, making sure they're kosher. Especially the deals Terry initiated." Terry had left a tangled web of intrigue and deceit behind when he died. I had no doubt Emma needed help untangling it, for a number of reasons, and was glad Gus was there to help.

"Gus wants to meet with Eric and me tomorrow," Emma continued. "Eric's going to Skype in. Then Gus and I are meeting some folks for drinks. The meeting shouldn't impact you, but I did want you to know he may be around a bit."

"Are you going to the Cunningham event tomorrow night?" I asked, avoiding the topic of my ex-husband.

"I am," Emma said. "The reception is to celebrate a new building development that just opened. Everyone will be there, so I need to make an appearance. We have some money invested in the project. Tell you what—come as my plus one. I'll make sure you have a chance to say hello to Jerry and Mimi. That way you won't have to owe Hal a favor."

"Thanks, Emma. I appreciate it." For a million reasons, I liked having Emma take me under her wing for this, rather than relying on Babs or Hal or someone else. Particularly if there was bad blood flowing among the parties involved. I made a mental note to try and find out more about Martin Samuel's disappearance. I told myself it was routine due diligence, but I was lying. I was curious. What had happened last winter on that boat?

I heard the key in the apartment door—somebody rattling it, turning the key again, and finally opening the door.

"I assumed it was locked," Harry said. "I'll never get used to open doors in the city." He shuffled his boots along the door mat and slipped his feet out of them. He hung up his coat and headed toward the kitchen area, and I stood up as he walked over to me.

He gave me a huge hug and hung on. "All I can say is thank heaven you're here, Sully." He pulled back and kissed me on the forehead. "You'll never guess who's playing Romeo as of three o'clock this afternoon?" He let go and walked over to the kitchen sink, washing his hands.

"You?" I said, pouring him a glass of wine. Harry had confided to me that he'd always wanted to play Romeo but was afraid he'd missed his window, since Romeo is supposed to be a teenager and Harry was well into his thirties. I'd caught him mouthing the lines with our Romeo from the wings on opening night at the Cliffside. "That's terrific. Isn't it?" I asked.

"'Terrific' is a loaded word. You're going to have to help me run lines—"

"Of course," I said. Not my favorite activity, but for Harry? Anything.

"First we eat, and drink," Emma said. She stood up and turned up the heat on the pasta water. "No shop talk for at least an hour. Deal?"

"Keep the food and wine coming, and you've got a deal," Harry said. He gave Emma a kiss on the cheek and sat down. I reached over and grabbed his hand.

"It's going to be fine," I said, squeezing it and letting go.

"Please let it be so," he said, drinking his wine in one gulp and holding his glass out for a refill. I obliged, and filled up my glass as well.

• Four •

We'd stayed up late, too late. Harry didn't have to go in until noon, so I let him sleep. I went out to a local coffee shop and had a breakfast sandwich and several cups of French roast coffee. Harry had no coffee in the house. Either his New Year's no-caffeine resolution was still holding firm or he hadn't been shopping for a while. Getting dressed before coffee was not my jam, so I made a note to stock up. I took another sip, watching people gingerly try to avoid patches of black ice, and then looked back down at my computer. I spent a few minutes reviewing changes I'd made to the grant application narrative. I hoped Babs would let me use a printer at the theater. Dimitri needed to look the proposal over, and he only read paper.

I considered leaving my car in the garage, but decided to drive over to the theater so I could stop and get groceries on the way home. I started a list, putting coffee in the first position. Added eggs, milk, cheese, bread, and bacon. I'd build up from there. Once I did the shopping I'd dump the car in the garage for the rest of the week. The stress of driving and parking in Boston was something I did not miss.

Taking the T would more than suffice to get me around town. After all, where was I going except to the theater and back?

I circled around for a few minutes, but then gave up and parked the car in a parking lot near the theater. It was about nine thirty. After signing in at the stage door, where Babs had left my name, I walked inside. I hadn't been to Bay Rep for years. As I stepped into the building, I paused to take it in and to get my bearings.

The theater was circular, and, depending on where you were in the loop around the theater itself, you were either backstage, in the box office area, near the bars, or heading to the bathroom. I walked to my left, toward an open door. I poked my head in and realized I was at the back of the house, where the audiences came in. I didn't step in too far, but I did stop and examine the set. Harry's reports of an iceberg stranded on the stage were not far off. Everything was bright white. There was a forced-perspective ceiling on the set that made it look as if there were a shiny white prism pulling the audience forward. There were a couple of ladders on the stage, and some miserable technicians holding up gels, focusing lights, and swearing into the dark void of the theater. Lest I interrupt this creative enterprise, I backed out of the theater and walked up the side, taking a left into the lobby.

Connie was talking to Babs Allyn. Babs was a few years older than me and had that casually elegant, put-together look I admired but would never even attempt. For one thing, my bank account couldn't take it. But it was more than that. Babs took her average height and frame and did them up, showing off a toned body with expensive clothes and topping it off with perfect makeup. She had obviously been a great beauty in her youth, and I couldn't blame her for trying to hold on. The thing was, she looked like a million other women, fighting age with blond hair and little bits of Botox that kept her lips from moving too much.

I was being unkind. But since I had no intention of holding on to my own past, I didn't understand the compulsion. As I moved into middle age, I felt that I was coming into my looks, finally. No youthful beauty to hold on to here. I hoped to become a striking old woman in the future.

Babs turned toward me and smiled. "Sully, so great to see you again." She gave me the requisite air kiss, which I returned. "I understand Dimitri is down to a dull roar this morning. Must be because of you and Connie coming down. I really appreciate it."

"Connie is the lion tamer. I'm just along for the ride," I said.

"Speaking of which, back to it," Connie said. "Let me know about the budget when you can, all right, Ms. Allyn?"

"Babs, please. And yes, of course. You've convinced me."

"Sully, you coming in to say hello to Dimitri?" Connie asked.

"In a few minutes. Let me catch up with Babs first," I said. Connie gave me a small smile and went back into the theater.

"I'm grateful to you both for making the trip. Dimitri is already easier to deal with now that Connie's here. From what I can ascertain, they were up half the night at his place working on the show. You're sure she's not some sort of magician?"

"Stage managers are magicians, you know that. Connie's better than most, since working at the Cliffside requires her to be well versed in all aspects of theater. And to think outside the box."

"Well, she's helping Dimitri and the technical director try to salvage the set and lights."

"What are you doing about costume design?" I asked.

"Pierre was the set and costume designer, but since he lived in France, we hired a local coordinator to do the fittings and oversee the production. Cassandra Ryan is a designer in her own right, so we've moved her up."

"I know Cassandra," I said. "She works at the Cliffside a lot."

"Having her on board has helped Dimitri's stress level but not taken it away. And it's added to mine. She's a bit of a handful, isn't she?" Babs gestured at one of the chairs in the lobby. There were several, all clustered around small tables. I looked toward the other end of the lobby and noticed that there were several seating areas spaced about.

I sat down. The chair was surprisingly comfortable. "Cassandra is a bit of a handful. That's one way to put it. But she's also a bit of a genius, and she works really well with Dimitri. They meet on the same wave length very easily."

Babs took a chair herself. "Listen, I know Dimitri is in a tough spot, taking over a production this far into the process. I appreciate his willingness to come in like this. I wish we had more money to throw at the production to give him a better chance of putting his stamp on it, but we're tapped out on this budget. This disaster should have been the jewel of the season. Oh well, sorry. I don't want to bore you with our war stories."

"Bore me? After *A Christmas Carol*, I'm grateful to hear other people's tales of woe."

"I look forward to swapping stories, maybe over drinks? Speaking of which, would you like some water? Or I could put the tea kettle on?"

"Water would be great, thanks."

Babs walked over to the screen and went behind it. She came back to the chairs with two bottles of water. "It'll be nice to tell the story to someone who gets it. We'd gone to France to see a Chekov production by Pierre a year and a half ago, and we were mesmerized. It was so original, and redefined the text for a modern audience. We were hiring outside directors for this season, and his work was highly regarded. We offered him a deal to come over here and direct what he wanted. He decided on *Romeo and Juliet* and told us he'd design the set and costumes. His assistant would design the lights and sound.

We hired Cassandra to oversee the costume fittings and build here, since Pierre was in France until the first rehearsal. All seemed fine. He came over, did a meet-and-greet with some donors. He described his concepts for the show, which sounded great.

"We trusted him with the production, did check-ins over the past year or so, and then the preliminary designs came in. Cassandra voiced some concerns, I have to give her credit for that, but we didn't listen to her. The concept was going to cost a lot, but since we weren't hiring other designers, we figured it out. We started the set build early, since it was so complicated. When Pierre finally came over, he was a different man. Not sure what happened to him, but his aesthetic changed over the year. He'd gone from warm to stark. Romeo and Juliet as written no longer interested him. He was looking for darker subtext, and adding it where it didn't exist. He decided that a lack of color supported his new vision."

"As if *Romeo and Juliet* isn't enough of a tragedy?"

"I know, right? You heard about the Capulet-as-sex-predator angle? And the Lady Capulet and Nurse affair?"

"Not about the affair." I shook my head. "What did you do?"

"As you know, the Bay Rep is going through changes. Our artistic director left last summer. Honestly, we were sort of auditioning Pierre for the role, but that obviously won't work. The company is working together on next season, so we can take our time before we make a decision on hiring a new AD. The collective is working well, but not having an artistic director was a problem for this show. There was no single voice in the room with the authority to question Pierre's judgment so that he'd listen. When the cast started doing table work, we realized that he was adding a lot of blood, and nudity. He even wanted Montague to simulate urinating onstage. The company balked, and Pierre pushed back. He had a 'my way or the highway' approach to his work."

"Don't most directors?"

"Yes, but they also allow the actors to have process. Pierre just wanted them to say the lines using his line readings. You know how much actors love feeling like robots regurgitating text. Pierre was also slashing scenes and planned on replacing them with projections he'd developed for another production."

"Of *Romeo and Juliet*?"

"No, a new piece. He was using German archival footage from World War II."

"Wow."

"Yeah. Quite the context to layer in. So anyway, we decided to part ways. His assistant is still here, though he's useless. Thank god I remembered seeing Dimitri's *Romeo and Juliet*. I knew he understood the play and hoped he could figure out how to do it on this set, with these costumes. He's meeting with the technical director and the crew right now to talk about changes. Our TD is thrilled about Dimitri's aesthetic and committed to making this work."

"Looks like everyone's got their work cut out for them. Are you still on the same schedule for opening?" I asked

"No, we've delayed it almost a week. You know something about delayed openings, don't you?"

I did and do, though despite everything, we'd only delayed *A Christmas Carol* by a day. I felt for Babs. It was always hard when money was being torched in a production. I was frustrated that I couldn't do anything to fix it for Dimitri. Or Harry. Or Stewart, if he was going to be part of the picture.

Babs turned on her phone and stood up. "I have an appointment downtown. A personal issue. I'd love to touch base again this afternoon. Might that work for you?"

"Of course," I said. "You've got my number. Happy to help however I can." My phone vibrated and I looked down at it. It was a text from Connie.

Where are you??!!??

"Starting now," I said. "I'm going to go say good morning to Dimitri. Run while you can, Babs."

Babs pointed me back down the hall and told me to go in the third door on my right. I landed onstage, entering upstage right. I still had to think about that every time I walked onstage. I wondered if the Greeks realized that so many of their conventions would live to this day. Their theaters were built on the side of hills, so upstage was to the back of the stage, and downstage was the front. Stage right and house left were the same thing, since when you were standing onstage your right was opposite of the people sitting in front of you. My purview as a general manager was the front of house, from the edge of the stage, or apron, on. I never liked being onstage. Almost getting killed backstage in December hadn't helped.

From where I stood, I saw the stairs to the dressing rooms on the other side of the theater. Normally the sides of the theater, the wings, are masked from the audience by flats or curtains, but there was no masking today. Just a wide expanse of shiny white with cube-like levels everywhere and a ditch, which I presumed to be the water feature, down the center. There were two bridges over parts of the stream. The theater seats were on three sides of the set, and raked sharply. Sight lines at Bay Rep were excellent even when you didn't want them to be.

I hugged the edge of the stage, trying to avoid stepping on the white set with my slush-covered boots. I walked down a side staircase into the house. I heard Dimitri before I saw him, and recognized the tone.

"What do you mean, it can't be painted? The scenic painter has come up with a scheme to help..."

"Help? This design needs no help. It is perfection."

"Was perfection. For another show. Not this one," Dimitri said quietly.

"It is no matter. The materials Pierre specified, they cannot be painted. They repel the paint. It helps keep it clean. Attempt to change it if you can, but it is folly. Never mind. I grow weary of dealing with your limited imaginations. Please remove my name from this debacle. I take my leave, and bid you good day." And with that an intense, bespectacled, very young man gathered up his ground plans and harrumphed offstage, knocking me in the shoulder as he did so. I almost tripped him, but decorum stopped me. This wasn't my theater.

I walked toward Dimitri and put my hand on his arm, squeezing it briefly. He gave me a pained smile and then turned back to the matter at hand. I hung back while he talked to the other man and Connie.

"How about if you rough up the finish? Might it take paint? Or at least dull it?" he asked a middle-aged man wearing a plaid shirt and low-hung jeans.

"We built this set and created finishes to last for the run. Sorry to say, but we're really good at our job, Dimitri. I don't think there's a lot we can do. Still, we'll run some tests in the shop and get back to you with some ideas later on today."

"Thanks. At this point a bare stage would be preferable. Is that possible?"

"Sorry, no. This was a bitch to install, and it required a lot of Tetris-type building that's going to take a long time to undo. And since our rehearsal space is being used for the next show, you need to keep everyone in here. I really am sorry, man. I tried to tell them way back." The plaid-clad techie ran his hand over his tool belt and shook his head.

"Thanks, Ron. Sorry, where are my manners? Ron Crystal, Sully Sullivan. Ron's the technical director of the Bay. He's trying to salvage this. Sully's the managing director of the Cliffside."

I didn't take it personally that Ron didn't look thrilled to see me. Technical directors never liked the "office types," a direct quote from our new technical director at the Cliffside.

"Good to meet you, Sully. I've heard good things," he said, giving my hand a firm shake, which I returned. Ron looked impressed. "Dimitri, give me a couple of hours to test out some ideas. I'll get back to you, I promise."

"Good enough for me, Ron. I know you're doing what you can."

Ron walked onto the set and exited stage right. Dimitri and Connie stepped back to look at their set. I joined them.

"I asked if they could burn parts of it to distress it, but it's been fireproofed," Dimitri said. "There isn't a single playing space more than nine square feet. There are traps, which are always fun, but none of them make sense for staging this play. At least not to me. That little twerp resigned from the project because I'm intent on bastardizing the designs. Would that I could."

"How about the costumes? I hear that Cassandra has been moved up to designer."

"She has, but we can't start from scratch. The costume design is white. Modern dress. White jeans. White boots. White T-shirts with *C* for Capulet or *M* for Montague. Nothing else to differentiate the characters. Everyone looks the same, men and women."

"Cassandra must hate that." I'd sat through enough production meetings to know that Cassandra took color seriously.

"She was here to coordinate, not design. She's willing to change the designs, but the budget isn't there."

"She's so talented and has an amazing shop. She may be able to pull the show from her costume stock. Cassandra works miracles, Dimitri. You know that. Remember what she did with *Six Characters* last summer? That show barely had a budget, but it was gorgeous. Genius." I was laying it on thick, but not too thick. Cassandra really was amazing. She sat on my last nerve, but I was learning to cope with it, and her. In this case, talent won out.

"Lights and sound need a rethink as well ..." Dimitri sighed. "The entire production needs a rethink. At least they got Robin in for lights. That just happened. They're still looking for a sound designer. One thing about the set, there's some interesting speaker placement."

"Robin's great. She must be freaking out a little about shiny white—"

"A little?" Dimitri barked a short laugh.

"But it sounds like Ron's working on that."

"He's doing what he can," Dimitri agreed.

"Worse comes to worse, you can do the sound," I said.

"I'm not a—"

"Dimitri, don't start," I interrupted. "You know that's the one area you micromanage on every production. I'm sure you've thought it through already."

Dimitri sighed and gave me a half smile. "I did call Liana to see if she'd do a soundscape for me," he said. Liana was a jazz musician and one of Dimitri's old flames. He had a knack of keeping former girlfriends on as friends. Liana was a great musician and also a good influence on Dimitri. Music soothed his savage beast.

"Perfect. You can worry more about sound later," I said. One of my Dimitri skills was helping him prioritize. I noticed that Connie was taking notes and nodding while I was talking. "What time does rehearsal start?"

"We pushed it back to this afternoon. We have to wait for our new Capulet to come in. I moved Harry up to Romeo yesterday afternoon."

"He told me," I said.

"He's a little old for the part, but he can pass for young. He's always wanted to play Romeo. I felt bad I didn't cast him in our Cliffside production."

One thing about Dimitri, he'd never cast a show based on loyalty. When you worked for him, you'd earned the role. Our Romeo had been a brilliant choice for that particular production. As Harry would be for this one.

"He'll be terrific," Dimitri went on. "Besides, our Juliet is hardly in the blush of youth. But she's good, and from the company."

"And there isn't a Capulet?"

"No, not in the company. Given Pierre's take, the character has felt a little cursed for this production. So I called Stewart. He's taking the train up today."

"Speaking of which," Connie said, "I need to go and talk to the company manager about his housing."

Stewart Tracy. My good friend, ex-lover, and current emotional confusion was in fact coming to town. He'd come to Trevorton to help save our production of *A Christmas Carol* and almost got killed in the process. We hadn't veered from the friendship path over the holidays, but I'd thought about it. Especially since the other object of my affection, my ex-husband, Gus, was dating the formidable Kate, one of the partners in his new law practice. I assumed Kate was formidable. We hadn't met. Yet.

"Isn't Stewart a little young to play Capulet?" I asked.

"A little. But he plays older, and wants the work. Bay Rep is a good resume credit. Or it was until this production."

"Now, Dimitri—"

"How long are you here, Sully?"

"I think I'll stay for a couple of days. There's a show at the MFA I want to see. It also looks like I may have a chance to say hello to Jerry and Mimi Cunningham tonight."

"The decision-makers themselves?"

"We've met a couple of times. I want to remind them of that. Their foundation money could seriously boost our building fund. New construction would be good for Trevorton. There are a lot of people who could use the work."

"You don't have to sell me, Sully. Let me know what you need me to do to help," Dimitri said. "It's impressive that the Cunninghams are still funding projects at this great pace. And that there are so many new Century Projects on the docket."

"It is, I guess," I said.

"You guess? You getting one of those gut twinges again?"

I hadn't thought about it, but Dimitri knew me too well. "Yes. No. From everything I can find, the Century Foundation seems to be funding at the same level they've been funding at for the past few years. Thankfully. A lot of other foundations have dried up."

"So that's the reason you're in town? To meet with them?"

"No, that's a bonus. I thought I'd check in with the Bay Rep. See for myself what you've gotten yourself into."

"Thanks, Sully," he said, putting his hand on my forearm and giving it a light squeeze. "Just seeing you here calms me down. It really does."

∞

I thought I was on my way to the front of the house. I'd gotten turned around a bit and found myself in a sea of beer cases and boxes of snacks. The door into the lobby was locked, which was as it should be given the value of alcohol. I walked straight ahead and another door was ajar. I walked through and found myself in the back hallway.

"Hello? Babs, is that you?" a voice said from the office on the left. A young woman came out the door and stopped short. She was tall, with black hair that was shaved on one side and swooped over her eye. Her black eyeliner was cat-eyed, and she wore deep red lipstick. Part Goth, part '40s pinup. "You're not Babs," she said.

"No, I'm not. I'm a friend of Dimitri's. Sully Sullivan. So sorry, I got lost getting out—"

"You run the Cliffside Theater, don't you?"

"I do," I said.

"I love that place. I went there with my father at least once every summer. It was always magical," she said. I saw the glimmer of a smile flicker across her face, followed quickly by a shadow.

"Thanks for sharing memories of the Cliffside. I always love hearing them," I said. "I went there a lot with my parents when I was a kid. My mother was an amateur actress and volunteered in the front of house when she wasn't cast. I didn't think she'd passed the theater bug on to me. But here I am."

The young woman smiled and blinked a few times. "Sorry, I've forgotten my manners. I'm Holly Samuel."

"Hello, Holly, nice to meet you. You work with Babs?" Holly Samuel, daughter of Martin Samuel?

"I interned here when I was in college. They offered me a job this fall. Working here is so different than interning. It's more…"

"More real?"

"Yes, that. I always took it seriously, but now I feel so responsible."

"Well, Babs knows what she's doing. You're learning from the best. But you're right—it is a lot of responsibility. Sounds like you've all had quite the ride these past few weeks."

"That's one way to put it. Babs promises we'll laugh about it all before the year is out, but right now I don't see how. I'm sorry, I should have offered you a cup of coffee. Would you like one?"

My years as a cop helped me read people. Holly wanted to talk. I forced myself not to look at the time and nodded my head. "A half a cup would be great. Black. I'm pretty caffeinated already." That was a lie. Before noon there was never too much coffee.

"Just a sec," she said. She walked over to a small kitchenette in the hallway and poured two cups of coffee into BRT mugs. She handed me one and I took a sip. Good coffee.

"Why don't we go out to the lobby?" she said.

"That's where I was heading, but I got turned around."

"Easy to do here," Holly said, guiding me past the cases of beer through a narrow path that led to a hallway. In front of us was a small office with desks crammed in. "That's my office. I share it with the house manager and box office manager. I'd invite you in, but there isn't room to put down your coffee. The door's right here." Holly pushed open a panel I hadn't noticed and we were back in the lobby, this time near the bar. There were several high-top tables with stools. We sat at one.

"These are great," I said. I'd spent a lot of time considering lobby furniture lately, and I admired the utilitarian elegance of Bay Rep's. The bucket seats were comfortable and the table tops were a good size.

"We put up a screen during the day, to hide this from view of the box office. We have a lot of meetings out here, which is why there are so many chairs and tables. We're sort of mid-renovation, working on making access to the theater universal. You know, taking out steps that aren't necessary, widening doorways. A ton of stuff. It requires shifting storage around, and our conference room is jammed.

That's why there are so many of us sharing an office, though I doubt that'll change. There's never enough room."

"That's so true," I said. "We're raising money for a new production facility, and I'm learning a lot about how to make the space functional for everyone. I'm also forced to figure out where the compromises need to be. No one is going to be completely happy with the space they're given, but that's the way it is. I will say, figuring it all out is easier to do with new buildings than old. It's like a puzzle."

Holly laughed. "Babs says the same thing."

"We learn that in general manager school," I said. "I'm joking, of course. I wish I'd been able to take some arts administration classes before I started my job. I jumped in the deep end and have been playing catch up ever since. I'm still learning all the time, which makes the job more interesting."

"Glad it isn't just me," Holly said.

"Not just you, no. I've got a group of advisors I call on when I've got questions. I couldn't do this without them. It's so different from my old job."

"Which was?"

"I used to be a cop."

"Really?" Holly's eyes got wide. She leaned forward in her seat.

"Really. A few years back I made a career change. Long story. But anyway, the Cliffside needed a general manager, and I needed a job. As I said, I had to learn on the fly, which was tough, but I had folks helping me along the way."

"Do you like the job, or are you doing it because you feel like you should?" Holly asked.

"Interesting question," I said. It was clear she wanted a real answer, so I gave it some thought. "Honestly, at first I did it because I needed a job. But now I do it because I love it. It's challenging to run a theater, as you must be finding out." Holly nodded, and I saw the hint of a smile. "But I've come to realize how important the work is, and how rewarding it can be. The one thing I hate is having to raise money, but even that I'm getting good at."

"For whatever reason, the raising-money part isn't too difficult for me," Holly said. "My dad runs—ran—his own business, and he was constantly having to pitch his work. I learned a lot from him, even when I didn't think I was."

"We all learn a lot from our parents. My mother's been gone a long time. I'd love her to know what I'm doing now. I think she'd be thrilled."

At that moment, I heard Dimitri yell. I couldn't hear the words but recognized the roar. It was how he let off frustration. Holly looked pale and her eyes glistened.

"He's harmless," I said, reaching across the table and patting her hand. I made a mental note to talk to Dimitri about his decibel level.

"Promise?" she said softly. "He's a pretty spectacular yeller. I have to tell him we don't have enough money to completely redo the costumes. I feel like puking."

"You want some advice?" I asked.

"Yes, please."

"Don't wait to tell him. Make sure Connie's in the room. She's a good buffer and will help him focus. Do listen to him, even if he's being loud. Also, be more worried when he's being really quiet and you think he should be yelling."

"Thanks. I need to meet Connie. I mean, I met her briefly, but I need to talk to her."

"Do that first. She's on your team. She's really great at her job, and about a dozen others."

Holly's phone pinged and buzzed, and she looked down at it. "Sorry, this is how Babs gets hold of me." Her brow furrowed while she read the texts. Her phone kept pinging, so it must have been a long text. "Babs says to find some money to put Connie on payroll. We're going to make her assistant director since we have a stage manager already." She glanced up at me. "Marcia Bartusiak was already hired as assistant director, part of our mentoring program."

"Right. The plan is for them to work together. I know Marcia. She's great, has a different skill set than Connie ..."

"I'll need to figure this out. Dimitri will be okay with two assistants, right? Do you think Connie will go for that?"

"I can't speak for Connie," I said. But I was glad they were coming through with finding some funds for her. Negotiating jobs and job descriptions is always tough, and as wonderful as Connie was, she could be formidable. "Maybe just wait until Babs is back and you can talk to Connie together?"

"She says that something came up and she's not coming back to the theater until tomorrow," Holly said.

I didn't want to pry, but leaving Holly alone to deal with all of this? That was odd. And it also struck me as unfair to the young woman. But this wasn't my theater, so I needed to step carefully. "Tell you what, Holly. Here's my card. Do you have a pen I can borrow? Thanks. This is my cell phone number. Feel free to call or text with any questions, or if something comes up and you need my help. Happy to offer my advice if I can. I don't know your theater as well as I know my own, but some things are universal. Plus, I can give you hints about some of the people."

Holly put my number into her phone and sent me a text. "Now you have my information as well. Thanks so much, Ms. Sullivan. I really appreciate it."

"Sully, please. No worries at all. You've got this. I'm happy to help. And thanks for the coffee."

• Five •

I took my phone out of my pocket. It had been on silent, and I had a text from Babs waiting for me. She said she'd be in touch later. *I need your advice,* was how she ended the text. I texted back that I'd be around.

I texted Connie. *Be nice to Holly. She's in over her head and running things today. Loop me in if she needs help.* Normally I wouldn't step in, but I couldn't help but feel for Holly. This was a lot to deal with on her own, even if Babs was only a text away.

I sat down on a bench in the lobby. Deep breath. I looked at the center door to the theater and heard voices calling for a meeting onstage. I felt the pull of the room, but I fought it. Once I walked into the theater, I'd get stuck in the vortex and lose all track of time. I looked at my watch. Close to noon. I could get some grocery shopping done and then come back for rehearsal. Or head back to the apartment and do some work. I took out my phone and worked on my grocery list.

My cell phone rang, startling me. I turned the ringtone down and picked up the call.

"Hi Connie. What's up? Where are you?"

"With Dimitri."

"Keeping him calm?"

"Trying my best. I have a favor to ask. Can you pick Stewart up? He's coming into South Station in an hour and has his stuff with him."

"Sure. Where's he staying?"

"Harry invited him to stay at his place."

"With Harry?" And with me. Great.

My car was old but very functional, missing only a few accoutrements. One of them included being able to text through the car itself. I also was, for whatever reason, having trouble figuring out how to voice-text anyone. I looked forward to our new crop of interns, who could help me figure out how to navigate this new phone.

It was for that reason that I felt compelled to pull over and text Stewart that I'd be outside South Station to collect him. Keep in mind that "pulling over" in Boston sounds simpler than it is. For most Bostonians, it means double parking. But as an ex-cop, I didn't allow myself to stop in the middle lane. Or, to be honest, I tried not to. The easiest way, then, for me to pull over was to park at a convenience store. So I used the opportunity to go in, grab drinks for Stewart and myself, and get a bag of almonds.

I was a list maker in all things. When I was a cop, I kept many running lists of questions I still had, things I knew, next steps. For my home, I kept a running list of things that needed to be fixed or renovated or repaired or replaced. That list was perpetual, since I lived in an old carriage house. For the theater I also had dozens of lists, ongoing, and moving up in levels of importance depending on where I was in the season. I was perpetually looking for a list maker app that followed my train of thought, but the only thing that worked for me was putting pen to paper, purging my brain, and then transferring that information into the Keep app, a system of blocks of text I could organize. I really did need to learn how to do voice recordings, because my brain was full and I couldn't write and drive. If I didn't write something down, I was afraid I would forget it.

I opened my soda and texted Stewart. *Is your train here yet?*

Twenty minutes away. Why, are you coming to get me?

I am. Come out to the Atlantic Ave side of the building. I'll pull up.

Looking forward to it! Steward texted back.

I felt a tingle in my belly. So am I, I thought. What exactly that meant I pushed aside for the moment. I headed toward South Station, which was just a couple of miles away, but there was Boston traffic to navigate.

∞

I did a slow crawl into the station, driving up behind the taxi line. Sure enough, Stewart was outside looking around, waiting for me. He was pulling his small black suitcase and wearing his gray knapsack. Under his arm he held a large loose-leaf notebook. I knew from having worked with him for years that this was his rehearsal bible, where he put his scripts, kept his notes, and stored research he found helpful. Stewart had his own system, and some of his research included things that might not make sense to anyone else but helped him build his characters. Maybe it was a picture of a place, or a costume, a meal, or sometimes even a character from a book or movie that helped spark his imagination and allowed him to get into the head of the character he was going to play.

Even when he explained his process to me, he could never explain the alchemy that gave him his brilliance. I imagined that the role of Capulet hadn't been on his radar before, so I wondered what was in the notebook. Like many actors, Stewart had an ego that was both healthy and fragile. I suspected he still thought himself as more of a Romeo. I wondered if he'd ever played that role. He would have been great. Actors, male actors, could measure their careers in terms of Shakespeare's characters: Romeo, then Macbeth, the Henrys, and finally Lear. Stewart wasn't at the Lear stage of his life yet, but he was past his Romeo stage.

I tapped the horn once and Stewart turned to his left. I gave him a brief wave and got one of his dazzling smiles in return. He came over and threw his knapsack and suitcase into the back seat, then climbed into the front, automatically reaching down to push it all the way back. My front seats were always all the way back, but I understood Stewart's rote reaction to getting into a car. Those of us blessed with long legs were always desperate for more room. He leaned across the console and gave me hello kiss on the lips. It was warm, gentle, and familiar. And lasted a little too long to be merely friendly. Someone behind us tapped his horn and Stewart leaned back.

"Sully, what a nice surprise your text was. When I heard Connie was going to Bay Rep to be with Dimitri, I wondered if you were coming down to join in on the fun."

"Fun is one word for it," I said. Driving around South Station was a little bit like playing bumper pool with lanes, and I focused on getting into the middle lane before I turned back to give him a smile. "I know they'll all be glad to see you. Stewart to the rescue yet again."

"I had some movie work last month. Not a big role, but the money was good. It kept me busy. But happily for all, including me, I have a stretch of time available. Glad to be here. You know me well enough, Sully—I love feeling wanted. Actors thrive on being wanted. Plus this does sound like quite the production. I'd rather be part of it than hear about it secondhand next summer when we're all back at the Cliffside making magic."

"Yeah, I stopped by the theater briefly this morning, but I suspect there will be stories," I said. "This may end up being a new legend. Hopefully it will help us forget *A Christmas Carol* and all that happened then."

"I look back on *A Christmas Carol* with great fondness," Stewart said. I laughed, but he didn't join me. "No, really, I do. When all was said and done, it was a helluva production. I'm proud to have been part of it."

"Even though it landed you in the hospital?"

"A few bumps and bruises. Part of the story. I'm just glad that it ended up raising some money for the Cliffside."

"Our *Christmas Carol* is always supposed to be a money stream for the upcoming summer season," I said while looking over my left shoulder for a place to merge. Taking turns going into one lane wasn't actually how merging worked in Boston. Rather, it consisted of winning the game of chicken with the other driver. I hadn't lived in the city for a few years, but having driven in it for so long, my muscles were quick to remember. I merged into the lane and drove into the underpass.

"But you're right—that last week of performances helped a lot," I continued. "Especially that fundraising performance. It put us in a good place to start this building project for the summer."

"Nice when it works," Stewart said, opening the notebook on his lap. He took a highlighter out of the front pocket of the notebook and turned to the page in his script he'd put a Post-it note on.

"What are you doing, learning your lines already?"

"No, just marking them. Dimitri sent me a copy of the working script last night. I had the copy center run it for me this morning so

I could bring it on the train. I've read it, and now I'm marking my lines so I can get a sense of the rhythm of this part."

"Have you ever done *Romeo and Juliet* before?" I asked.

"As Romeo, yes, three times. It's a pretty tough play to do, since it's so well known. How do you raise the stakes? How do you tell the audiences this old story in a new way? How do you play the tragedy so that it's really tragedy, not a stereotype? I've never played Capulet. Before now, never thought I was old enough. But I guess I've crossed that Rubicon to playing fathers."

I glanced over at Stewart and noted that he was staring out the window with a faraway look on his face. "Hey, sweetheart, you're here to help Dimitri," I said. "Nobody who spends five minutes with you thinks you're in the father stage of life, whatever that means. Besides, aren't there some great father roles? More than for mothers, that's for sure."

"Yes, of course. You're right. Being an aging male actor isn't as hard as it is for other folks in the theater. I get it. But still, I can't help but feel old. The roles they're calling me in for these days aren't the dashing leading men anymore. They're the dads. When did I cross that line?"

"For TV?" I asked. Stewart nodded. "Listen, ages on TV are all screwed up. Don't worry about that. As for this, Dimitri needs somebody he can count on, a leader to help with the rest of the cast. Since he's thrown Harry into the role of Romeo, Harry needs your help too. I think the ages of this entire production are all over the place. But that's the least of the problems." I told Stewart about the white concept, and he laughed. Sort of laughed. It was more of a horrified laugh than a "boy is that funny" laugh.

"I know Connie's a magician, and the Bay Rep has money, but this sounds like it's going to take a little bit of a miracle to pull off," he said.

"Stewart, if I've learned one thing working at the Cliffside it's this: all of theater is a miracle. Really. Getting all these people together and focused on one goal, opening night, working with budgets, personalities, space issues, and every other challenge. Making the director's dream come true. There's a point during every production when I'm convinced that this is the show where we won't be able to pull it off, but then I sit in the theater on opening night, with people in the audience, and actors walk onstage fully dressed, on a set, in lights, speaking words that make sense and that everyone can hear. That moment of realizing we pulled it off? That's magic to me. Don't laugh."

"I'm not laughing," Stewart said. "I just love that you still feel like this, and you help me remember what the magic is."

"To know your lines, not be naked onstage, and have lights on?"

"That, and trust the process."

"Well, if I was going to sum it up, I would say that's the challenge for this production. To get trust back in the process. I know you'll help Dimitri with that. You helped on *A Christmas Carol*, and you'll help with this. I'm glad you're here."

"I am too. Terrified, but glad. So, Harry tells me I'm going to be staying with him on Beacon Hill? Are we going there first? Or straight to the theater?"

"I'm staying there too. We can go there and drop your stuff off, give you a chance to freshen up. Or I can bring you right to the theater and I'll take your stuff to the apartment. Which do you prefer?"

"If you don't mind, I prefer going right to the theater. I'd rather get started sooner than later. But I'll see you in a bit?"

"Absolutely. To the theater we go." I glanced over at Stewart. He was looking down at his script again, highlighter in hand, searching for his lines. He was breathtakingly handsome, and had that spark of personality that gave him special powers onstage. That spark was both exciting and trouble. Good trouble, but trouble nonetheless.

∞

I texted Emma, letting her know I was on my way back to the apartment with Stewart's bag. She texted back that Stewart would be staying in Amelia's apartment, unless I wanted to move down there and let Stewart stay with Harry. I was fine with staying with Harry. Besides, Max was settled in.

So I wasn't going to stay in the same apartment as Stewart after all. Just as well. I found a space on Charles Street and brought his belongings in, leaving them outside the front door of Amelia's apartment. I took the car back to the garage and went to the market on my walk back to get coffee, fruit, eggs, and some more bread for the morning. I tossed in some cookies and chocolate while waiting in the checkout line. The day had gotten away from me and I needed to get ready for tonight. I texted Holly and Connie to let them know I wasn't coming back to the theater today but would be reachable by text or cell.

I half expected to see Emma when I let myself into the apartment, but Max was the only one home. *Am I all set to be your plus one tonight?* I texted Emma.

All set. Crazy day, will fill you in later. I'll need to meet you at the University Club. 7 p.m. Tonight is dressy and/or business dress. You have something to wear? Emma texted.

I do, I replied. And I did, but it needed to be ironed. That was the story of my life: rumpled but ready. I pulled out my serviceable black suit, a houndstooth shirt, some tights, and my black boots. I'd wear my mother's triple strand of pearls and some diamond and pearl earrings Gus had given me as a wedding gift. I fingered the earrings. I loved them, but hadn't worn them for a long while after our divorce. Now that there was a bit of a détente, I'd started wearing them again. I tried not to read too much into that. I put a brooch in my pocket just in case I needed to fancy it up a little. I went in to take a quick shower and brought the suit with me. Maybe the steam would let me forgo the iron.

Raising money had started off as the least favorite part of my job, but I'd moved it up to the "don't mind" level. You never just outright asked for a donation. Instead, you developed a relationship with a potential funder and figured out when to make the ask. And *if* to ask, since sometimes donors weren't a great fit. Basically, it involved being nice, schmoozing, and remembering details. I'd learned how to be nice from my mother, how to schmooze from my father, and how to remember details from my days as a cop. They all served me well while raising funds.

I didn't differentiate between big donors and small ones, since for an organization our size, every little bit counted. But the Cunninghams and their foundation were bigger than big money. For the Cliffside, the money could change our whole operation. Making improvements while not going into the crazy debt that hobbled so many theaters who'd added space—that was my goal. It was a leap for the company in many ways, and I was determined to make it happen. I ran my hands down my legs and took a deep breath. Today was about touching base and starting to build a relationship.

I looked at my cell phone. I was doing fine for time, so I put the kettle on for tea. I felt a head-butt at the back of my knees and looked down. Max came around and gave me a plaintive meow. Less of an "I'm starving" and more of a "since you're feeding yourself, how about feeding me too?" I squatted down and lifted his front end up so that I could kiss the top of his head. Max obliged for a second, but then he scooted backward, out of reach.

"Okay, buddy, I'll give you an early dinner. Not sure what time I'll be home, but don't try to sweet-talk Harry if he gets home before I do. You're good at getting double fed when we've got company."

Max put on his best innocent look, complete with the sideward tilt of his head.

"Don't give me that look. I'm on to you." I bent down and rubbed behind both his ears. I went into the refrigerator and got his wet food, put a tablespoon into a dish, and set it down for him. I added a bit more dry food to his bowl. The wet food was gone in no time, but I left the plate on the floor, hoping that Harry would understand that the cat had already been fed if he got home before I did. The vet had given me the "Max needs to lose some weight" talk, and I was doing my best. We both had gained some winter weight, and I needed to do what I could do to help us both lose it.

I took out my laptop and put it on the kitchen table. This was probably verboten most of the time, but living alone had given me bad habits, which included working while I ate. The battery was running low, so I plugged the laptop in and sat down to do some web surfing. I logged into my *Boston Globe* account and put in the words "Martin Samuel."

He'd had a long, high-profile career, and there were a lot of articles about him. Since the return was so overwhelming, I simply read the titles of the articles for several pages. But these headlines, along with the type of press he'd garnered, were enough to give me a sense of who he was as a person.

I hit the images button, and a man I could vaguely recognize filled the screen. Martin Samuel was a large man, not fat but definitely a presence. Brush-top hair styles for years, the only variance being the color and the hairline. Sometimes he wore a goatee, other times he was barefaced. He rarely wore a smile. Hal Maxwell had been the public face of their marketing firm, schmoozing customers and prospective clients. But Martin had had a role to play, and I thought about that role. Was he more of the creative force behind Maxwell and Samuel?

I got up and poured the tea water into my mug. I thought about eating something but my stomach was in knots. I always felt this way before an event. Work would help. I went back to the list of articles on the *Globe* site and added the word "disappearance" to the search. These articles I didn't go through as quickly. I started with ones from a year before, when the boat accident first happened, and moved to the present. I actually didn't need to move quickly, since there were so few articles. Then I went on to the web itself and put in the same search terms. Not much more than what the *Globe* had displayed. Only that Martin Samuel had been with a group of friends on a boat tour of the Caribbean, there'd been a party, and at some point during that night he'd left the boat.

I had to wonder if anyone was looking for him. Someone must have been, right? Looking either for Martin or his body. Like so many topics I explored, this really was none of my business. But it did make me curious, and I'd learned the hard way that to ignore my curiosity was only to help it grow.

I took my notebook out of my bag and started a new page. I wrote the initials *M.S.* at the top and added three questions: *Who was on the boat with him? What happened? Who was looking for him?*

I had nothing more to add. But at least now that it was written down, Martin wouldn't be rattling around in my brain.

At the front of my notebook I had an index. I added *M.S.* to the table of contents, along with the hand-numbered page I'd started my list on. Then I looked at my entries for the Cunninghams and went to those pages. I reread all my notes. For some, many, who were looking at prospective donors, my notes wouldn't make much sense. Alongside who else they'd funded, what else they owned, and any other altruistic facts I needed to know, I always added in as many personality details as I could find, either by meeting the donors or by doing some research.

Jerry Cunningham was a self-made man who'd started his fortune in real estate. He married Mimi Evans, a small-time heiress who'd built her own little empire by flipping properties in Chicago. They'd moved to Boston about twenty years prior and together continued to build up their empire, the Cunningham Corporation, and to expand it. Some of that expanse was under the Century Project banner. They were also part-owners of sports teams and high profile partners in other projects. Various parts of the empire were developed under their philanthropic wing, the Century Foundation. It was there that they established scholarships. Donated to museums. Created research labs. Supported theaters. Their contributions were large and flashy, and garnered national attention.

I had met some donors who wanted their contributions to remain anonymous or without fuss. Not so the Cunninghams. Big tangible projects were more likely to get their funding. My board at the Cliffside wanted me to be willing to give them naming rights if they helped fund our production center, but I was holding out. The Cunningham Pavilion, the name the board had suggested, didn't have a healthy ring to it for me.

One of the most interesting things I'd found out about the Cunninghams was that you rarely read something about one of them without a mention of the other. If Mimi Cunningham was dedicating a research facility, Jerry Cunningham was there cheering her on. If Jerry was at a game, Mimi was sitting beside him wearing a team hat, cheering just as loudly. They were huge supporters of arts and culture, and always attended events together. The few times I'd met them, they had in fact struck me as a team. Not quite speaking for one another, but never contradicting one another either.

Suddenly I remembered that I needed to get moving. I took a deep breath and checked the time on my computer. Five thirty.

I put my dishes in the dishwasher and went to get dressed. Tonight's reception required more time in my typical five-minute makeup routine. The last time I'd decided to focus more attention on my makeup, I'd stuck a mascara wand in my eye, which had somehow caused me to sneeze, which created raccoon rings on top of a bloodshot eye. It had taken me twenty extra minutes to fix that. So I'd learned not to rush when using implements near my eye. Besides, I wanted to look my best. You never knew who else might be there.

My heart skipped a beat and I paused, thinking about what I was anticipating. Would Gus Knight, my ex-husband and probably the love of my life, be there? Would Kate be there with him? I couldn't help but wonder what his girlfriend looked like. At the same time, I didn't really want to find out.

Not even a list in my notebook could help me sort that out. Instead, I focused on not blinding myself while I put on an extra coat of mascara.

• Six •

One step out the front door made me rethink my footwear. Could I get away with my rubber-soled shoes? Not tonight. Carrying my shoes wouldn't work—all I'd brought with me were dressy boots, Bean boots, and slippers. I made my way down the hill in my fashion-first boots, holding railings and sides of buildings along the way. A fine film of ice covered the sidewalks, now that the sun was gone, and walking was treacherous. But my stubborn streak and deep Yankee frugality wouldn't allow me to call a cab for a few blocks. At least going. Coming home, I might change my mind.

Once I was on the flat part of Beacon Hill, walking was much easier and I began to go through my mental Rolodex, refreshing the names and faces I might see tonight. Searching for a name mid-conversation was a sign of weakness, or so my father had taught me.

The University Club was a private club on Commonwealth Avenue. It was a membership-only organization, with reciprocal memberships in other cities throughout the world. Though not affiliated with a particular educational institution, its mission was to create learning opportunities for its members. All rentals had to support that mission as well, though the club was a popular, albeit tony, wedding site. I supposed members could learn about event planning by hosting weddings. The Cunninghams' event was a benefit/announcement for the Century Project's newest endeavor, a mixed-use development in Boston that promised affordable housing, nonprofit office space, several retail outlets, and a cultural center in addition to million-dollar condos.

After I was confirmed to be on the guest list, I was directed to the coat check. From there I was pointed toward the grand center staircase that led to the ballroom. My constant search for suitable rehearsal space had me in the habit of exploring every site as a potential theater venue, so I took a good look at the beautifully framed map to the left of the staircase, which confirmed this was the way to the second floor. I wiped my shoes one more time and started up the stairs. As I veered to the right to enter the ballroom, I stopped to take it in. With its understated elegance, high ceilings, and open floor plan, this stunning room was built for show.

It was crowded, and people were moving slowly, so I took a closer look around. There were fireplaces at either end along the exterior wall, and both were lit. Bars were set up at each end of the room. Along the wall facing the doorway, between the fireplaces, was a table of food. There were also wait staff offering food, and trays of wine glasses as well. The glow of the room was warm. I looked up at the sparking chandeliers overhead and then took note of the understated small lights tucked into the crown molding, which provided specific pools of light that added to the ambiance of the room.

Before joining the theater world, I never would have noticed what made a room feel warm; I would merely have experienced the warmth. These days I always noticed the colors that were used, the lighting, the floor coverings, the palette of the paint on the walls, even the smells. The candles on the tables must have been slightly scented, because there was a faint vanilla smell that belied the number of warm bodies jammed in the doorway.

After a large man moved to the side, I realized the reason for the slowdown. The Cunninghams were greeting people as they came into the room. They were expertly moving people forward, and in short order it was my turn to say hello. I started to introduce myself but was stopped by Jerry Cunningham.

"Sully, so good of you to come! Mimi, look who's here."

"Lovely to see you again," Mimi said, leaning forward and kissing the air next to my cheek. "I think we're expecting some paperwork from the Cliffside?"

"Yes, we're submitting a grant for our new production center—"

"Of course, of course!" Jerry said. "I've been looking forward to hearing more about that ever since Hal told us about it. Tell you what—once everyone is in, I'd love to grab a couple of minutes to hear more about the project."

"That would be great," I said, moving along into the room so that the next guest could be greeted. I let out my breath. I didn't have to break the ice anymore about the project. I was glad I'd come and very prepared to talk. It was just a question of when. Given the stream of people entering, I realized it might be a while.

I've always found the problem with these sorts of events to be the food or drink question. Walking around, you can't balance a plate and a glass. So, do you drink, and then eat? Given my empty stomach, I thought the eat-and-then-drink option was safer. Safer still was staying away from foods with leafy green, tooth-sticking substances. Cheese and crackers were a safe option. Happily there were other options as well, including canapés and mini quiches. I grazed for a while, then got a plate and worked the room. I saw Emma and made my way over to her, slowing down so as not to interrupt her conversation. Instead, she used me as a reason to stop hers, gesturing me over.

"Hey, cousin! I didn't see you come in," she said.

"I've been hiding out at the food table. Hello, Hal, good to see you." I leaned over to give him an air kiss.

He didn't return it; instead, he looked a bit distracted. "Sully, I didn't realize you were in town. What brings you to Boston?"

"I'm visiting with Dimitri. He's working on *Romeo and Juliet* over at Bay Rep."

"Babs's swan song with the company," Hal said.

"Swan song?" I asked, forcing my most innocent look to take over.

"Whoops. Too much wine. The news isn't public yet. Babs is making some changes, decided to move on." He didn't say any more, instead drinking the rest of his glass in one gulp. I have to admit, I was impressed that he didn't cough.

"Babs is here too, isn't she? I thought I saw her when I came in," Emma said.

"Is she?" Hal took a deep breath and looked around, then down at his empty glass. "I'm going to get another drink. Anything for you ladies? No? Well, I'll see you later."

Emma and I watched him walk away, and once he was out of earshot, Emma leaned toward me. "Thank heavens you came over," she whispered. "I like Hal a lot, but I wasn't holding up well under his hard sell."

"Hard sell?"

"One of the reasons I didn't make it home before coming here was my meeting with Gus. He suggested we pull out of a deal with Hal's company and the Century Project, at least for the time being while our company is being restructured."

"What kind of deal? If you don't mind me asking?"

"Investment, mostly. We would be providing capital in one of their new development projects, in return for office space and preferred vendor status for the future. It wasn't much, at least not in their world. But you know how things have been going. With the changes at the Whitehall Company we decided to play it conservatively for now, and keep our cash handy."

"Is everything okay?"

"Gus has a bee in his bonnet. That's why he wanted to meet this morning and have a drink with Hal. But yes, everything's fine. Or it will be, according to Gus. He feels like we should keep our cash liquid, and part of the deal with the Cunninghams was a substantial escrow account that we were going to renew terms on. Gus wants us to cash out, step back."

"A lot has happened this year," I said. Like half of your company's executive staff dying, I thought but didn't say aloud. Sometimes I marveled that Emma could get dressed in the morning, never mind help run a company. Time to change the subject. "I picked up Stewart Tracy from the train station. Thanks for letting him stay, by the way. It's way nicer than actors' lodgings normally are."

"Amelia's apartment is a little more utilitarian than Harry's, or even mine, but he should be comfortable. I'm so glad Dad bought the townhouse all those years ago. I'm also glad Brooke preferred modern buildings, otherwise Dad would have probably taken it back over. So anyway... Stewart Tracy. I'll have to pay more attention to what I wear to breakfast."

"Emma, do you have a crush on Stewart?"

"Don't be daft. Of course not. It's only been a ... he's a handsome, charming man. I really enjoyed having him around over the holidays. He helped us all take our minds off everything. That's all."

"I'd believe you if you didn't blush when you said his name," I teased.

"Well, do I remember correctly that you and he had a thing a couple of summers ago? Or so I've heard?" she asked.

"In the past. We're just good friends now. Well, not just friends. 'Just' undermines it. Good friends."

"I wouldn't mind being good friends with Stewart," Emma said, elbowing me gently in the ribs. She looked over my shoulder and swore softly. "Damn, I've got to rescue Gus. Hal's got him cornered. Come with me."

I really didn't have a choice as she took my hand and pulled me across the room. "Gus, look who's here," she announced. Both men stopped talking and turned toward us. I could tell that the conversation hadn't been pleasant.

"Hello, Sully," my ex-husband said, leaning in to give me a quick kiss on the cheek. Gus didn't air kiss, and I felt a surge of happiness when I felt his cheek stubble brush against me. Gus smelled great, damn him.

"Good to see you, Gus." Actually, it was sort of a bag of mixed emotions to see him, but the next introduction helped to focus them.

"Have you met Gus's partner, Kate Smythe? Kate, this is Sully Sullivan," Emma said.

So, this was Kate. Kate was in her early thirties, with a hundred-dollar haircut and the perfect makeup that comes from expensive lines and lots of practice. Her outfit was similar to mine but a better fit, and much hipper. Though we were less than a decade apart, she made me feel very, very old.

Kate had called Gus several times in December when he'd been at my house, but we hadn't ever talked. She was supposed to come with him to see *A Christmas Carol*, but it turned out that he came up alone and left right after the show. Gus and I hadn't spoken since.

I put my hand out, but Kate hesitated before taking it. She must have known who I was, and I wondered exactly *what* she knew. One thing was for sure—she didn't look happy to meet me. I ignored that and shook her hand heartily.

"Nice to meet you, Kate. I've heard so much about you," I lied, letting her hand go. I'd heard very little about her. I'd rectify that later, with Emma.

"Nice to meet you too, Sully. I've heard a lot about you as well." Kate snaked her arm through Gus's and smiled at him. He had the good grace to look uncomfortable. This soap opera, I didn't need.

"You know, I think I need a glass of wine after all," I said. "I don't see any waiters around—I guess I'll head over to the bar. Emma, do you want anything?"

"I'll take a red wine, thanks."

"Here, I'll go with you," Hal said. "I need another one too."

He was quiet as we walked over but had regrouped by the time we got to the bar. "Have you had a chance to talk to Jerry and Mimi?" he asked.

"Just to say hello when I first came in. I'm hoping they can grab a couple of minutes to talk some more, but they seem really busy."

"Jerry's always busy. I'd offer to help, but not sure how much good it would do this week." Hal glanced over and gave me a weak smile. "Never mind me. Just feeling old and worn out. I hired a new person to help with digital marketing, and I met with her this morning. I was supposed to be teaching her the business, but it ended up the other way around. Some of the principles of marketing are the same, but the delivery system? It's a changing field. I can barely keep up. It hit me this afternoon—this is getting to be a young man's game. Young person's game. If you don't stay up on it, you may as well resign yourself to being a buggy whip factory when cars were invented. Useful one minute, outmoded the next."

I smelled Babs's perfume before I turned around to see her approaching us. The transformation from how she'd looked a mere eight hours earlier shocked me. Her makeup was smeared and her shirt was half untucked. Her necklace was slightly askew. Hal absently went to straighten it, but she recoiled at his touch.

"Darling, at some point you have to come up with a new metaphor. That one is getting tired. And besides, didn't you steal it from that play? What was it?" Babs said, intentionally keeping space between herself and her husband.

She was unsteady on her feet, and Hal reached out to put a hand on her elbow. She shook it off. "Sweetheart, your cold medicine seems to be affecting you more than usual," he said.

"Cold medicine. I needed much more than cold medicine to come here tonight after ... but I'm here, my pet. You can't ignore me here."

"Babs, please, for God's sake."

"You owe me, Hal. Don't forget it. You owe me." And with that, Babs wrenched her arm out of his grip and stalked away.

I'd been stepping back slowly during the diatribe. Hal looked down and around slightly. I removed myself from his line of vision and went to the other bar to get the wine. As I waited for them to open a new bottle of Malbec, I watched Babs sashay with a drunken swagger through the party. She stopped for a moment and said something to Jerry Cunningham, poking him in his chest. He clutched her hand in his fist and squeezed it before noticing that folks were paying attention. He let Babs go, then turned and walked away.

Mimi Cunningham stepped in and tossed her drink in Babs's face. Babs said something that I couldn't hear, and Mimi flushed. It was quite a standoff. Two women of the same echelon. Blonded and botoxed to fight the ravages of age. Suited in the latest uniform of pants, silk shirts, fitted jackets, and high-heeled boots. Both of them were far too cultured to let it get past a thrown drink. But for a moment, just a moment, I could almost hear someone whisper "girl fight." Then Mimi laughed and said, "Sorry, Babs, I tripped." Everyone giggled, pretended they believed her, and moved on.

"Bitch, you'll get yours. That's a promise. You'll all get yours," Babs said. She turned to leave. I started to go after her, but Hal appeared by my elbow and held me back.

"Don't bother. Not while she's like this."

"I've never seen her like this," I said.

"It isn't a usual occurrence," he said. "But she's a mean drunk. I've learned to stay out of her way."

Emma walked over to us and took Hal's elbow, steering him toward the food before he got another glass of wine. I watched as Gus went after Babs. She fought him off for a few seconds, but then she let him take her arm and guide her out of the room. I noticed Mimi watching them go.

"Quite the show, wasn't it?" a voice said. I turned to my left and realized Kate had come up and was standing next to me.

"Yes, quite. Not sure what it was about."

"It could be a million things. Babs and Hal are finally breaking up. I thought it was amicable, but obviously not. I think Hal got the Cunninghams in the divorce, which doesn't bode well for Babs and her theater. Bet you know something about that. Sucking up for money, I mean. Isn't that what you do?"

"Some of the time, yes," I said, plastering on a smile. The way Kate was staring was off-putting. "So, does your firm ... do you and Gus work with the Cunninghams?"

"Only when our clients have business with them. I wish we had more direct contact. Since we're working with the Whitehalls, Gus won't let us work for Jerry and Mimi. Conflict of interest. Or so he says. He can be such a stickler sometimes."

I realized that Kate had used the opposite of my eat-and-then-drink approach, and perhaps hadn't bothered with eating at all. She seemed to be a little drunk. One glass of wine and a very warm room and I was feeling the effects of the alcohol myself. But I knew when to switch to water. Kate grabbed another wine glass from the waiter's tray as he passed and took a healthy swig.

"Tell me, Sully, has Gus always been so strident about rules?"

Was Kate always this gregarious?

I thought for a moment before I replied. "Yes, I guess he has been." So was I, back when I was a cop. But I wasn't going to share that insight with Kate. "That's why I was surprised when Gus went into private practice. Working in criminal law, on both sides of the aisle, suited him. I thought he'd even run for District Attorney one day."

"Yeah, his old superhero complex. Well, maybe he feels the same way today. Hell, all of our clients need to pass a morality test. It's exhausting. And ridiculously limiting. Ah well. In for a penny, in for a pound, I guess. He's quite the combination of looks, charm, brains, and money. Plus he's pretty good in the sack." Kate smiled sweetly, and I did everything I could to keep my face neutral. Unfortunately, I couldn't control the blush that rose up on my neck.

"Sully, glad to find you," Emma said, inserting herself between Kate and me. "What say we bid goodbye to the Cunninghams and get out of here? It's getting crowded, too crowded."

"Sounds good to me—"

"Where's Gus?" Kate broke in.

"Gus? I think he left with Babs. Not my turn to mind him, Kate. You should pay more attention."

Kate turned and harrumphed away. "Nice to meet you," I called after her.

"Liar," Emma whispered.

"Shut up," I said. I looked around but didn't see Jerry Cunningham anywhere. "Let's get out of here."

∞

"Well, that little scene with Babs sure broke up the party, didn't it?" Emma asked while we were putting on our coats.

"It really did. I'm sorry I didn't get a chance to talk to the Cunninghams—"

"For the best. They weren't in the best frame of mind after that," Emma said. "I saw Hal say something to them before he left, probably tried to apologize, but they blew him off. I'll call them tomorrow, see if we can all meet for a drink this week."

"Emma, you don't have to—"

"I know I don't have to. I want to. Besides, it will give me a chance to smooth things over. Jerry and Mimi seem to understand why we're stepping away from the Century Project work, but I want to make sure." We stepped out of the front of the University Club. "Wow, is it cold."

"And icy. Be careful," I said. "You mentioned that stepping away was Gus's idea? Do you know what spurred him on?"

"Gus plays it pretty close to the vest, but he's been carefully going through our business records since Dad died. He's also been trying to track what Terry was in charge of, since that tends to be shadier."

I noticed that Emma's tone changed when she referred to her late husband. It was the family business that had kept their marriage together for so long, and it must have really rankled her that Terry's deals could be tainted on top of everything else.

"Did Gus give you any examples of what he's worried about?" I asked.

"No, he wants to make sure he's got all the information straight. But he was pretty firm in his recommendation that we step back from a number of deals, most of which were with the Cunningham Corporation. Tell you what—I'm not going to worry about it tonight. How about if we walk down to the cross street and try to hail a cab home?"

"Sounds good to me," I said. "These boots were not made for walking, at least not on ice." As if to demonstrate, I slipped on the ice a bit and Emma caught me by the elbow. We linked arms and slowed down a bit.

"Meeting Kate must have been interesting," she said as we made our way over icy sidewalks.

"She made Gus sound like some kind of Boy Scout," I said. "Right before telling me he was pretty good in the sack."

Emma stopped short, almost making me collide with her. "She said what?"

I told her about the conversation I'd had with Kate. "I think she was a little tipsy."

"More than a little, I think. We went out before the reception and she slammed back a couple of vodkas."

"No food?"

"No food. She doesn't eat. She only drinks clear liquids, mostly vodka." Emma shook her head. "Gus insists she has a great legal mind, and I agree. She's pretty sharp. But still, I don't know what he's thinking. Sorry, Sully. Is this weird?"

"A little, yes. I didn't know anything about Gus's life for so long, so catching up with it is odd. Especially since it really isn't my business, you know?"

"But you still care. Don't bother to deny it. I can see it when you look at him."

I didn't bother to deny it, or to say anything. We walked another block and then stood at the corner of Commonwealth Avenue and Arlington Street, across the street from the Boston Public Garden. There wasn't a cab in sight, and it was cold.

"I don't have one of those apps on my phone," I said. "How about if we cut through the Public Garden and head back?" I hit the walk sign, then looked over at Emma as she backed up a bit.

"What's the matter, Emma?"

"Rats."

"Rats?"

"Last time I walked through the Public Garden at night there were a ton of rats running around. I guess they come out in the dark."

"They do." I didn't love rats, but I'd gotten used to them over the years. I'd worked a lot of cases at night back in the day. Rats were part of the city. "Would you rather we walk around it? I'm freezing and I need to keep moving."

"I don't even like walking on the sidewalk next to it. Tell you what, how about if we head right instead of left and go to the Bristol for a burger, and then cab it home?"

"Twist my arm," I said. The Four Seasons was one of the city's best hotels, with rooms overlooking the Boston Common. The Bristol Lounge was on the ground floor, and besides being a very nice, comfortable bar, it had great drinks and even better burgers.

Spending time with Emma was more fun than I'd expected. We hadn't spent a lot of time together since I'd moved back to Trevorton, and little of that time had been stress-free. I could tell the events of the past few months had taken their toll, but she looked better than she had before, and actually laughed when I told her about Dimitri's set for *Romeo and Juliet*.

"Well, Babs didn't seem too worried about it tonight, did she?" Emma asked. We were seated in gloriously overstuffed chairs at an intimate, marble-topped table that was full of plates and glasses. We were near the fireplace, and I felt warmer than I had in days.

"She was a very different woman than the one I saw at the theater earlier," I said.

"It seems official that she's quitting the Bay Rep this summer. She talked about posting the job after *Romeo and Juliet* opens. I wonder why she's been so close-mouthed about the move," Emma said.

"Given the way the production is going, she probably wanted to right the ship before she left. Is Hal going with her? It was hard to tell if they were together or not," I said.

"He indicated they were still together when we had our meeting, so I'm confused. Hal's crazy about Babs. She's his second wife, broke up his first marriage, did you know that? I think he'd do anything for her."

"Sounds nice," I said. "Having someone willing to move mountains for you."

"Does it really?" Emma asked. "I used to think it would be, but now I imagine it would be suffocating. I envy what Mimi and Jerry have. It isn't perfect, but they're devoted partners."

"They do seem like quite a team. Can any marriage be that good?"

"Boy, are you cynical," Emma said. "I think they're the real deal. Dedicated to each other and to their businesses. No one gets in the way of that. Ever."

I thought about that kind of love, and envied it a little. Our burgers arrived at that moment, so we took the opportunity to change the subject and move on to small talk.

"What makes these burgers so good?" she asked.

"We probably don't want to know. My father made great burgers—you know what his secret was? A frozen pad of butter in the middle."

"Wow."

"Wow is right. I dream of those burgers. What's great about these are that the fries are also good. Not as good as the Beef & Ale's, but good."

"You're a Beef & Ale aficionado, aren't you?"

"I am," I said. "My home away from home. Besides, cooking has never been my forte. I'm more than happy to have other folks do it for me."

Emma laughed. "I never had to cook, but since I've been living alone, I've taken it up. I actually enjoy it."

"Well, if that sauce you made last night is any indication, you're good at it."

"The sauce is one of the things I cook well. I'm working on building up my repertoire."

"Happily, sauce is versatile," I said.

"Good thing, since I make vats of it. Do you want another drink?"

"No thanks. I'd forgotten that the martinis here are served in fishbowls."

"I know, but they're also delicious. Ready to go?" Emma waved the waiter over and asked for our check. She paid the bill and we started gathering our winter belongings together.

I find winter, especially February, to be exhausting. All the layers of clothes, the ice and sludge, the darkness and the cold. Just exhausting. Add to that my very full day, and I was done in. I wasn't about to fight Emma about taking a cab the few short blocks back to the townhouse.

As I wrapped my scarf around my neck, I saw a blue-and-white pull up across the street and two officers get out and go into the Public Garden. An ambulance came up right afterward, and another police car arrived after that.

"Someone must have fallen on the ice," Emma said. "Or maybe the rats attacked."

I shuddered a little even though we were still inside the bar. We went outside under the heat lamps while the doorman called us a cab. That many police cars, and that hum of activity? It wasn't a slip and fall.

A gust of wind came up, and woke me out of my revery. I was curious about what had happened, but it was no longer my business.

• Seven •

Max was the only one home when I got there. I gave him a little more dry food and finished putting away the few things I'd brought that afternoon. I put the bag of coffee I'd bought right next to the coffeemaker. I took out my shopping list and added to it. Harry had little aside from protein powder and crackers in the cupboards. No junk food whatsoever. That would not do, not if I was going to stay here for a few more days.

I went to bed, intending to add a new note about the evening, but sleep thwarted me. At some point I must have taken off my glasses and turned off the light. Or Harry did it for me. The next thing I knew it was seven o'clock in the morning and Max was standing on my chest, requesting his breakfast. I pushed him off and spent a moment acclimating myself to the room before stumbling into the bathroom.

My room was on the alley side of the building, which meant that buildings blocked the low sun this early. One of the downsides of living on a hill. On the other hand, I couldn't see into other people's windows since the floors were staggered. I leaned forward. Change that. You couldn't see unless you tried. I made a mental note that I needed to close my blinds tonight.

I went to the kitchen and put on the coffee. I fired up my laptop. While it was booting up, I reached into my purse and took out the bottle of Advil. Burger or no, two glasses of wine and a martini took their toll. My father had always warned me not to mix the grape and the grain. I should have taken heed.

I opened up Boston.com and almost did a spit take when I saw the "breaking news" headline: *"Identity of Public Garden murder victim rumored to be Mimi Cunningham. Press conference to be held soon."*

Wait—what? Mimi Cunningham? A murder victim? I'd just seen her. Was that what the police car went in for? I shook the cobwebs out of my head and read the entire story. Not that there was much. Just a series of bulletins. Body discovered. White, middle-aged. Robbery suspected. Strangled. Identity pending informing next of kin.

Robbery and strangulation? Not likely, I thought. At least not in that order. Strangulation was a crime of passion. And hard to do. Overkill for a robbery. It left trace evidence. No, at night, in a park, a robbery would have been simply a bash and grab. Not to say that a victim couldn't end up dead, but still.

Death is always hard; murder just made it infinitely harder. Of course, I was making leaps. Educated leaps, but leaps nonetheless. Maybe it was an accident? Perhaps Mimi's scarf or necklace got caught in the robber's bike as he road away? If the robber had a bike. Or maybe he tried to grab her necklace and she got strangled in the process? I shook my head. The ghost of Isadora Duncan wasn't likely to show up here.

I was doing a Google search for any other information when I heard my cell phone ring. I went over to my coat and found it in my pocket. Down to twenty-five percent. I'd forgotten to charge it last night. Now where had I put the charger?

"Sully, did you hear about Mimi?" Emma asked as soon as I answered the phone.

"Reading about it on the web as we speak."

"Coffee made?"

"Of course."

"I'm on my way down."

She must have been on her way the minute I picked up, because a second later she was at the door. I hurried into my room and grabbed a fleece to put over my pajamas. I also checked to make sure Harry's door was tightly shut before I let her in. Emma had on yoga pants and a T-shirt, with a light jacket on top. She was wearing fleece slippers and had brought a coffee cake with her. Bless her.

"I was on the treadmill and had the TV on, and heard the news." She went into the kitchen and helped herself to a cup of coffee while I dished up the cake. "Can you believe it?"

"Remember when we were leaving the bar? The police cars? I thought something must be up, but I had no idea."

"That means it must have happened right around when we were having dinner." Emma shuddered. "How horrible."

"It really is." I was more concerned for Emma than anything. She'd been through so much in the past few months. But another murder? Too much for most to take. Emma was of tough Yankee stock, but still.

"Should we tell someone? About the timing?" she asked.

"I'm sure they'll be checking guest lists at nearby restaurants and will be in touch. I'm not even sure who we would talk to." That was a bit of a lie. I hadn't left the police department on the best of terms, and I didn't relish the idea of contacting old friends turned foes. "Tell you what, give Gus a call. He can reach out to them."

"Great idea." She took out her phone and hit one of the speed dial buttons.

"I hope you don't wake up Kate," I said.

Emma made a face and spoke into the phone. "Gus, it's Emma. Did you hear about Mimi? I think we should go to the police, don't you think? Help however we can? Get ahead of this. Call me."

"Get ahead of what, Emma?"

"Sully, another murder? And I'm close by? Again? It's only a matter of time before the press catches on and starts chasing me."

"You were with me at the Bristol. The whole time."

"Doesn't matter. The press is going to eat this up. And now is not the time." She sipped her coffee and sighed. "Sorry, I know that sounds harsh. But you know what it was like over the holidays. And there we were protected by the gates at the house. Here we're out in the open."

"You could head back up to Trevorton," I said, though I didn't think it was a good idea to leave town. "Maybe Gus could suggest a PR firm to help? Or Hal could? Though Hal will be pretty upset, I'd imagine—"

"Sully, you're a brick, you know that?" That was a phrase my mother had used as well. It meant strong, steady, and immovable. It also meant thick, but I deferred to context. "Does anything ever freak you out?"

"A lot freaks me out, but panic serves no purpose. And this doesn't come close to freaking me out. I don't know much about managing the press, but it seems to me that you'd only be a story for half a second. The Cunninghams have enough of their own story going on to keep the spotlight. Right?"

"Right. Right." But she didn't sound convinced, and as if to emphasize the point she hit redial. "Gus? Call me." She hung up and dialed another number. "Kate, it's Emma Whitehall. Call me when you get this." She hung up again and started to fidget. She started sending what I assumed were follow-up texts. "Would you mind if

I check my email on your computer? So much easier than on my phone and I'm too lazy to go upstairs."

"Sure, of course." I turned the computer toward her. While Emma clicked away, I went back in my room and found my charger and my notebook. I brought them both back to the kitchen, and plugged my phone in. I sat down with my book and started to write down notes.

"What are you writing, Sully?"

"Notes from last night, while they're still somewhat fresh. Just in case. Old habit, but you'd be surprised what details you forget, and how quickly."

"I do the same thing after meetings. Someone else takes the minutes. But I always write a meeting memo for my own files. I notice if someone seemed out of sorts, or nervous. Or was a particular jackass. Gives context to the official notes."

"Exactly." My notes were just that. Notes. Timelines. Some questions. Nothing too detailed, or reflecting too much concern. Just old habit.

Emma headed back upstairs to get ready for work. She tried to call Jerry Cunningham before she left. She got his voicemail and left a message telling him how sorry she was, and that she was available any time for anything he needed. I was surprised that Jerry's voicemail wasn't full. He either had a better phone plan than I did or he was keeping up with his messages.

Harry woke up at nine, and looked ragged. "I'm inviting Stewart up for breakfast, is that okay?"

"That's fine." And it was. But it also meant I was getting dressed. Women and gay men could see me in my flannel poodle PJs, but ex-boyfriends? Not so much. I took a quick shower and got dressed.

My day's outfit looked much like Emma's morning ensemble—workout pants, a T-shirt, and a warm fleece. A little makeup in honor of Stewart's presence and I went out to meet my public.

The boys were sitting around the table, scripts splayed and coffee cake demolished in front of them. They were deep in discussion, so I grabbed the coffeepot and brought it back into the kitchen to make another pot. Third of the day. I needed to buy more coffee, but then again, I might not be staying after all. Not much point, since I wouldn't be able to see Jerry Cunningham to talk about the grant. And hopefully Dimitri and the gang had things under control. I'd find out soon enough.

"More coffee, gents?" I asked. "Harry, you still caffeine-free?"

"Not since rehearsals started. Fill her up, Sully."

I poured Harry's, black, and then Stewart's. I handed him the cream. "How goes it?" I asked.

"Shh, Sully. We went out after rehearsal. For a couple of drinks. Then a couple more."

I grabbed the Advil and brought it back to the table. "I went out with Emma and had a bit of a headache myself this morning. Then I saw the news." I told them about the murder. I skipped the part about Babs being out of control at the reception. They were working with her, and I thought she deserved a little privacy, at least from me. They both murmured concern and then went back to their scripts.

"What time is your call?" I asked after a while.

"Not till noon. Thank God. Dimitri is doing some table work with Juliet and the Nurse this morning. Trying to undo some of the damage from Pierre," Harry said.

"How's it going?" I asked.

"How's it going ... how do you think it's going, Stewart? From an outside perspective."

Stewart looked over at Harry and shrugged. He turned toward me. "We're behind, of course. But it's a great group. They've worked together for a long time. Such are the benefits of a repertory company. I've worked with a couple of the actors before."

"A few of the Bay Rep actors—Ruth, Stephanie, Ray, Tina, Bob—they've worked up at the Cliffside several times when Bay Rep is closed for the summer. Are they all in this production?" I asked.

"Yes, Ruth is playing the Nurse. Stephanie is Lady Capulet. Ray is Tybalt. Is that right? Or is he Benvolio now? There were a couple more switches yesterday based on which roles they'd played before. Anyway, having a full cast is great. And Dimitri has rediscovered his footing, despite the set. Still…"

"Still?" I looked at both men. "Still what?"

"Still, I'm surprised they aren't doing more to accommodate Dimitri regarding the designs," Harry said. "I sort of get the set issues. But costumes? There should be some give with costumes. I know that budgets are tight, but still."

"Dimitri and Cassandra were going to talk to Babs yesterday—"

"But she never came back. Holly told them there was no more money, but they all agreed to talk to Babs together. Holly's on our side, which is great, but—"

"There are no sides in all of this," I said. "Babs is just trying to watch the budget, make sure the company takes the least amount of a hit it can. Don't pit Holly against Babs. That's not good for anyone."

"Duly noted," Harry said. "Thanks for reminding us all we're on the same team. Holly's in a spot, and I think she could use some help—"

"Babs is the managing director," I said.

"She's been gone a lot," Harry said. "I think that you could help Holly see the bigger picture."

"I talked to her yesterday, told her to call me."

"Yeah, well, she's not going to do that. You know how it is, Sully. Situations like this, the budget gets blown up a little. We were wondering if you could come in and talk with Holly again," he said as he poured me more coffee.

"Who's we? Why?"

"Stewart and I brought it up with the cast after Dimitri left with Connie last night. They agree it might be a good idea, especially if Babs isn't around today. Holly could use some 'how to deal with Dimitri' lessons. She just keeps saying no, or that she can't, and then he yells."

"I asked him to be quieter—"

"You might as well ask a bird not to sing," Stewart said. "He isn't yelling at her, he's yelling at the situation. But she's having trouble parsing that under the circumstances. She goes back to the office and cries. And comes back out and pretends she wasn't crying and says no again. I feel sorry for the woman."

Dimitri had gone through a number of general managers at the Cliffside before I came aboard. "So you want me to babysit Dimitri?" I said. I felt bad that Holly was taking it so personally. One of the things that made me a good managing director was that yelling didn't bother me. I'd dealt with far worse in my previous career.

"The yelling fits get in the way of the rehearsal process. Just when we're getting somewhere, Holly comes in and it's gone. If you could be a buffer, just for today? And maybe tomorrow unless Babs comes in?"

"What's in it for me? Aside from having to hear rehearsals of *Romeo and Juliet* for hours?"

"Come on, Sully, I know you love it. If you insist, I'll come up with other ways to make it worth your while." Stewart raised his eyebrows and smiled lasciviously. But the underlying smile was genuine, as was the tone. Ah Stewart. What was the term? Friends with benefits? Not a bad concept. Maybe.

"Promises, promises." I said, looking away and catching Harry's amused eye. "You both owe me. But happily for you, I have a lot of grant writing to do, and I can do it at the theater as easily as I can here."

"One more thing. Please, can we drive? I'll pay for parking," Harry said. "And can we hit Trader Joe's on the way? We need some rehearsal food and Connie is car-free. We need to do our part to bolster the company."

Getting Stewart and Harry through Trader Joe's was like herding cats. Such a great variety of junk food that you can pretend is a little good for you. We ended up with a very full cart. As I bagged the groceries, I tried to sort them. I'd stocked up on soy chips and nuts and coffee and other goodies to bring home. I packed a Dimitri bag, and Harry and Stewart grabbed some food for rehearsals. I made a bag for the office staff. I did a quick calorie count of the food in the car and shook my head. My step count was pitiful these days. I really needed to get a walk in, or better yet, a run. I always left a change of clothes in the car in hopes that I would get a work out in during the day. They'd been in the car since September.

We got to the theater around eleven thirty. I could hear Dimitri's bellows from the lobby. Both Harry and Stewart waved me into the theater, and Stewart patted my butt as I walked by him. Sure enough, Dimitri was holding court at the foot of the stage, lost in a dramatic tirade. Connie tried to interrupt but it was difficult, to say the least. He'd worked up a full head of steam. Holly was half sitting, half leaning on the armrest of a chair. I had to give her props; she was taking it. But I could also tell that she was struggling, either to get a word in edgewise or not to cry. She was wearing a suit today, but it was a far cry from Babs's designer piece. More of a Primark or H&M suit. More my kind of suit, frankly.

"I have never, ever had such a lack of support—" Dimitri started.

"Sure you have, Dimitri," I said, making my way down the aisle. "Remember two summers ago when you wanted to use a trampoline for the set of *Twelfth Night*? No one thought that was a good idea. We all said no." I walked over and patted his arm. My version of an embrace. Usually it worked to calm him down.

"Sully, no jokes. This is amateur hour around here, and I'm sick of it."

"I'm sure Holly is doing her best. Holly, sorry to interrupt. I need Dimitri to look over some grant applications, hope you don't mind the intrusion. Is Babs in yet? I'd love to say hi."

"I haven't seen her yet," Holly said, standing up.

"Maybe I'll hang for a bit. Is that okay with you? I'll just sit in the back."

"As long as Dimitri doesn't mind," she said, sidling over to the door.

"No, he doesn't mind. He loves having me in the room, don't you, Dimitri?" Dimitri glared at me, but I didn't break away from his glaze. The group around us dispersed. Connie winked at me and followed Ron backstage.

"Seriously, Dimitri, do you have a sec?" I asked. "I do want to run a couple of grant things by you."

"Harrumph."

"I bought you some orange gel sticks from Trader Joe's. It's a little early for candy, I know, but they're orange. Sort of a breakfast flavor."

"You know I love those," Dimitri said, following me to the back of the theater. We both sat down and I handed him his bag.

"I know. I bought several boxes," I said.

"Bless you." He took the candy out and opened the top of the box. He took a deep inhale, then closed the lid back up. Dimitri was a sensory person and believed firmly in delayed gratification. He'd have to earn a jelly stick. "All right, ask me your grant questions, Sully. Rehearsal starts at noon."

I handed him a bottle of water. "I also got you some breakfast bars, almonds, a bag of apples, some string cheese, and this water. Fill the bottle up three times today. You have to eat, Dimitri."

"Don't mother me, Sully," he said, rifling through the bag and finding the breakfast bars. He ripped one open with his teeth. "Thank you," he said, his mouth half full. "Are you here to babysit?"

"Yes and no. Just want to make sure you're okay."

"I'm fine, but frustrated. We can make two changes that'll be all the difference. I want Cassandra to change the costume designs. We need color on stage. She ran a dye test, but we feel that dyeing the white clothes will muddy it even more. She wants to build a few pieces and needs a budget for that."

"What's the second thing?"

"Ron thinks he has an idea of what we can do to enable us to paint the set. There's a place down near the Cape that sells sailcloth. We think if he cuts it, and slaps pieces on the shiny white, he can paint them to add more depth to the set. Sailcloth has more texture than muslin and will stand up to wear and tear."

"And the problem is?"

"Both of these changes cost money. Not huge money, but more money than Holly feels like she can authorize on her own."

"So you need Babs to be here."

"In this situation Holly is fairly useless. Apparently this production has been a money pit, and we can't add any more money into the budget to cover the costs."

"I just want to remind you, Dimitri, that Holly is in a tough situation. Since you're a guest director, she's trying to toe the company line while helping. You need to cut her some slack."

"Why should I—"

"I heard you made her cry, Dimitri. More than once."

"I did not."

"You did. Probably not on purpose, but I expected better. Remember, you're representing all of us down here. You want us to be known as the thugs from up on the north shore?"

"I cannot be held responsible for someone's emotional outbursts."

"You can when you cause them. Step back, Dimitri. How much can you do without affecting the budget? Are you and Cassandra on the same page?"

"We are. We don't even want period costumes. Just color. Hoping that from chaos she can create a design. We can pull from stock. Rent from other companies. We just need something to start with."

"So, start. You're the director. Get Cassandra to figure out a game plan and start. Don't look for approval. Just do it. And make sure it doesn't cost anything. At least not at the beginning. Better to ask for forgiveness than permission. Unless it's from me. Then you'd better have permission. Seriously, Dimitri, why so nervous? Bay Rep is a big company. An important company. And they asked you to step in because you're good. So show 'em. Figure this out. But try not to make people cry. Okay?"

"Cassandra has a lot riding on this as well."

"Her ability to change mid-stream sounds like a great behind-the-scenes story angle, doesn't it? Don't they blog here? We can make her out to be the hero. And if it doesn't work, or people miss the white on white, so be it. You take the hit. Regarding the set fix, let me go talk to Holly. Maybe there's a way to make it work and I can help her think creatively. How does that sound?"

"I'm going to take a hit on this no matter what," Dimitri said.

"Or get the glory. Stewart says it's a great company of actors. He and Harry are pretty excited."

"Are they?" Dimitri asked.

"Of course they are. They have faith. So do I, for what that's worth."

"It's worth a great deal, Sully."

"Then don't sweat the rest of it. Just tell the story. This is a great team, so let them help you. I'll talk to Holly."

"You'll stick around a bit this afternoon? Let me know what you think?"

"Of course. I wasn't joking about the grant applications. I can just as easily work here. It *will* mean that I'll have a computer in the theater." Computer and cell phone lights in the house were Dimitri's pet peeves.

"For this, and for you, I will make an exception." He stood up and stretched. I reached down and handed him the bag of food. He took it and walked up the aisle to the edge of the stage, where several people were standing over a board that had been painted to demonstrate the solution Ron had come up with. Dimitri turned to me and put down the bag. He pointed to the board and put both hands together as if in prayer.

"I'll do what I can," I yelled down the aisle.

• Eight •

Given what happened, we need to assume that the Century Foundation may not be reading grants anytime soon, my development director wrote in an email. My first reaction was disappointed frustration, but then I caught myself. A woman had been murdered and we were worrying about the grant. *Send in the application anyway, but here are the other applications you've been working on. They look good; I've made a few tweaks. I've got the board working on making connections at the foundations. Will you have time to look them over today?*

I'll make the time, I emailed back.

She'd attached three applications, ready to be printed out and proofed before they were submitted. I was glad there was a plan B. And C. And D. One way or the other, we needed to get this funding on track if the production center was going to be at least somewhat built by the summer season.

I carried my laptop back to Holly's office, hoping to borrow a printer. I found Holly at her desk, surrounded by piles of paper. She was staring at the wall in front of her, her shoulders slouched forward.

"Hi, Holly. Sorry to interrupt. I wondered if I could borrow a printer?"

"Um. Sure, I guess so," she said, straightening up a bit. "Do you want to send me the document and I can do it for you?"

"No thanks. I can just connect to this printer. Is that okay?" I pointed to a LaserJet in the corner. The model was very close to the one I had back in my office, so I was hoping it wouldn't require any new software. Fortunately, it worked. Unfortunately, each application was several pages long, and the printer was a little slow.

After a minute or so of Holly and I ignoring each other, I thought that I should try and break the ice. She must have had the same thought.

"No, you first," I said, after we'd done the double talk tango.

"I just wanted to thank you for talking to Dimitri. Harry says that he'll probably get a little easier to deal with. I mean, well … "

"Less of a pain is the ass is all I can help you with. Easier won't happen. That said, Dimitri's a good guy and a great director. And, I dare say, he's a little nervous. You guys are a big deal."

"Yeah, I guess we are. My first paying job in the theater was with Les Pathes. Do you know them?" I nodded. Les Pathes was a company that did interdisciplinary work and toured it. They operated on a small budget and spent long periods between productions raising money and rehearsing. "I loved the company, but it was hard work, and I didn't love worrying about my bills all the time. I thought it would be so much easier working here, with real budgets and a staff. But it's just as stressful except on a bigger scale. You know?"

"The Cliffside is my first theater gig, but I can imagine. Are you glad you made the switch?" I could see that she was struggling with the answer, so I let her off the hook. "At least you're getting lots of great experience. And Babs must be a good mentor."

I'd always heard good things about Babs Allyn and Bay Rep, but I was beginning to wonder how true they were. Morale seemed low, and this *Romeo and Juliet* situation would have kept me at the theater, not away from it.

"She was. Is. She's got a lot going on right now," Holly said, fidgeting with a binder clip she'd picked up.

I wanted to ask her more, but Holly was shutting down. I admired her professionalism, but I didn't want to pander to her and say so aloud.

"Holly, there is one thing that Dimitri mentioned. Not that this is my business in the least, and I know it's caused a ruckus. Has Cassandra spoken with you today?"

"No, not today. We talked last night, but she didn't like my answer. I still haven't been able to reach Babs, and Cassandra insists she'll only speak with Babs."

Of course she would only speak with Babs. Cassandra was a talented costume designer with an ego that eclipsed almost anyone else I'd ever met. In my life.

"I haven't spoken to her either," I said, "but Dimitri mentioned that they were talking about new designs, probably mostly pulled from her stock."

"I've been trying to figure out if I can throw them any more money. I have an idea, but I should check with Babs first. Don't you think?"

"Of course. Though if you can figure it out without it affecting the overall budget too much, maybe she'd be grateful that she didn't need to deal with it. Just a thought. Is there any room, anywhere, to move money around?"

"Well, I understand that Stewart is staying with you? Will he have housing for the whole run?"

"He and Harry both. Might that save some money?"

"Some." She showed me a number. "I heard that they're also looking at getting some fabric for the set—"

"So they can paint it, from what I understand."

"I'm making some calls, trying to see what I can do to get it okayed for set use, and get a better price. I'm really trying. I think I can get it for about half the amount we're saving on housing. So I'm wondering if the other half could go for costumes."

"That's good thinking," I said.

"Thanks. To me this seems like a wash. Am I missing something?"

I asked Holly a few more questions, and she had answers for each. It would have been easier for me to just look at the budget, but I didn't want to overstep. Besides, Holly being able to answer questions seemed to buoy her confidence. "Sounds to me like you've really thought this through," I said.

"I know the company doesn't think that's true, but I am trying," she said.

"Keep looking at the budget, see what you can do to move things around. My assumption is always that as long as the bottom line stays the same, you can play with expenses a bit," I said.

"That's what I thought, but I'm not sure if Babs will think the same way."

"Tell you what. When she gets back, why don't we meet with her together and talk it through."

"Thank you for the offer. I may take you up on it," Holly said. She smiled for the first time that day.

"You know, Holly, if I've learned one thing doing this job it's that few people are going to tell you you're doing a good job. Most folks think you exist to say no. So let me say this—you're doing a good job."

The last of the applications had printed out, so I unhooked my computer. "Do you have a couple of binder clips I could borrow? While I'm collating, why don't you draft an email to Babs and run it by me?"

"That would be great. Thank you, Sully."

"Thank you Sully indeed. Glad to see that someone is helping Holly run this ship. Where the hell is Babs?" Hal Maxwell leaned through the doorway, looking done in.

"Uncle Hal, how are you?" Holly ran up and gave him a quick hug around his neck. Then, as if she'd suddenly remembered I was there, she let go and took a step back. "I've been calling and texting. I even went by your house early this morning, but no one was there."

Hal looked pained. He turned his hand over and ran his knuckles along Holly's cheek. "Oh, my sweet girl, I'm sorry I worried you. I wouldn't do that for anything. You know that, right? I must have been home. Maybe I didn't hear the bell? But then Jerry called me in the middle of the night, asked me to come down—"

"Jerry? Is everything all right?" Holly asked.

"You haven't heard?" Hal turned to me. I hadn't made the connection, but of course Holly must have known Mimi Cunningham. I was doing too good a job at compartmentalizing my life these days.

"I'm sorry, Holly," Hal said. "I was hoping you already knew. I hate to have to be the one to tell you this, but Mimi Cunningham was found dead."

"Dead? What, did she have a heart attack or something?" Holly asked.

Hal was silent, so I filled in. "Holly, I don't know any of the details. From what I've read, they think it was foul play."

"I'm not surprised," Holly said. Aside from her initial reaction, she was very calm.

"You don't mean that, Holly," Hal said.

"Yes, I do mean that. You and I both know she knew what happened to my dad and never told us. Who knows what other secrets she was hurting people by keeping?"

"Holly—" Hal looked at me anxiously.

"Didn't you tell me she was the last person to see him alive? Did I tell you she threatened to call the cops last time I went to see her to ask about him? I'm not sorry she's dead. She was a terrible person. I don't even feel bad for saying that."

"You're in shock, sweetheart," Hal said. "We don't want to give Sully the wrong idea." He turned toward me. "Sully, Holly's been under a lot of stress this past year. I'm sure you can imagine."

"Of course—"

"The Cunninghams were, at best, secretive," Hal said. "They didn't do a lot to help us try and find out what happened to Martin. But I really believe with all my heart that they had nothing to do with his disappearance."

"Well, you believe more than I do," Holly said. "I think they know what happened. I wish that you or Babs remembered something. Anyway, maybe Jerry will have a change of heart now. I always thought he was the nicer of the two. I'll call him."

"Holly, maybe you should give him a few days to get his bearings. This must be a hard time," Hal said.

"I'll give him a few days, Uncle Hal," she said. "I've got some sense of the social niceties. I'll even go to the funeral if you think I should. That's what a nice gal I am."

Hal looked like he was going to say something more, but I interrupted. I felt as if I'd stepped into the middle of a family squabble, and I wanted to leave, but not before I asked Hal a couple questions.

"Hal, have you heard from Babs today? Holly hasn't heard from her and neither have I. Not that I need to, but she said we'd find some time to chat."

I looked at Hal and tried to read his face. He fumbled in his coat pocket and pulled out his phone.

"She sent me this text. We had some words yesterday. Last night, after the unfortunate incident at the University Club, she made it clear she needed some time to think. Here's the text—she says she's going to go up to our place in Vermont for a few days. That she's going to reach out to you as well. Holly—"

Holly went over to her desk and picked up her phone. "Argh, I turned the volume off earlier. Yes, here it is, she texted me around five o'clock in the morning—"

"That's when she texted me," Hal said.

"Yup, told me the same thing. 'Heading up to Vermont.'" Holly took a deep breath and put her phone in her pocket. "I thought you closed your house down for the winter?" she asked Hal.

"No, we keep it open for ski weekends. Bring clients up, let them stay for the weekend. We did shut down the phone, though. Cell phone is spotty up there—"

"I remember," Holly said. "Last summer I had to go way down to the end of the dock, loop my arm around the piling, and lean out over the water. That was the only way I could get any cell reception. I can't believe she'd leave without talking to me first."

"She's not herself these days," Hal said. "We've been arguing a bit, trying to figure out what the next steps look like for both of us. I also think—Holly honey, I'm sorry to say this, but the anniversary of your dad's death is coming up soon, and that's affecting Babs more than she wants to let on. I know we've all been thinking about him a lot lately. She always thought he'd come back, that he just went away to get himself together—"

"To dry out, you mean," Holly said quietly. "I thought that must be it, especially after he sent that postcard. But it's been almost a year."

"Your dad had his demons, but he was a good man. Anyway, maybe she's feeling some kind of delayed grief. I'm sorry she left you in the lurch." Hal turned toward me. "Sully, I hate to even ask—"

"You don't have to ask anything," I said. I reached over and grabbed Holly's hand, squeezed it gently, and let it go. "Holly's got this. I'm happy to talk it through with her. I don't know the ins and outs of Bay Rep, but I do know how to manage a budget. We won't screw anything up too badly, will we Holly?"

"I hope not," she said quietly. "Hal, if you hear from Babs, please have her call me. I just want to hear her voice."

Hal's phone buzzed. He looked down at the message and frowned. "It's the—listen, I'm sorry, I need to take this. I'll check in with you later, okay, Holly? Sully, thanks for pitching in. I'm glad you're here." He gave Holly a brief half hug as he answered the phone and scurried out of the room.

"I'm glad you're here too, Sully," Holly said. "You must think I'm terrible, what I said about Mimi. Of course I'm not glad she's dead. It's just that—it's been an awful year. Now that Babs isn't here ..."

"Listen, do you have Babs's address up in Vermont?" I asked.

"I do somewhere. Why?"

"I know some folks up there. They're around Woodstock, right? I remember Babs mentioning it once. I'll ask somebody to go by the house and have her call in. I don't want to intrude. I mean, that's a long way to go to be alone. But it's hard to believe she'd leave you in the lurch like this—"

Holly sighed. "Uncle Hal's right. The anniversary of my dad's disappearance is affecting us both. Maybe he really is gone."

"What do you mean?" I asked gently.

"A couple of weeks after he disappeared, I got that postcard from him. He told me to hang tight, he'd be in touch."

"Do you have the postcard?"

"No, Babs asked to borrow it a few weeks ago. She told me she was going to try and find out what really happened, and that she needed to show it to someone. Maybe that's what she's doing."

"Maybe," I said. "Or maybe it's affecting her and she needed to take a break. I'd still like to talk to her and get her blessing to help you."

"I'll text you the address of the Vermont house when I find it. I'm sure I've got it somewhere," Holly said. She took a deep breath and her eyes got watery. "I need to get some fresh air, clear my brain a little bit. Would you do me a huge favor?"

"Sure. What you need?" I asked.

"Would you go talk to Cassandra? Float the number we talked about by her?"

"Sure, of course. I'll be happy to talk to Cassandra," I lied.

How did I get myself in these situations? Even off-duty, I had to go talk to one of the most difficult people I knew.

"Well, Sully Sullivan, as I live and breathe. Thought you were trying to ignore me. I was starting to take it personally."

"Now Cassandra, why would I be trying to avoid talking to you?" I said. Cassandra stood in the middle of the theater, draping pieces of fabric on the backs of the seats in front of her.

"Let me count the ways, right, Sully?" Cassandra set the bag of fabric on the seat next to her. She stepped out into the aisle and opened her arms wide. I stepped in and gave her a big hug. She let go, stepped back, and looked me over from head to toe, shaking her head. I knew I disappointed her. I always did. I made no effort to dress to impress, barely wore makeup, and owned enough accessories to fit in a gallon-sized baggie. Scarves included. Cassandra had never met an accessory she didn't like and always used scarves to add a splash of color, either as a headwrap or around her neck. Sometimes both. Her bangles jangled and her earrings were always a work of art. She made them herself, and also made necklaces and other pieces of jewelry. She sold them on Etsy, one of the many ways she kept revenue coming in, helping her to live her artist life. She made more money working on movies, but her heart was in theater.

I knew she felt about Bay Rep as Dimitri did, that it was an amazing opportunity she didn't want to take lightly.

"I was only planning on being here for a couple of days," I said, zipping up my fleece so she couldn't see the grease stain in the middle of my shirt. "I'll admit it, it's all yoga pants and sweatshirts from here on out."

"You're killing me slowly. You know that, Sully?" Cassandra said. "I'll try to pull some scarfs together for you, other things to brighten you up. You look like a college student, and a badly dressed one at that. It just won't do. You should represent the Cliffside a bit better than that, my friend."

"You're right, of course," I said, pulling my fleece down. "I'm in off-season mode. You must love working with Babs Allyn. She dresses to the nines."

"She does dress beautifully, but honestly? I prefer working with you. At least you answer my questions and let me know where I stand, even if it doesn't make me happy. Babs has been ignoring the entire situation, if you want my honest opinion. She's given up. Who in their right mind would let a production of *Romeo and Juliet* happen with all-white costumes when the set was going to be all white? I'm asking you now. Who?" Cassandra shook her head, her braids gently clicking together in disbelief. "I tried to ask questions, but I was told to shut up and do my job. So I did. I was hoping someone would come to their senses at some point."

"That set is a challenge, isn't it?"

"In the original design, the set had a bit more color, but then Pierre changed it. The costumes have always been what they are, but I was hired to coordinate their creation, not design."

"How's the process been?" I asked.

"The paycheck here is better than the Cliffside, but it's been a rough couple of months, for a lot of reasons. I'd love to work with the company when they're less stressed, but I'm not sure that's going to happen anytime soon."

"The idea behind the design is sort of interesting," I said. "But if Pierre wanted monochromatic, why didn't it include black, white, maybe some grays? But all white, with letters for the families?"

"You see, you've got the instincts," Cassandra said. "Even if you start *Romeo and Juliet* with one family in black, one family in white, and then put Romeo and Juliet in grays at the end, that's something. Obvious storytelling—too obvious—but at least it makes sense. But this plan? He said everyone should be a blank slate, no storytelling with the costumes. Can you imagine? That just doesn't work for me. But like I said, I was more of a hired hand, so I made it work."

Cassandra fingered her notebook, where I imagined she'd been doing drawings since Dimitri had called her and told her he was coming aboard. "Are those your ideas?" I asked.

"Some of them, yes. I was trying to build on the white jeans and T-shirts, since they're all in the shop ready to go."

"They must've saved some money on the budget that way—"

Cassandra sighed. "You'd think, wouldn't you? But these weren't just any white jeans. Pierre insisted on specific jeans, imported. From Europe. I don't even want to tell you how much each pair cost. It would make your heart ache, honestly it would."

"Can you dye them?" I looked through Cassandra's drawings, which, as always, went from her ultimate dreams down to the realities of the production. She always showed me that range, helping me see what would be possible if we found a bit more money. Cassandra had designed our production of *Romeo and Juliet*, and I recognized some of her dream costumes as ones she'd shown me back then. Back when she still thought she had a chance of talking Dimitri out of the dystopic version of *Romeo and Juliet* he eventually put onstage.

Ultimately, she'd risen to his concepts, delivering futuristic costumes that gave us all a thrill under the summer lights.

Someday Cassandra would be able to design her dream production of a *Romeo and Juliet*. But not this time. I flipped to the end of her drawings and saw what she had come up with for this production. I recognized some of the pieces from previous designs for other shows, many of which she'd done for us. Reusing pieces made a lot of sense, given everything about this production. I noticed that both Romeo and Juliet wore white jeans, but with different tops, of course. I suspected that these were the pieces Cassandra was mostly focused on; the pieces she would make for this production. The pieces that would be the Cassandra signature. They both looked ornate and complicated. And expensive. I suspect they were all three, but that Cassandra would do what she could to mitigate the cost.

"Okay, Cassandra, bottom line. Tell me what you need. I'm helping Holly navigate these waters since Babs is out of town for a few days. We could go back and forth, play the games. But neither one of us have time for that. I suspect you want to get moving on this design. Not sure how you can pull this off in such short order, but you are a bit of a miracle worker."

"Don't blow smoke, Sully," Cassandra said. "It doesn't suit you. You know I'll do what I can. My name's on the line too. I'm not going to leave Dimitri hanging. I do need some money, though."

"Do you have a piece of paper I can use?"

"Sure." Cassandra tore a piece off the back of her sketchbook and handed it to me. At the top I wrote *budget increase for costumes* and below that I wrote a figure.

"Will that help?" The figure I wrote was a little bit less than the figure Holly was considering. Cassandra always enjoyed a negotiation. I looked up at the set—still a bright, shiny white. I imagined actors in costumes, lights, maybe with some props. There was a lot that could affect the set. I couldn't make a decision for the company, but if push came to shove, I'd counsel Holly to pour more money into costumes if possible.

Cassandra wrote down another figure, a little over what Holly had had in mind. I wrote down Holly's figure.

"I think I might be able to talk them into this. Afraid that might be it."

"Then that will have to do. Trust me, Sully. The audience will be grateful that we're telling a story with the costumes. Folks pay attention to what you wear. That's why it matters. They pay more attention to that sometimes then anything else. Which is why"—she looked at my yoga pants with disdain—"you need to let me get you some pizazz."

"All right, you win. I'll try to jazz it up while I'm here in the big city." I got up and walked down the center aisle, out into the lobby. I texted Holly: *Cassandra's all set*. I sent the budget number.

Great, thanks, she replied.

I'm going out for a bit, I texted. *I need to buy a scarf.*

I also needed some fresh air. To clear the cobwebs. Theater folks live by the adage, "The show must go on." No matter what, the job takes precedence. Come to think of it, cops work by the same adage. No matter what, the work gets the attention. And what was I doing? I'd put Mimi's death into a box and ignored it.

I put my coat back on and set out to the shops on the next block. A little window-shopping, a realignment of my humanity. I sighed and thought about Mimi Cunningham. A woman was dead, and I'd only been thinking about how that affected my grant application. I needed to do better, to be better, than that.

• Nine •

The thing about a walk in February is that the clear blue skies always make it seem like a good idea while you're inside. But once you set foot outside, you realize you need a destination. The bone-rattling cold is not to be suffered for long periods of time without reason. Today it was a damp cold. My father would've said that it smelled like snow. I hoped not. Getting around was hard enough without the white stuff to add to the challenge.

I went into the first store I came upon rather than going the extra block to the bookstore. This was the type of shop I normally avoided like the plague. Full of accessories, jewelry, tchotchkes, and pocketbooks, all grouped by color. But it was warm, so I decided to stay and look around. I gravitated toward the sea of black but then forced myself to walk over to the mountain of red. I found a scarf that I liked: deep red and muted white painted cabbage roses interspersed amongst sage green vines. It was long and very wide but could be scrunched up to a much smaller size. Happily, it also came with a diagram that showed me the different ways of using it. I saw a necklace with black and white flowers and shiny silver leaves.

Dangle earrings with a black ball on the ends. I put them all in the basket and continued to wander around. I was choosing accessories with my gut because my brain was otherwise occupied.

I thought about Holly's reaction to Mimi's death, and her implication that Mimi had somehow been involved with her father's disappearance. I remembered Hal's pale, drawn face. He'd lost a friend. Babs's sudden disappearance indicated that perhaps Hal had lost a wife as well. Babs. I needed to follow up with her, make sure she was okay. Holly was going to text me the address in Vermont. I checked my phone. No text from Holly yet, so I sent one asking for the information.

I checked my phone ringer and realized I'd turned it off. It had become habit to turn off my ringer whenever I walked into a rehearsal room or theater. Problem was, I often forgot to turn it back on, giving me unexpected respites from the cacophony of daily life. I walked up to the counter and put my basket down. The woman at the counter asked if I had a shopping bag with me.

"No, sorry to say. I usually do, but I used them all up for groceries. I might be able to fit it all in my purse," I said.

"You'd hate to lose anything," the clerk said. "You can buy one for ten cents or would you rather get one of our cloth ones for a dollar? They're wicked cute."

I looked at the bags, thought of all the ones in the back of my car, and decided to add one more to the collection. I put a black and red one on the counter. "Great choice," she said with a smile. The perky clerk then announced the total of my sale, and I was a bit shocked at the figure. That was the last time I'd go shopping after a pep talk from Cassandra. I took a picture of the bag and texted it to Cassandra. *Your fault.*

While the clerk was wrapping every item carefully in tissue paper, I checked my voicemail.

"Sully, it's Gus. Assuming you heard about Mimi? Horrible news… *garble garble garble*…Need to talk…Doesn't make sense…Call me as soon as you get this."

I handed the clerk my card and called Gus back. He didn't pick up his cell phone, so I called his office.

"Good morning. Knight, Smythe, and Brown," a well-modulated voice said.

"Hello, this is Sully Sullivan. Could you connect me to Gus Knight?"

"It's Kate. I was hoping he was on this call. That's why I picked up," she said. She didn't even try not to sound annoyed. "Gus should be here. He's blown off two meetings already this morning. We have a conference call in five minutes. I know things are crazy, but you'd think he'd keep me in the loop."

"In the loop? What do you mean?" I signed the credit card slip and picked up my bag, mouthing "thank you" to the salesperson. She nodded and cheerily started refolding scarves at the front counter. I walked toward the front door but stepped to the side to finish the call in the warmth of the store.

"I came in this morning to find out he'd dropped all of our Century Project and Century Foundation clients. Without talking to me. You just don't do that— you just don't cut off twenty-five percent of your income—"

"I thought the Cunninghams weren't clients?" I asked.

"They aren't clients. But there are concentric circles, six degrees of separation. I was negotiating deals with, working with, companies who are working with the Cunninghams. But he decided we need to separate those as well. Without talking to me. It's a mess. People got letters of separation this morning, phones are ringing off the hook, email is blowing up."

I didn't know what to say. I could defend Gus, but I wouldn't. I assumed, based on the Gus I knew once upon a time, that he had a very good reason for doing what he was doing. But not to talk to Kate about it? I didn't blame her for being angry. I would've been too, even if he was in the right.

"Kate, I don't know what to say. I'm trying to track Gus down; he left me a message—"

"Which is more than he did for me. I've been trying to find him all morning. I have no idea where he is."

"Well, I'll try to find him too, and if I get hold of him I'll make sure he gives you a call."

"Like he'd listen to you more than he'd listen to me. Actually, strike that. He probably would. Bastard."

"He certainly can be. Hang in there, Kate." I ended the call and left the store.

I called Gus's cell phone, got voicemail again. This time I left a message. I walked outside and took a deep breath, feeling the knife of the freezing cold air slicing through my lungs. Waking me up. Forcing me to be worried. I felt my phone buzz in my hand and quickly took my glove off so I could accept the call.

"Hello?"

"Sully, its Gus." He was shouting. Not really shouting, just speaking loudly. It sounded like he was near a construction zone of some sort.

"Where are you? Are you all right?" I asked.

"In the tunnel. There's construction going on. What else is new? There's construction everywhere these days."

"Gus, focus. What's going on?"

"You heard about Mimi Cunningham?"

"Yes. Terrible news."

"Terrible, of course. Terrible. It's just that...I don't know, the timing is too perfect."

"The timing? Of a murder? What are you talking about?"

"Dammit, I don't know what I mean. Yesterday I decided to..." His phone broke up. I was afraid I'd lost him, but then he came back on the line. "Don't you think that's odd?"

"Think what's odd? Gus, I lost you for a minute. Gus. Gus? I lost you again."

"Sorry. Damn tunnel. Where are you? Can we meet?"

"I'm near Bay Rep. Of course we can meet. Where?"

"Can you get to Harvard Square? How about Cambridge One? In an hour? That'll give me time to check with...call you if ...but I..."

"Gus? I've lost you again! I'll see you at Cambridge One in an hour."

I went back to the theater to talk to Holly. I explained that I was going over to Harvard Square for lunch.

"I'm going to take the car. Will you let Stewart and Harry know? I'll check with them on my way back, and if they're done with rehearsal I'll come by and pick them up. You sure you're all right? Everything under control for now?"

"So far so good, knock wood," Holly said. "Cassandra and I had a great talk. Thank you for that. I'm still working on the set fabric, figuring it out. I think I have a good lead. Anyway, I thought I had the Vermont address in my contacts but I don't. I must have put it in my car GPS. When I get a minute, I'll see if I can find it in an email and text it to you. Are you still willing to—?"

"Of course I am. I think we'll both feel better if we know Babs is up there and all right. It doesn't seem like her to just leave like that, does it?"

"No. But like Hal said, this anniversary has thrown us off our game a little bit. I've put off having a funeral for my dad until…we agreed that after a year went by, if we hadn't heard from him again, we'd have a memorial service. I never really thought we'd get here."

Impulsively I reached over and gave Holly a hug. Before I started working in theater, I was not a hugger. But being around theater people, living in the heightened reality of emotion, I'd realized the power of human contact even from relative strangers. Holly returned the hug, giving me a squeeze at the end.

"Thanks, I needed that," she joked with a watery smile.

"Holly, you know what I was thinking about when I went out to buy a scarf?" I pulled the scarf out of the bag and tossed it around my neck. She picked up the end and pulled the tag off gently. "Thanks. I thought about how good theater folk are at compartmentalizing. When we're in the theater, or in rehearsal, we focus on the work at hand. Real life doesn't intrude. But sometimes, maybe it should. I wonder if Babs got tired of real life not intruding. Anyway, I'm not going to make excuses. She shouldn't have left you in the lurch like this. But some unsolicited advice. Okay?" Holly nodded. "First, ask me anything. If I don't have the answer, I'll help you figure it out. Don't hesitate for a minute. Second. Write a note to the Bay Rep board, let them know what's going on. Better to keep them in the loop. Third? Take care of yourself. Let life intrude. Mourn your father. If you don't, it'll pop up on you. Okay?"

"Okay," Holly said. "Thank you, Sully. Now I know why Dimitri is so glad you're here."

"We'll get through this," I said. "All of it."

∞

When I was in college, Cambridge One was a Chinese restaurant. It may not have been great food, but it tasted wonderful after an evening of carousing in the Square. Raising the drinking age had affected a lot of restaurants that catered to drunk, cheap undergrads, and the Chinese restaurant had closed several years ago. In its place was a grilled pizza place with polished concrete floors, cherrywood booths, and a large window that overlooked a cemetery. Gus and I had eaten there a lot when we were together, but I doubted that it was sentiment that made him choose it. Instead, he just wanted a place I would know but where not many folks would know me. Harvard Square had changed a lot in the past five years. I put my car in a parking lot. More expensive than a meter, but less expensive than a ticket. Who knew how long this would take?

I got there a little early and was shown to a table in the back. I sat on the outside so that Gus could see me and I could see him. I ordered a soda. No Gus. Then I ordered a pizza—steak, tomatoes, arugula, and Gorgonzola. I ate my half and started to nibble on his. By the time I was down to the last two pieces and had checked my cell phone for the hundredth time, I was officially worried. That was cemented when I saw Antonia Vestri walk through the door and head right to my table.

"Sully."

"Toni." So much for small talk. You'd think I'd have more to say to my ex-partner, one of the best cops I knew, after six years.

"Where's Gus?" she asked.

"Dunno. We're divorced. But you knew that." Gus got Toni in the divorce. She'd decided to stay on the side of law and order, and Gus was that. Not that I'd put up much of a fight. I was career poison to be around those days, and I didn't want Toni to get infected. I'd given up most of my friends from my former life. But I still missed some of them. Especially Toni.

"He was going to meet you here at two. Did he leave already?"

"He never showed. How do you know he was supposed to meet me?"

"He told me. When he called to arrange a time to come to the station, to talk about his relationship with Mimi Cunningham."

"Relationship?"

"Business relationship. Apparently it had been fractious of late. Things are escalating quickly in the Cunningham case. That's to be expected; she was a VIP. So I thought I'd come in and talk to Gus off the record. Give him a heads-up. Folks want him to come in for questioning this afternoon."

"About the murder?"

"Shhh. Jeeze, Sully, you're still loud. You going to eat that piece of pizza? What the hell is this, lettuce? Who puts lettuce on pizza?" Toni took a bite, then finished the rest of the piece in two bites. She picked up the second piece and gestured at me. "Damn, woman, you did a good job getting rid of the rest, didn't you?"

"Help yourself. And yeah, I was hungry. What's up with this questioning crap?"

"Gus was one of the last people to see Mimi Cunningham alive. And the department got a tip that he had information. Anyway, we called Gus's office, found out he was out. I called his cell. He called me back on my personal cell, and I explained the situation."

"That you were going to question him?"

"I wanted to give him notice, as a friend. Believe it or not, he appreciated the call. He said he had something to tell me. We had a bad connection, but he mentioned he didn't have a lot of time since he was meeting you here at two. So, where is he?"

"I don't know. Honestly. He never showed. And hasn't called."

"And you tried him?"

"Yeah. Between calls and texts, at least a dozen times. No answer."

"Just a sec." Toni tried Gus's cell and left her own voicemail. Then a text. Then she called Kate and had a quick conversation. From what

I gathered, Kate hadn't heard from him either. Finally she called someone else, presumably at the station. No one had heard from him.

"And you have no idea why he wanted to talk to you?" Toni asked. The waitress brought her a glass of water and asked if she wanted to order anything. Toni said no and took a sip of water.

"No. His cell phone kept breaking up. He said he was in a tunnel. He asked if I'd heard about Mimi Cunningham's murder. Then he said that something seemed wrong, and something about wanting to wait until two to meet with me so he could have time to do something. I didn't hear what."

"Sounds like our conversation. In and out, in and out. Any ideas?"

"About what it meant? No," I said.

"Did you know the victim?"

"Mimi Cunningham? We'd met a few times at different functions. But we'd never had a conversation that was about anything more than the Cliffside. That's my theater."

"Yeah, I'd heard you were working for a theater. Gus said you were doing well. Interesting career change."

"Well, you know how it was."

"I don't, actually. We never got around to that conversation." Toni took another sip of water and put the glass down so hard that water bounced onto the table. She didn't move to wipe it up.

"C'mon, Toni. I was persona non-grata at work. I wanted to keep you clean."

"We were friends, Sully. I tried to be there for you."

"I know you tried." I'd pushed her away when she'd tried to get me to see Gus's side of the story. I wasn't ready for that conversation until a couple of years later. "I'm a jerk, what can I say?"

Toni sighed. "A lot more than that, but we'd need a good meal and a decent bottle of wine. What's say we wait until Gus can be there too."

"You're worried about him?" I asked.

"Yeah, a little. He sounded like he was confused about something. Gus doesn't confuse easily."

"You think it had something to do with the murder?"

"Yeah. But who knows what it was? Gus is running in pretty tony circles these days. And his girlfriend, Kate, is useless. He's probably just stuck somewhere and his cell died." The way Toni had said Kate's name summed up her opinion, and it wasn't good. We'd worked together for a long time, and not only had a shorthand but also understood tone. Made working cases a lot easier.

"That must be it," I said. "How about if I call you if I hear from him?"

"Great. Let me give you my numbers."

"Have they changed? Because I still have them. Do you need mine?"

Toni had the good grace to look embarrassed. "Yeah, I do. You know how my temper is, Sully. Gets the best of me sometimes. I can be quick on the delete button."

"Neither one of us was at our best back then. Here's my card. And this"—I wrote down my personal numbers—"is my cell and home. Use my cell; I'm staying in Boston for a few days."

Toni's phone vibrated and she checked the display before putting the call on hold. "I've got to take this. Call me, okay?"

Seeing Toni wasn't nearly the ordeal I'd feared. Instead it was a relief. She was one of the last people I needed to make amends with. Of course, I had little doubt that Gus had paved the way with Toni, told her that he and I were back on speaking terms. It would always hurt that she had taken his side in the divorce, but I'd come to realize that I hadn't given her much choice.

I left the restaurant and walked around for an hour, in case Gus ended up in Harvard Square. I went into a stationery store and perused the notebooks. It should have been nirvana for me, but I was distracted.

I was worried about Gus. I tried his phone again, and this time got a "full mailbox" message. Damn. That didn't take long. Suddenly two texts came in, even though they'd been sent over an hour ago. They were from Gus, one text that was split in half. The second part came in first, and I was confused for moment:

night, but a few things seem odd. Talked to Kate re time. Problems. Mimi dead doesn't make sense. M heading to CC to see. LU.

Sorry to be cryptic but am concerned that I might not make it to C1. Hoe a call from KC that I need to return. H wants to see me asap. Not sure what happened last

Hoe a call? Must be had. Between autocorrect and the need to wear glasses, texting could be torturous for folks over forty. KC? Who was KC? Kate? Kate's last name was Smythe. And why would he spell it out Kate later? H? Could the K in KC be a J? Jerome Cunningham? Made sense. H for he? That made sense too. Talked to Kate re time. Mimi dead doesn't make sense? Did he mean death? M heading to CC. Am heading to CC? CC? Cunningham Corporation?

LU. Love you?

No, not possible. I'd figure that part out later.

I hit reply, but I wasn't sure what to say so I kept it short. And sweet.

RUOK? I'm here. Toni says hi.

The text said it went through, but I didn't get a delivery notice. Gus, where are you? I left the store without buying anything, a first for me. I decided to head back and sit in a dark theater and let rehearsal wash over me. Or at least that was the plan. Until Emma called and told me she might be under arrest.

· Ten ·

Emma was at the police station. I supposed I should have been pleased that I was her first call, but then I remembered that Gus was incommunicado, so I may have been her second choice. Had she heard from Gus? There was so much going on. Mimi's death, Babs leaving, Gus's going off-line. One of my strengths was being able to connect things in unexpected ways. But in this case? I was missing some dots and didn't know what they were. What connected and what didn't? I'd always found that if I forced ideas, I made a mistake. Better to let the story come to me and let the connections become clear. I had to trust that they would become clear, because right now it was all just a murky muddle.

I pulled my car into a meter and added enough quarters for a couple of hours. I needed to download that parking app. But if I needed to feed the meter, it would be a good excuse to leave the station to take a walk. I took a deep breath before entering the police station. I'd spent a lot of my working life in this building, and I still wasn't coping well with how much I missed it.

Luckily, the desk clerk was new since my time and I didn't see anyone I knew. Yet. Emma had told me she was on the second floor, so I went up to find her. Now, this was trickier, since I likely knew at least one person. Deep breath, move forward. I asked at the front desk for Emma and was directed to a conference room at the other end of the hall. I felt a few eyes on me but didn't look around. Instead I knocked where I was directed and waited for the terse "come in" from the other side.

Toni Vestri, twice in one day. But the look on her face precluded me from mentioning that. She tipped her head to her left, and then I saw him. John Engel. A blast from the past that I could have lived without. He was still a sweaty ball of human flesh, rounder and with less hair on the top of his head. The site of him made my skin crawl.

"Well, look who the cat dragged in," John smirked. "I thought that they said your lawyer was here, Ms. Whitehall."

"I never said I was her lawyer. Just that I was here to see her," I said, pasting a fake smile on my face and looking right at that sentence-parsing pain the ass. "Does she need a lawyer?"

"No, she's not under arrest. We're just asking some questions. Toni joined us a little while ago, as a matter of fact. Kinda handy that you're here, since you might be able to back her up."

"Back her up?" I asked. John was talking tough, but I could tell he had nothing. He was fishing. Trying to get Emma off her game by making her think she needed an alibi. He must've already known she had one, otherwise he would've separated us, taken separate statements. "Timeline wise?"

"Sully, would you mind going over your timeline once you left the University Club yesterday evening?" Toni asked.

"Of course not. We left at about eight o'clock, eight thirty maybe. We walked down to the corner of Commonwealth Ave and Arlington and decided to go to the Bristol for a burger. We walked on the opposite side of the street from the park to the hotel, had dinner, and then took a cab home."

"Home?"

"Emma and I are staying in the same townhouse on Beacon Hill. Different apartments. As we were leaving the bar, we saw a unit pull up and double park. That was about ten o'clock or so. Both officers went into the Garden."

"Can anyone confirm the time you left?"

"Emma paid with a credit card, so it's probably time-stamped. And the doorman who called us a cab knew her, but I'm not sure if he checked his watch."

"You didn't walk through the Public Garden? Wouldn't that have been shorter?" John asked.

"Ms. Whitehall is afraid of rats, so we avoided it," I said.

"Well, we all know you're not afraid of rats, are you, Sullivan? Kindred spirits." John Engel didn't try to hide his disdain. I stared him down but didn't rise to the bait. What was the point of giving him the satisfaction? It was all a lifetime ago. I forced my face to remain neutral.

"Is that all?" I asked.

"You both alibi each other. We confirmed it earlier," Toni said. She shot a glance at John, daring him to contradict her. "Ms. Whitehall was just telling us about the party itself. Maybe you could supply more details?"

"Sure. Do you want to talk to us together?"

"Yes, this is an unofficial interview. It could just as easily be done at her office or her home, but Ms. Whitehall volunteered to come down to talk about the timeline for last night. Which we appreciate," Toni said. "She was just describing an altercation between a Ms. Allyn and the victim. She mentioned that you were there. Why don't you tell us what you remember about that?"

"Okay," I said. I hoped Emma had gone the route I planned to take: tell the entire truth as I remembered it. "Babs—Ms. Allyn—confronted Jerome Cunningham first. I couldn't hear what she said. He turned away, and his wife stepped in. Babs said something to her. Again, I couldn't hear it. And then Mrs. Cunningham threw a drink in Babs's face."

"And then?"

"And then Babs left. Gus went out after her. Gus Knight."

"And Ms. Allyn's husband? Hal Maxwell? He was there?"

"He was. Hal didn't go right out, but I think he left before we did. Didn't he, Emma? At least I thought I saw him leave. There was sort of a mass exodus."

"Did you see Mrs. Cunningham leave?" John asked.

"No, but Emma told me that she and her husband had stepped out."

"But you didn't see them go out or come in again?

"No."

"And did you see Gus Knight come back in?" Toni asked.

"No, sorry."

"Did you pass him on the street?"

"No."

"Because he said Babs wouldn't let him walk her home. So he came right back in and stayed in the front hallway," John said. "Since there's only one way out, you would have passed him on the way."

I shrugged and looked at Emma. "I don't remember seeing him. Do you?" She shook her head. "There were a lot of people leaving, and we were trying to get our coats. I don't know what to say. It was dark. We were talking."

"And you'd been drinking."

"Two glasses of wine. But I still was in control of my facilities."

"I'm sure you were," John said. "So, you can't provide an alibi for Gus? Would you if you could?"

"If I could, I would. But I can't."

"Do you know where he is now?"

"Gus? No, sorry. We were supposed to meet for lunch but he never showed. And he didn't call." I didn't mention the text. I'd tell Toni about it later, when John wasn't in the room. I knew she was already looking for Gus, and wasn't sure whether the text would help or hurt his case. I'd let Toni figure that out.

Part of me wanted to ask for more details, but this wasn't the place for friendly conversation. John and I went back and forth for a bit longer, but neither of us had much more to offer. After several minutes, Emma and I left and went to my car. "Have you heard from Gus?" she asked me.

I showed her the text.

"What does that mean?" she asked.

I gave her my translation, which really didn't help much. "I've got to say, I'm a little worried," I said.

"Damn. So am I," she said. "I haven't been able to reach him for hours. Where to now?"

"Let me text Harry, see if they're done for the day and I can pick them up. Otherwise, we'll head home?" I sent a text to Harry and waited. After a few minutes, I texted Holly and asked if they were done. *Another hour,* she texted back.

Tell Harry and Stewart I'll meet them at home.

Will do. Talk to you tomorrow.

"Let's get some dinner on the way, what do you say? We'll figure out how to find Gus." I pulled out into the traffic and eased my way into the righthand lane. We'd be taking back roads over to Beacon Hill, and that would cut down on traffic considerably.

"I'll call in for a couple of pizzas and a salad from down the street. We can pick it up after we drop the car."

"Sounds like a plan. I keep meaning to go grocery shopping but haven't found the time yet," I said.

"Then what's all that?" Emma pointed to the bags in the back seat.

"Rations, not groceries. More on the junk food side of the food pyramid than the healthy side."

"Works for me," Emma said. She sighed, and I looked over at her. Her lips were pursed and her brow furrowed. "When you came in, I was hoping you wouldn't be worried—that Gus would have talked to you and you could talk me down a bit," she said.

"Sorry. When did you last speak with him?" I asked.

"This morning. He asked me for Jerry Cunningham and Hal Maxwell's cell numbers, which I gave him."

"He didn't have them?"

"No. He had to get a new phone recently. Kate dropped his old one in a sink or something. Anyway, he lost all his contacts."

"He didn't have—"

"You sound like Eric," Emma said. "He couldn't believe that someone we knew didn't have all of his records living in the cloud. Gus was, is, very conservative about privacy. I do know he was very upset about losing the info on his phone, and he was hoping to get it back soon."

"He had my cell number," I said.

"One of the first ones he asked me for," Emma said. "Anyway, he didn't tell me why he wanted Jerry's number."

"I talked to Kate this morning. Did you?" Emma shook her head. "She was wound a little tight. Said that Gus had broken off his business relationship with folks in any way associated with the Cunninghams. Did you know he did that?"

"Yes. Sorry, I should have mentioned it. Gus was diving deep into a lot of issues and decided to extricate us from a few more deals. He sent out a couple of emails to Eric and me late last night."

"What were the issues?"

"Not sure. I know he was investigating a few threads that gave him worry. His phrasing. Yesterday afternoon, he let me know he was cutting off business ties with another four clients who were working with the Cunningham Corporation. He was concerned about some conflicts of interest. He didn't explain more."

"Conflicts of interest? Not because of their involvement with the Cunninghams?"

"He said conflicts of interest. We were supposed to talk about it more today. He said some of it would involve the Whitehall business directly, so he wanted to talk it through with me."

"Were you worried that it would be bad for your business?"

"In Gus I trust," Emma said. "Plain and simple. I trusted that he knew better than I did because of the work he was doing. I also know he knew how much I valued my relationships with the Cunninghams, and he wouldn't risk that without good cause. One of the reasons he kept me out of the loop was so I could keep my business and personal lives separated as much as possible."

"His text was cryptic, to put it mildly. 'Mimi dead doesn't make sense'?"

"I don't even think he knew Mimi that well, but I could be wrong. Maybe he was distraught?"

"Maybe. 'Heading to CC'? What do you think that means?"

"I'd assume the Cunningham Corporation, to work out details? We had a meeting scheduled for later today but it got canceled. What are you thinking, Sully?"

"I'm thinking we need to find Gus."

∞

We need to find Gus. For some reason, that was making my gut ache. I had no idea how we were going to find him. But I had no idea about a lot of things. Time to go to work.

I called Toni's cell and got voicemail. "Toni, Sully. Listen, I'm going to cut to the chase. I don't know where Gus is and I'm worried. His voicemail is full, and the phone doesn't even ring anymore. I got a text from him. I'm going to forward it to you now. Give me a call."

"Why did you do that?" Emma asked. "It was obvious the police think Gus had something to do with this. You just gave them proof."

"Not them. Toni. And maybe it is proof, but of what? In Gus we trust, right? I've known Toni a lot of years, worked with her for a while. She's friends with Gus. It won't hurt to keep her in the loop. She has more juice and can try to trace his cell."

"You're that worried?" Emma asked.

"I guess I am, yeah. Just seems that when someone like Mimi Cunningham dies like that, there's probably more to it than a random mugging. Why wasn't Jerry with her, anyway?"

"From what I understand, Jerry went out for a drink with some other people after the event. She wanted to go home, so she took a shortcut through the Public Garden. You don't think it was a robbery?"

"I don't know of many robbers who strangle their victims. They tend to use guns and knives, and mostly for show. Strangulation shows passion. And at ten o'clock at night? Even this time of year there are people around. Even with rats keeping citizens at bay."

"Okay. So, if it isn't a robbery…maybe Gus saw it happen?"

"No. If Gus saw something happen, he would have called it in himself and waited for the police. But if he heard about the murder this morning and thought about something that didn't make sense?"

"And wanted to check it out? Or double check something? Maybe he's doing his own investigating?"

"Maybe," I said. "It doesn't sound very Gus-like, unless he was really uncertain about something."

"What should we do?" Emma asked.

"Let's go home, write down what we know, and compare notes."

While Emma called in our food order, I thought about Gus doing investigating. Maybe he was following a hunch. If that was true, I needed to make it easy for him to find me. I checked my phone, which needed to be charged. I would stay put at the apartment and keep trying to reach out to him.

Emma and I dumped the car in the garage and grabbed the shopping bags. I did buy a lot of food. Yeesh. We made our way down Charles Street and stopped to pick up the pizza and salad. Three pizzas. They threw in some rolls for good measure.

"Leftover pizza is perfect for any meal," Emma said. "Can you grab the groceries if I grab the pizza?" I put the salad and rolls into the grocery bags and picked them up. Not too bad. I shoved my accessory shopping bag into my knapsack and put it on. I could do this. Besides, pizza twice in one day? I needed to step up the exercise somehow.

We were juggling pizza and Trader Joe's bags and my knapsack and her briefcase as we approached the door. Emma handed me the pizza while she pulled out her keys. Out of the corner of my eye, I noticed a couple getting out of a car. She had a camera and he was holding a mic.

"Ms. Whitehall, Ms. Whitehall! We have a couple of questions for you. What's it like knowing someone else who was murdered? Do you have any comment?"

I saw Emma fumble a bit with the lock. I physically stepped in front of her, blocking their path. I didn't say anything, I just stared. The pizza boxes took away from my penetrating look, but I still had it. Mr. Reporter stopped in his tracks.

"Ms. Whitehall, it's better for you to talk to us now, get your story out."

Emma had opened the door. "Puh-leeze, I said.

"Who are you?"

"Greta Garbo. I want to be alone." I followed Emma in the door and pushed it closed. The heavy wooden door had windows near the top, but the glass was old and hand-blown. There were side panels of glass to let light in, but these were fairly opaque. And likely shatterproof for security reasons, or at least I hoped so. I resisted the urge to turn around and look out the door, even when a light went on. Probably from the camera—were they really doing a report from outside the apartment?

"You should text the boys, tell them to use the alley entrance," Emma said. "We should have used it but I didn't want to walk the extra block." She took the pizzas and headed up the stairs to Harry's apartment. She waited on the landing while I moved past her with the key to open the door.

"I don't know. Maybe we should have them come in the front door. Handsome men coming in at all hours? It could divert their attention," I said.

"Very funny. Text them. They don't deserve to be hit by this."

"Deep breath, Emma. You knew this could happen, you said it yourself. We'll just start using the alley door—it's blocked by a gate, right? No big deal."

"You're right. More important things to worry about. Let's put the pizza in the oven to keep it warm."

My cell phone buzzed and dinged. I checked the text. It was from Stewart, not Gus.

Late rehearsal. Going out afterward. Don't wait dinner for us. See you tomorrow.

"We're on our own tonight," I said to Emma.

"Probably just as well. Making small talk when I'm thinking about Gus and Mimi—not sure I'm up to that. How about if we have the fig and blue cheese pizza, some salad, and put the rest away?"

"Let me go get some tools of the trade so we can do some work while we eat." I walked toward my bedroom.

Emma called after me, "Tools of the trade?"

"Index cards, highlighters, sharpies, tape," I responded over my shoulder. I grabbed the small bag I took with me always, my mobile office full of those supplies and others. "We want to find Gus, right?"

"Yes, and—"

"No 'and.' Not right now. It won't survive the test of the cops if they think we're trying to figure out what happened to Mimi Cunningham. We need to have clarity of purpose. Let's focus on Gus and try to figure out what he was doing, what he found out. Let's search for Gus and see where that takes us."

Emma put a plate with a piece of pizza down on the table in front of me, and one in front of herself. She poured two glasses of water and put them down as well. Two wineglasses followed, along with napkins, forks, and knives. "I figure tonight we should be better about water-then-wine-then-water. Keep our heads a little clearer."

"We do need some clear heads," I said, unpacking my office bag.

"Now show me these tools of the trade." Emma poured us each a glass of wine and sat down. I took out the index cards, a brand-new pack, and handed her a stack. Then I handed her a marker and laid the highlighters out in front of us.

"So, today's Wednesday. I got a text from Gus around three o'clock this afternoon but I don't know when he sent it. I think that's the last time anyone's heard from him." I wrote down *Wednesday* on one card and *text from Gus 3 p.m.* on another card and laid it under the Wednesday card. I highlighted the *3 p.m.* in yellow. "Yellow indicates we can't confirm what's on the card. Let's go backward in time, figure out what we know."

"What we know about Gus's disappearance? Or about everything? Are you making us a crime board?"

"I'll admit, this is a tool I used when I was a cop. No piece of information is off-topic when you're trying to solve a mystery. The mystery we're trying to solve is 'where is Gus?' But there's a lot more to that story. We don't know what pieces have to do with anything. So let's work backward, fill in the gaps we know, try to figure out what he was thinking. Where he was going."

"You really think this will help?"

"It can't hurt. Besides, I don't know what else to do right now. And I need to do something."

· Eleven ·

We kept working until after midnight. We took the cards and put them up on Harry's cabinets with painter's tape. We both stepped back and looked at the work.

"Now what?" Emma asked.

"Now we think about what questions we have, and who we need to talk to. Write down the questionable facts—the stuff highlighted in yellow—and try to get them confirmed one way or the other. Write down every question you have, no matter how random it seems."

We both sat with index cards in front of us, pens poised above them, waiting for brilliance to flow. Nothing came. I wrote down four names on the tops for cards and laid them out in front of us. *Kate. Hal. Babs. Jerry.*

"These are the folks who I think can help us figure this out," I said. "Tell you what. I propose we both get some sleep and come at this fresh in the morning. We may come up with the wrong questions because we're tired and have been thinking about this too long. A path may be clearer in the morning."

"Sounds good," Emma said. "One quick thought about how to talk to Jerry—how about if we drop off your grant application tomorrow? It would give us an excuse to go in. Is it ready?"

"It is, but that seems in bad taste, don't you think?" I asked.

"Jerry Cunningham is a businessman, first and foremost. It wouldn't surprise me to hear he'd been in the office today. Let me see if I can set something up. We can ask him questions about Gus. Just have to think through what those questions are before we go." Emma stood up and loaded the dishwasher. I put the leftovers in the refrigerator. Neither of us spoke, but we both kept looking at the cards on the cabinets. Emma finally drained her wine glass and put it on the rack.

"See in the morning, Sully. Sleep well."

I turned on the dishwasher and wiped down the table. I gathered up my belongings and went into my room. Max was waiting for me and gave me a side-eye as if to say "go to sleep."

I did get some sleep. Not much, but some. I got up at five thirty and did some stretches. Max watched me from his side of the bed, but after a while he closed his eyes and went back to sleep. He never was an early riser.

There was a treadmill in the corner of the living room, and I moved the pile of magazines off it and plugged it in. I stepped on and started a run. It was a nice treadmill and gave me choices about the terrain I'd be running on. I chose flat, with occasional hills. No need to overdo it. I went fast enough to clear my mind and work out some of the adrenaline in my system. As far as I could tell, Gus had been missing for almost sixteen hours. I was hoping that he had taken himself off the grid. I didn't like the alternative.

I put on the pot of coffee and showered. Now the question was what to wear. I channeled Cassandra and decided I needed to look presentable but still accomodate my need for comfort. Again with the black stretchy pants. They were boot-cut, long, and new enough to still be black-black, not grayish with black splotches. I wore a black cashmere sweater over a white silk T-shirt. Added my new jewelry and a dash of makeup. Presentable, if I did say so. I'd still wear my Bean boots, but Boston was forgiving in the footwear department in February.

I emptied out my knapsack and repacked it with the day's gear. A fleece. Some protein bars. My water bottle, which I filled. My computer, the recharging cord for it, and my phone. Some other odds and ends that my sleep-addled brain thought might be helpful.

Harry was pouring himself a cup of coffee when I came out. He handed it to me and poured himself another. I noticed that he'd already fed Max, who was happily chomping on a large dollop of wet food.

"I see you've been decorating," Harry said. He took a sip of coffee and looked at the cards all over the cabinet. "What's going on? You're not investigating that murder, are you?"

"No, of course not," I said. "Really. Emma and I are looking for Gus. He seems to have gone off the grid. That's what this is all about. We aren't investigating the murder. Leaving that to the police," I said, taking a sip of coffee and not meeting Harry's eyes.

"Gus is missing? Do you think he's okay?" Harry asked.

"I'm sure he is," I lied. "I just want to find him."

"Understandable. Sully, I know we're all in rehearsal mode, not dealing a lot with real life. But if you need me, you know I'm here, right? For whatever you need. Always."

"Thanks, Harry, I do know that," I said, giving him a quick hug. "I promise I'll keep you in the loop."

"Why are you so dressed up? And up so early?" he asked.

"I couldn't sleep. Thinking about Gus. Plus, I'm going to drop off the Century Foundation grant and try to talk to Jerry Cunningham, see if he knows anything. I need to track Dimitri down to get him to sign the application first, though. I wanted to look presentable for that. Dropping the application off, not meeting with Dimitri. As you know, I'd be comfortable wearing yoga pants and a hoodie to meet with Dimitri. What are you doing up so early?"

"Believe it or not, Stewart and I are going to the Boston Public Library this morning. They have some Shakespeare folios we want to take a look at. Hoping that maybe seeing the original work will give us a little divine inspiration."

"How's it going?"

"Not bad. Pretty good, actually. That's part of the problem. Before Stewart came, earlier in the week, the goal was just to get through. Now? The cast is jelling, and committed. We see the potential. And realize we don't have enough time, enough rehearsal hours, to get there. So Dimitri gave us the morning off, told us not to come until two. Clear the cobwebs, get our heads in the game."

Rehearsal periods for shows were always fraught. They started off with great expectations and hit bumps along the way. Despair came in for Dimitri usually just before tech rehearsals started, and then things evened out. It was an emotional, predictable timeline. But this timeline was truncated, and I knew it must be wearing on Dimitri.

"You know where he is this morning? Is he meeting folks at the theater? I'll text him; maybe we can meet for breakfast. He must need a sounding board. I haven't talked to him since—"

"Yesterday. You talked to him yesterday. He's doing well; Holly's dealing with him on equal footing. Probably your doing. If you need to talk to him this morning, he's downstairs on the couch. We got in late last night and decided to keep talking. By the way, if you're hoping for cold pizza for breakfast, you're outta luck," Harry said.

"There are rolls—" I said, with a bit of hope in my voice.

"Nope. No rolls. But there are eggs and cheese. How about if I make some scrambled eggs, you want to go down and let Dimitri and Stewart know I'm making breakfast?"

"You mean wake them up? Sure. Do me a favor—let Emma know you're cooking breakfast. She's going with me this morning."

∞

I went down the back staircase and let myself into Amelia's apartment. Emma was right; there wasn't a lot of personality in this place, no sense of Amelia. Amelia's life, her place, her center of being was in Trevorton at the Anchorage, their family home. I doubted she'd even left the grounds since New Year's. She probably hadn't left the greenhouse except to eat and sleep. I made a mental note to go visit her soon.

Amelia's apartment appeared to be a one bedroom, which made sense given the first floor entranceway into the building. The furniture was utilitarian, the walls were bare. It wasn't homey, but I imagined that it was used more for guests than for family. Even though it was, technically, the first floor, the windows looked out at the top of cars. Amelia had bottom-up shades that didn't keep the light out, but they did make the place feel like a cocoon with only a sliver of real life seeping in.

I looked at the lump on the couch and recognized it immediately. Dimitri was a power napper, and I'd found him in the same position several times on our office couch. Another selfish reason I wanted to get the new production facility built. With more space, maybe I could finagle my own office space. Who was I kidding—that wouldn't stop him. Dimitri tended to sprawl himself and his belongings wherever he was. I walked over and touched his shoulder, whispering his name.

"Damn, woman, what time is it?" he growled.

"Early. Sorry," I said. "Sign these. Then you can go back to sleep."

He sat up and fumbled for his glasses. Though still handsome, he looked exhausted. I couldn't imagine what he'd look like by opening night. He glanced over the application and signed where I told him to. Then he flopped back on the couch pillows dramatically, closing his eyes again.

"Seriously, Dimitri, go back to sleep," I said quietly.

"I'll sleep when I'm dead," he said. Then he winced. "Sorry, I'd forgotten for a moment. Awful thing that happened to Mimi Cunningham, isn't it?"

"It is. Confession, it may be getting worse. Gus—Gus Knight, my ex-husband, you remember him from last winter?" Dimitri nodded. "Gus was supposed to meet me yesterday for lunch, but he never showed. He sent me a text and mentioned Mimi. I'm a little worried. I'm trying to figure out why he's gone off the grid."

"Could something worse have happened to him?" Dimitri said, opening his eyes and looking at me.

"It could have," I said quietly, swallowing. Dimitri could drive me crazy, but I wondered if anyone understood me as well as he did. He always cut right to the chase, had enough respect for me to do that. "I really hope not. The police are looking for him too, which is of some comfort since they have more resources. Of course, they're looking for him for another reason."

"Do they think he had anything to do with Mimi's, um, you know?"

"They have questions. So do I, though I know he had nothing to do with her death. Murder … he doesn't have it in him. Being a jackass, yes that. But not murder. Anyway, while I drop this off I thought I might say hello to Jerry Cunningham if he's there."

"Ask him some questions about Gus?"

"Only if it comes up naturally in conversation," I said.

"Sully, I know of no one who can force topics to come up in conversation with quite the flare that you do. Be careful, though, and let me know if I can help with anything. Not that I can—"

"Well actually, you can. If you hear from Babs or if she shows up, let me know right away, okay?"

"Has she disappeared as well? I thought she just went away for a few days?"

"Yes, that's right. I'm feeling the need to check in with folks, that's all. No worries. By the way, Harry is making a mysterious egg concoction with various cheeses and other leftovers. Upstairs. There's coffee too."

"Ah, sustenance. Bless his heart. A fine actor, and an even better human being."

"Should we wake up Stewart, let him know about breakfast?"

"He's been up and out for a while," Dimitri said. "I heard the door close. Probably went to get some breakfast food, or fruit, or something like that. I don't know. We can all meet upstairs in Harry's apartment. I'll be up after I take a quick shower. I assume that's where you're staying?"

"It is. I'll see you there. Take the back staircase; it's easier."

If I'd left a quiet apartment with Harry at the stove, I came back to a hubbub of activity. A washing machine was doing its thing. Stewart, Harry, and Emma were sitting on one side of the table looking at the timeline she and I had created the night before. When I walked in, the talking stopped. I went over and got my old coffee mug, pouring the cold dregs into the sink and then refilling it with fresh, hot brew.

"What's going on?" I asked, leaning up against the sink and staring the three of them down.

"Just filling them in on our day yesterday," Emma said. "Oh, and they're doing Dimitri's laundry."

"He was thinking of going to a laundromat this morning. Seemed that was a colossal waste of time, considering we have a washer and dryer in our unit," Harry said.

"Is he on his way up?" Stewart asked. "I assume he's awake?"

"He is, taking a shower. Good idea, bringing his laundry here. As you know, he never would've made it to a laundromat. And clean clothes are important."

"I've got to admit, it's like doing Johnny Cash's laundry," Harry said. "Black shirts, black jeans, black socks, black underwear—"

"Too much information," Stewart said. "Especially this early in the morning."

"But it's okay to talk about dead bodies and missing ex-husbands? Does it ever occur to any of you that we're all a little screwed up?" Harry asked.

"Every day, in every way," Emma said. "And I couldn't be more grateful for that. If the three of you had stopped asking questions back in December, who knows where we'd all be today. By the way, Sully and I are looking for Gus, nothing more. We owe it to Gus. He's a good guy, and my friend."

"He is a good guy," Harry said. "Hope you can find something out when you're at the Cunningham Corporation."

"Sully, about that," Emma said. "Looks like first we have to go have a cup of coffee with Hal Maxwell. He texted me this morning and wanted to set up a time to talk about the business. I would have said no, but we want to talk to him, right? After that we'll go drop the grant application off."

"I hope—"

"I called Jerry this morning, left a message telling him I'd be in the neighborhood and asking if he could give me five minutes to say hello. His secretary called back and confirmed that he was in the office and would have a fifteen-minute window around ten o'clock."

"You've been busy," I said. "What time are we supposed to meet Hal?"

"Eight fifteen. He's got a window of time right before a meeting in Union Square. I thought we'd take my car, make sure we get everywhere in time. That okay with you?"

"Fine with me."

"Then we should plan on leaving in about five minutes. I'm going to go up and brush my teeth. Fix my lipstick. Try to look presentable."

"You're always presentable, Emma," Stewart said, flashing his best smile.

Emma blushed and went up the back stairs.

"Do you ever not flirt?" Harry asked. "Honestly, it's exhausting."

"Exhausting for you, maybe," Stewart said. "It gives me life. Anyway, Sully, we're going to hang out here and do some housework, then go to the library before rehearsal. If you need us, or need anything, text or call, okay? As a matter of fact, text or call every couple hours just to check in."

"You're being ridiculous—"

"Just do what he asks, okay Sully?" Harry said. "Trouble tends to follow you around. Don't make us worry too much about you. Be careful."

"Will do, my dear friends. Now to make my escape before Dimitri ascends and adds to my to-do list."

· Twelve ·

Emma's car was a mini-Cooper. Off-white with a black stripe. I was surprised that I could fold my six-foot frame into the car, but it was comfortable. And very sporty.

We met Hal in a diner in Union Square. On weekends the wait to get in was at least an hour. Today we found a seat right away. It probably helped that Hal was waiting for us. The waitress came over and we ordered breakfast. Their French toast was made out of Portuguese bread. Why would I even try to resist it?

"We're going to stop by the Century Foundation later and drop off Sully's application," Emma said. "We plan to say hello to Jerry."

"He's at work? Well, I guess he's got a lot of things to take care of." Hal stirred his coffee vigorously but didn't take a sip. "Mimi's memorial service is today, did you know that?"

"Today?"

"Jerry wants to do it today. He'll plan a larger memorial for later this spring."

"I suppose I can't really blame him for that," I said. "Better to get it over with."

"Precisely what I advised," Hal said. "I suspect he would appreciate seeing you there, Emma. If it isn't too painful."

"Thank you, Hal. Too painful? Hopefully not. I may bring Sully with me for moral support. She helped me through a lot this winter."

"Friends are important during difficult times," Hal said. "Emma, I know this is terrible timing, but we've been wondering if you'd reconsider your Century Project involvement. I only ask because Jerry is trying to wrap some things up before he leaves."

"Leaves?" I asked.

"He's going away for a few weeks. To try to get over this. Of course, the way things are nowadays, he's almost always reachable."

"I'm not sure what you are asking, Hal," Emma said.

"We both know that a continued investment by Whitehall and Associates would be a tremendous vote of confidence in the projects. It always would have been, of course, but it's even more important now. This sort of, um, situation makes investors uneasy. And I'd hate for Mimi's legacy to be the death of this next set of projects. Gus has our newest proposal. Unless he gave it to you to look over? Did he? Leave the proposal with you, I mean?"

"The last time I spoke to Gus about this, he was advising we pull back even farther," Emma said quietly. "Sorry, Hal."

Hal sat back and toyed with his coffee mug.

"We haven't been able to reach Gus since yesterday afternoon," I added. It wasn't an elegant way to ask the question, but it was the best I could do. "You haven't spoken to him, have you?"

"Me, no. But I have spoken to Kate," Hal said. "I got the distinct impression they'd reconsidered and she was recommending reinvestment. Presumably because she'd spoken to Gus."

"I haven't spoken to Kate," Emma said. "I'll try to connect with her later. I'm sorry, Hal. Without speaking to Gus, I don't feel comfortable moving forward. I know you understand. Maybe we can revisit this when Jerry gets back?"

"Here's an idea. Let me share the most recent set of documents with you, so you can look them over before you speak with Kate. Gus suggested most of the changes. He agreed on a more moderate withdrawal timeline. Here, the documents are in this folder. I just sent you a link," Hal said.

"Hal, I don't know how to make that work—"

"I do," I said. "I'll help you figure it out. Maybe we can give Kate a call and she can talk you through it?" That way I'd also be able to look at the documents. Something was hinky. Was this one of the reasons Gus had gone off the grid?

"Okay, but I'd rather wait until Gus gets back—" Emma said.

"Yes, a good idea," Hal replied. "To wait until Gus gets back. But the timing is getting tricky, what with Jerry leaving…tell you what, we'll talk about this later. After the service. How does that sound?" Hal didn't wait for an answer. He took out a couple of bills and tossed them on the table. "The service is at three at the Boston Synagogue." He stood to leave, but I interrupted him by putting my hand on his arm.

"Hal, have you spoken with Babs?"

He almost turned purple, but his tone remained well-modulated. "Not since her last text. Maybe Holly has." He turned and left the diner without looking back.

The waiter poured me another cup of coffee and I sipped it gratefully. I took out my notepad and started writing.

"What was that?" Emma asked. I looked up and she was looking right at me.

"What?"

"Asking about Babs. You don't think she's missing too, do you?"

"I wanted to see how he reacted. It's probably nothing," I said. "So, about the agreements Gus had, and then canceled. What exactly are they?"

"They were letters of agreement. Prospectuses on different Century Projects. A ton of paperwork that Gus generated. Seriously, it's a ton of paper. It must all be in that file. Things were flying back and forth between Gus's office and the Cunningham Corporation and Hal's office. I wasn't keeping up with them, especially after Gus put the brakes on. I think Gus shared a folder with me already. I'll check on that later. I'll forward you Hal's link so you can help me look at the documents."

"Do you know why Gus put the brakes on?"

"No, not really. It was less about the Century Projects we were partnering with and more about the other companies they were aligned with, or so Gus said. He talked to me about it last week, and then we had that meeting on Monday with Eric with his final recommendations. As I said, we told Hal and the Cunninghams on Monday. They asked us to go to the reception anyway, let bygones be bygones. I think the plan was to get us to change our minds, but Gus sent the letters of dissolution out late that night. I should have asked him more questions, but I thought we'd catch up yesterday."

"It's weird he didn't tell Kate, isn't it?" I said. "Aren't they partners?"

"This is Gus's story to tell, but my impression is that he and Kate are on the rocks, professionally and personally. Kate has great ambition. I think she's considering going to work for the Cunninghams as an in-house lawyer. That might have been one of the reasons Gus seemed to be thinking about ending the relationship last time we talked. Their relationship is complicated."

"Maybe there were some other side deals that Gus didn't like?" I asked, trying not to get distracted by that interesting tidbit. For someone who didn't like gossip, Emma was a font of information.

"Possibly. I know we need to talk to Kate," Emma said. "But first, we need to get downtown to see Jerry. Hold on to your hat, I'm going to take a shortcut."

∞

"So where exactly is the Cunningham Corporation?" I asked Emma as she zipped through traffic. She'd texted Eric before we left, asking if he could come to Mimi's memorial that afternoon.

"Park Square, in that new building with the spire on top."

"How much of it is given over to the Century Foundation?"

"The corporation and foundation occupy the top floors of the building. When specific projects are underway, teams come in and share office space as well. The Century Projects are quite the brand throughout New England."

"They sure are," I said. "That was probably Hal's doing. There's a new project opening this spring, the Century Art Center up near the New Hampshire border—"

"They're doing a second Century Cape Project. You're right, Century was all about branding. At least that's what Terry always used to say," Emma said. Her jaw clenched as it always did when mentioning her late husband. "Eric emailed this morning and said he wanted to hire a private investigator to look at the business projects we've invested in with the Cunninghams."

"Didn't your company do that work before you signed any contracts?"

"The Cunningham partnership was a Terry deal," Emma said. "We assumed he did the work—maybe he did? Or he just ignored what he found? He probably leveraged it for his own benefit." Terry'd had a very tangled relationship with the family business.

"Gus would have—" I began.

"Gus didn't come in until late last fall. He's been untangling the spaghetti that my father's paranoia and Terry's duplicity built ever since."

"Huh," I said. "Well, if the Century branding was done to hide something, they did a good job. There are Century Projects all over New England, and the Century Foundation has funded some great work."

"I know that the foundation has contributed a great deal to the region," Emma said. "But Gus said he's been hearing that a couple of the Century Projects have run into some snafus, with projects being delayed or stopped midway. Have you heard anything?"

"No, but I don't travel in the same circles you do," I said.

"It's probably nothing. You should hear what folks say about the Whitehalls," Emma said. "Seriously, trash talk is part of the business. Anyway, we're here. Let me valet the car."

Emma and I made our way up to the main offices. Traveling with a Whitehall had its benefits. For one thing, when we walked into the Cunningham Corporation, someone recognized her. We dropped off the grant application and then walked to the other end of the hallway and opened a black-glass door.

"Ms. Whitehall?" the woman sitting at the desk at the other end of the room asked. The space looked more like a living room than a reception area, and I had to wonder if it was usually full of people, or if it was always a bit empty and mostly for show.

"Sherry, hello. So good to see you. I didn't expect that you'd be in today. My friend Sully needed to drop off a grant proposal. Thank you so much for getting us in to see Jerry. I don't want to intrude, but I did want to pay my respects. This must be a terrible time for all of you."

"Thank you so much. Yes, it is terrible. I still can't believe it. It's so...difficult. But he insisted we come in today and get some things done before the service."

"Coming into the office helps keep the mind occupied. I know that firsthand."

"I know you do," she said. "Perhaps it will be good for him to see you, since you've been through the same thing so recently? I'm so sorry, that was inappropriate—"

"No, its fine. I'm happy to say hello and let him know I'm thinking about him."

Ironically, Peter Whitehall's death had brought Emma and me closer together, which was a sliver of a silver lining in a very dark cloud. Sherry was right—murder forged a common bond between those left behind. I looked over at my second cousin. She was a stoic Yankee, but no one was that stoic. Much as I was grateful for the opportunity to see Jerry Cunningham, I was sorry that the situation raised the specter of loss for my friend. It hadn't been nearly long enough for her grief to not cause tremendous pain. I reached over and rubbed her arm gently. She smiled at me and went over to take a seat.

Sherry disappeared into the next room and closed the door behind her. My phone vibrated and I stepped aside to answer it.

"Sully, its Harry. Just wanted to tell you that Holly still hasn't been able to reach Babs Allyn. Rumors are flying."

"What rumors?" I whispered.

"That she killed Mimi Cunningham. Because she was having an affair with Jerry. Just thought I'd let you know."

"Whoa. Damn. Listen, we're going to go in and see Jerry Cunningham any minute. I'll check and let you know how that goes. Call or text me if you hear anything else."

My phone manners, which were never stellar, had completely gone out the window with the advent of cell phones. No hellos, no goodbyes. Just on and off. But now I had an excuse for my abrupt hang-up beyond bad manners. My mind had started to whir, and I needed to process a couple of new ideas before I saw Jerry Cunningham. Could Babs have strangled Mimi? It wasn't impossible. But why? Was the affair rumor true? Why was I just hearing about it now?

I sat next to Emma on the couch in Sherry's office while we waited. Emma was busy sending an email or a text on her phone, so I didn't interrupt. Besides, I wanted to wait until we were out of the building to share the rumors about Jerry and Babs. I needed to clear my mind, so I looked around. Although the building was new, the office had an old Boston air about it. Cherry wainscoting, desks, and built-in cabinetry. The couch was mid-century with gold upholstery and brick red, avocado green, and slate blue squares and dashes. The area rug was the same palette. The décor made the office feel both old fashioned and modern. With money.

I didn't have time to process much more than initial impressions because Sherry came back to usher us into the inner sanctum, Jerry's office. Emma seemed right at home there. The man himself stood up and came around his desk. He looked sallow beneath his tan, and bags sat under his eyes. His hair wasn't perfectly coiffed, nor was his suit pressed. To the right a door was slightly ajar, showing a bathroom. I saw a suit bag hanging on the door.

"Emma, thank you for coming by." He took both of her hands in his and held them.

"Jerry, I can't tell you how very, very sorry I am. I know how hard this is."

"Yes, I know you do. I was just thinking about how inadequate I was in December…"

"Don't. Don't." Emma griped both of his hands. When she turned to me I saw tears in her eyes. Maybe she wasn't as stoic as I'd first thought.

Jerry turned to me. "Thank you, Sully, for coming by."

"Mr. Cunningham, I'm so sorry about your wife. I hope they catch the person responsible."

"Jerry, please. The police have been very good about keeping me updated on the investigation. Not that there's much to keep up with at this point."

"I'm sure there will be a break in the case soon." And I was. Socialites like Mimi Cunningham getting murdered in a public park? Not tolerable. I was trying to figure out how to tactfully ask if they had any leads, but that was a tough conversation to jump into.

"Well, I hope they make the right assumptions. From what I understand, I think they're focusing on Gus," Jerry said. "I have an alibi for Mimi's murder, but last night they started asking a lot more questions about Gus."

"Gus isn't responsible," I said, sounding harsher than I meant to.

"I agree, but the cops don't," he said. "Apparently there was some contract discrepancy regarding one of the Century Projects—the office building on Newbury we started working on together. Some funding discrepancies because of Gus's paperwork. I'm not sure where they were headed with their reasoning, but I think he may be in trouble." The phone buzzed and Jerry picked it up, grunted twice, and hung up. "Sorry, ladies. I have a few phone calls I need to make before I fly out."

"Are you going somewhere?" Emma asked, feigning ignorance.

"Yes, I'm heading out of the country for a bit right after the service to get my bearings."

"Of course. I often wish I'd taken some time after…but you'll be at the meeting tomorrow, won't you?"

"Meeting tomorrow?"

"Eric just texted me about it. Given everything, the changes we made in our business dealings, we have that escrow account that can be closed."

"My flight is tonight, late. Perhaps my proxy can fill in?"

"Jerry, your proxy was Mimi," Emma said gently. "Under the circumstances you, Eric, and I need to be there."

"If we don't sign the paperwork tomorrow?"

"The money stays in escrow and some of the penalties kick in."

"Any way we can move the meeting up?"

"No, sorry. Eric won't be in Boston until tomorrow afternoon. Late. He won't be able to make an earlier meeting. We could postpone until you get back, but you'll need to cover the cost of the—"

"No, no. That won't work. Let's get the money moving to the right places. Can Kate fill in for Gus?"

"I guess so," Emma said. "I'll ask Eric to check on that."

"Let's assume so, and meet tomorrow to get this taken care of. I know you Whitehalls could use your funds being freed up. I'll reschedule my flight."

"If you're sure."

"Of course. A few hours delay. No big deal."

"Thank you, Jerry. We've taken up so much of your time." Emma got up to leave. I'd have liked to ask a few more questions, but I followed Emma's lead and stood up as well.

"Please, Emma, it was wonderful to see a friendly face," Jerry said. Emma hesitated, then walked over and embraced him.

"Anything you need, Jerry. Anything. Just let me know."

"Thank you. That means the world to me." He stepped back and wiped his eyes.

∞

We waited until we were in the car before we spoke. There was something about the building that made you feel as if you were being watched all the time. Because you probably were. Once we were on Storrow Drive and she could shift into gear, Emma pushed a button on her steering wheel.

"Call Eric's cell," she instructed. I listened while the phone connected.

"Eric? You can't come to Mimi's funeral this afternoon after all. I told Jerry you were out of town until late tomorrow afternoon. Call me when you get this." She disconnected the call.

"So, he could have had Jerry sign papers?"

"And conveniently left Gus holding the bag. Listen, Sully, Jerry was lying. Gus and I specifically talked about the Newbury building contract specifics, and I signed off on them. There's no possible malfeasance. Unless someone changed the contracts."

"To make it look like Gus was guilty. Which he couldn't fight because he isn't around right now. Convenient, isn't it?" I said.

"Right. So I bought a few hours for us to figure out what the hell is going on," Emma said. "I don't think Jerry killed Mimi. But I wouldn't put it past him to cover it up if it was in his best interest."

"Even the murder of his wife? I don't know them well, but they seemed devoted."

"They were. I have no doubt that Jerry will find justice for Mimi, even if he has to pay for it."

"Great. Vigilante justice. More common than I like to think about," I said.

"Really? You must have some interesting stories, Sully."

"Here's one. Harry said that there's a rumor going around the theater that Babs and Jerry were having an affair. And that Babs killed Mimi."

"An affair with Babs? Really? Huh."

"Huh? You don't seem surprised."

"You know, maybe it's because of what I went through with Terry, but I'm more sympathetic to unconventional unions than I used to be. I do think Jerry and Mimi were devoted, but they'd been married a long time. But still, Jerry and Babs? I wouldn't have guessed that."

"That could explain the scene the other night," I said, remembering drinks thrown in faces.

"It sure could. Maybe Jerry is going to meet Babs somewhere? Nah, I don't believe it. I've heard that Babs was going through changes, but I don't think she left Hal for Jerry."

"But she did leave Hal?"

"Still trying to pin that down, but the latest I've heard is that they've been separated for a while. She may have filed for divorce."

"Emma, you are a font of information."

"Eric's bored in Trevorton. He fancies himself a private investigator. He's been asking around, looking at public records."

"I'll talk to him about privacy laws later. So, Babs filed? Not Hal?"

"No, not Hal. He couldn't."

"Couldn't? Come on, spill. There's a cone of silence in this car. Tell me what you know."

"I've known Hal for years. He has a summer house the next town over, did you know that?"

"I do. He's a donor to the Cliffside." Sometimes I felt as though I'd been close to Emma for years, but other times I was reminded that we still had to figure out how our adult lives intersected.

"So do you know him well?" she asked.

"I know him like I know a lot of our donors. He comes to events, always writes at least two checks a year. He's advised on a couple of projects. We tried to get him on the board last summer, but he declined."

"That was right after Martin disappeared."

"Right. Hal talked about needing a change of scenery. Come to think of it, Babs wasn't with him, but I just assumed she was back in the city working," I said. "He was around a lot last summer. He's a nice guy who picks up the bar bill at the Beef & Ale. But he'd always leave alone."

"You know, one of the things I always liked about Hal was that our business life and our friendship didn't overlap. But lately he's been off his game a bit—pushing more. I've been giving him space, but it's getting uncomfortable. Part of what made him so successful was that he knew when to walk away and come back another day. But not so much lately."

"Yeah, he's been pushing me a little too, wanting to do rebranding on the Cliffside," I said. "I'm surprised he hasn't brought it up these past few days, but we're small fry compared to the other things going on. Anyway, bad marriages can screw you up. We both know that."

"We do indeed," Emma said.

"Do you know Babs well?" I asked.

"Not as well as I do Hal, but pretty well. She reminds me of myself, actually. Born Yankee. Pretty tightly wound. Married to a charismatic man."

"And successful on her own. We were on the same panel at the last StageSource conference and ended up going out to dinner. She is really, really good at what she does, and she's kept the Bay Rep running despite the challenges with changing artistic directors the past couple of years. I'm really surprised she left the company in the lurch this week."

"Who's running things?" Emma said.

"Holly Samuel."

"Martin's daughter? I forgot she was back working for Babs."

"Hal came in while I was in the office yesterday. When he told Holly about Mimi, she didn't seem too upset. She made some accusations about her father's disappearance. Can you remember anything else about what happened with Martin? There wasn't much real information in the articles I found online."

"Not anything more than I told you already—" Emma began.

"Please, Emma, you travel in those circles. Guaranteed you know more than I do."

"Okay, let me think it through again. It was last March that Hal, Babs, Martin, the Cunninghams, and a few other people chartered that boat in the Caribbean. They went to bed one night, and when they woke up Martin was gone. So were the lifeboat and his overnight bag."

"Was anyone questioned?"

"I'd imagine they all were, but no one was arrested. No one talked about it. The assumption was that Martin had taken a powder for a while, but it's been almost a year."

That's the problem with Yankee stock, especially among the upper crust. Minding your own business is ingrained into their DNA. Not that they don't gossip, but it's hard to make them break ranks and tell you what they know. Of course Emma was making an exception for me, but I was family. This all makes it really, really hard for investigators. Rich people justice. I ran into it last fall when Peter Whitehall was killed. They deal with their own.

Was that what had happened to Mimi Cunningham?

∞

Emma and I decided to go back to the townhouse before the memorial service. She wanted to get some work done, and I wanted to do some more research. I walked into my apartment, or what I had started to consider my apartment, and was surprised to see Eric sitting at the kitchen table working on his computer. I gave him a big hug.

"When did you get here?" I asked.

"When Emma first called, I jumped in the car and headed down. I was here before I got your message. I planned to visit Harry soon anyway. I figured I would hide out and you could catch me up."

I texted Emma, who came downstairs and brought her laptop. The two of us told Eric what had been happening over the past few days, concluding with our visit to Jerry Cunningham.

"So let me get this straight. I'm not going to the funeral this afternoon because we don't want to sign the paperwork with Jerry and free up the assets that our company needs?"

"I know, I know," Emma said. "But I want to figure out what Gus was worried about before we sign anything. I've looked over the numbers, the paperwork, everything a million times. It's all in order. We sign the papers, our money is freed from escrow and we walk away. This is what I want. But considering that Hal asked me to go forward with the business, and then less than an hour later Jerry basically told me he's going to cut and run—I don't know. Something is going on. What do you think, Sully?"

"I don't know the business ins and outs, but I've been listening to the conversations. And everyone is hiding something. The fact that we have a dead body, and Gus is missing, makes that statement pretty obvious."

"By the way, ladies, I like what you've done with the cabinets," Eric said.

"I hear you've been fancying yourself a private investigator lately," I said. "Surely you know the technique."

"Someone's been spilling secrets, I see. I'm just trying to catch myself up," Eric said. He glared at Emma, who refused to look up from her computer. "I'm ashamed at how little I knew about how the family business ran. Gus keeps uncovering things, and I'm sick of being surprised. So I'm preparing myself for any other skeletons in the closet by doing some background checks. I hire professionals when it gets too tough."

"You couldn't have mentioned this to me the other day?" I said.

"I was trying to figure some things out on my own. I'm getting reports together, and I'll share them when I'm able, okay? I doubt they have anything to do with what happened," Eric said. "Tell me about the cards on the cabinets."

"We'll tell you about the cards but you have to promise to fill in any information we haven't put up there already. Promise?" I said.

"I promise," Eric said.

"We're trying to find Gus. He's missing," Emma said.

"Gus is really missing? Or is this the way you're investigating Mimi's murder while pretending to look for Gus? I mean, how can he just disappear?"

"Great question," Emma said. "He's been gone almost a day. Have you heard from him?" Eric shook his head.

"Maybe we can try and see Kate before the funeral," I said.

"Kate? What does she have to do with anything?" Eric asked.

"Kate told me that Gus was dissolving any business remotely tied to the Century Project and the Cunningham Corporation. He apparently sent out official notices to folks on Tuesday."

"Gus told me he was planning to do that," Eric said. "At first I thought it was extreme, but he convinced me it made sense. He talked me through the business implications, the paperwork he needed to follow up on, legalities of dropping clients. Most of the clients were Kate's, honestly."

"When did you last speak with Gus?" Emma asked.

"Wednesday morning," Eric said.

"Do you know what time?" I asked. Eric picked up his phone and swiped through a screen.

"Seven o'clock. We spoke for fifty-two minutes." Eric put his phone back down on the table. "Everything seemed on track, but he did seem a bit distracted."

"Distracted?" I asked.

"Well, it was to be expected, given Mimi's death and all. His plan was to go after Jerry and Mimi a little harder, try to get us extricated from all Century Project activities, but that was going to take a lot more work. It would burn some bridges too. We agreed to wait until this weekend when I came down, so he, Emma, and I could discuss all the options in person."

"Were you going to get yourself out of the Newbury Street project?" I asked. "That was the project Jerry seem to imply Gus had mishandled in some way."

"Gus mishandled? Gus? There's something going on with that project, but Gus and I were both in the dark. I spent the better part of yesterday trying to figure it out. All I've found out so far is that its bills haven't been paid and companies are putting a lien on the property. I was hoping to talk to Jerry about that too."

"What does Kate have to say for herself?" Emma said. "She isn't returning my calls or texts or emails."

"Her voicemail is full," Eric said. "Both on her cell and at the office. She isn't returning my calls either. Emma, do you remember if she took the lead on the Newbury project, or was it Gus? I know Gus was the end-product point person, but why do I remember Kate playing a bigger role in this particular project?"

"I honestly don't remember," Emma said. "That was right around the time…right around the holidays. I know I sat through meetings, but I don't really remember much. For all I know I dropped the ball on something important. I'm so sorry, Eric, I haven't been holding up my end of the stick very well lately, have I?"

"Emma, don't. You falling behind is one hundred percent better than most people's best work. You didn't miss anything. This is all a little squiggly. Listen, while you're at the funeral, how about if I add some index cards to your timeline? Some details about the projects?"

"Eric, Hal shared a Dropbox folder with Emma this morning that he said had all the paperwork in it," I said. "And Emma, you said Gus had shared a similar folder with you. Maybe it would be worth comparing the two? I wonder if there are some answers in there."

"Sounds like my kind of project," Eric said. "Emma, can you give me access?"

"Tell you what, brother, I'll do you one better. Here's the password to my email. Don't judge, but it's the same password for everything. Have at it, see what you can find. Forward the email to Sully so she can look at it too. Just remember to add notes to the index cards. Meanwhile, Sully and I will go to the funeral and represent the family."

· Thirteen ·

Emma Whitehall was a very punctual person. I, typically, was not. But she was a good influence on me, and was my ride to the service, so we found ourselves arriving a full forty-five minutes before the event started. We were not, however, the first. In fact, we had to park two blocks away, since the synagogue's parking lot was already full. We found a spot, and Emma and I were both going through our larger bags trying to take only what was necessary with us to the service. Tissues, cell phones, lipstick for Emma, cough drops for me. Emma also slipped some of her business cards into her pocket. One good thing about winter coats is that they are full of all sorts of hidden pockets, making a purse almost obsolete. I checked one more time to make sure my lipstick was on straight, and noticed that the vehicle parked behind us also had two passengers, both sitting in the car, neither moving. I recognized the bouncy brown curls of Toni Vestri and saw the sun bounce off John Engel's bald head.

"Emma, wait here for a second. I just have to check in with somebody."

I got out of the car and walked back to the unmarked vehicle behind us. I knocked on Toni's window, and she had the good grace to look embarrassed.

"Hey, Sully," she said.

"Hey, Toni. Hey, John. You following me or staking out the service?"

"Following you?" John said. "Don't flatter yourself. We've got bigger fish to fry. The only reason to follow you would be to find your ne'er-do-well ex. But we'll find him soon enough. Unless he's really taken a runner. Wouldn't blame him if he did. Evidence is really piling up against him—"

"John, shut up." Toni said. "We need to follow the evidence, but we can't assume we know where it's going to take us."

"Listen, I know you're friends with Gus," John said. "Hell, I know him too. We go way back. He's a good guy. But you can't tell me—"

"John always was very good jumping to assumptions without evidence backing him up. His famous gut," I said to Toni.

"It only failed me once," John said. "I never would've taken you for a snitch, that's for sure."

"A snitch? That's what you call it? Fine, at least I wasn't closing my eyes to what was going on around me—"

"Talk about no evidence—"

"Stop it, you two," Toni said. "Seriously, I've had it. Believe it or not, we're all on the same side."

"What side is that? The rat squad side?" John said.

"God help us," I said, "he's been watching old gangster movies again, hasn't he? That's never good—"

"Don't provoke him, Sully, please. Hey, will you do us a favor?"

"Not us. *You*. I wouldn't ask her to spit on me if I were on fire—" John began.

"Don't worry, Engel, I wouldn't. What do you need, Toni?"

"I assume you're here for the Mimi Cunningham service?" she asked. I nodded. "It's private. Jerry Cunningham won't let us in. It would be great if you could keep an eye out, take note of anything that draws your attention."

"See if Gus shows up, for one," John said.

"Thanks, John. Yes, see if Gus shows up. But also see who else shows up, who doesn't. You know Babs Allyn, right?"

"I do. She runs Bay Rep and I have some friends working there right now. She hasn't been around for the past couple of days. Apparently she's up in Vermont."

"Where in Vermont? Do you know?" Toni asked.

"Holly—that's her assistant—Holly was supposed to send me an address, but she hasn't. Honestly, I forgot to ask her today. I'll text her again, forward it to you."

"Why did you want the address?" Toni asked.

"I don't know." I rubbed my hands together and looked around at the additional cars that were parking. I needed to get inside. "It just seemed odd that Babs left out of the blue like that. I never like it when things seem odd. Especially when somebody's died."

"Well, if you see her, or Gus, or hear anything, or see anything, let me know, will you? Come to think of it, just call me later. Okay?"

"I'll call you later, Toni. I won't call you John. That's probably for the best, for both of our sakes."

As I walked back toward Emma's car, she got out. Together we headed toward the synagogue and Mimi Cunningham's memorial service.

∞

"Isn't there usually some sort of reception after these sorts of things?" I whispered to Emma.

The service was over, and Jerry was greeting people at the rear of the synagogue. The Rabbi had made an announcement that a celebration of Mimi's life would be held at a later date "when things are more settled." For now, she welcomed us all to give Jerry Cunningham our respects on our way out. Needless to say, the line was long. Emma and I had been in the middle, toward the side. We hung back, didn't force our way into the line. I did take the opportunity to stand up and look around. See who was there and who wasn't. I noticed Hal toward the back. He must've come in late. He was alone, no Babs in sight. I cast another quick look around, hoping to see Gus's silver head. There were plenty of silver heads, but none belonged to him. I wasn't surprised, but I was disappointed. Where are you, Gus?

I looked to my left and saw Kate staring right at me. I returned her look and forced a smile and small wave. She made a point of turning away and scurried out the side door. I was tempted to give chase but thought better of it. Maybe Emma and I would stop by the office on our way home. I took out my cell phone and dialed. I got a voicemail greeting that told me the office was closed for the week and calls would be returned next week. So much for that idea.

We made our way into the receiving line to give Jerry our respects for the second time that day. I took the opportunity as we got closer to look at him closely as he was greeting guests. He looked tough, exhausted. But grief-stricken? Or scared? I couldn't tell. He did look like the weight of the world was on his shoulders.

Walking back out into the February chill and the setting sun was a bit of a shock. So much had happened already today, it was hard to believe it was still daylight. Emma must've felt the same, because we both stood there for a second getting our bearings.

"Nice service," I said.

"Not really. This was just a placeholder."

I looked over at her and remembered her father's funeral. That had felt like a placeholder too. I realized they'd never had a follow-up memorial service after his murder was solved. Given everything, that was probably bad form, but I made a mental note to think about some way to honor Peter Whitehall this summer at the theater.

"What do you think that's about?" Emma asked. I followed her gaze and looked to my right. Kate and Hal were standing toward the side of the road, having an argument. More than an argument. From their body language, it was more of a fight. I looked to my left quickly but realized that Toni and John were out of the line of sight. I took out my cell phone stealthily took a quick picture. I couldn't hear what Hal and Kate were saying, but it was clear that Kate was furious and Hal was defensive. He was trying to calm her down, and put his hands on both of her upper arms. She shrugged him off and twisted away from him.

"I told him Friday, and I meant it," Kate said. That was loud enough for us to hear, along with a few other folks nearby. I turned and saw that Jerry had heard her too. Kate stalked off, got into her small red car, and drove away. Emma and I watched her weave in between mourners making their way up the side street, back to their cars. We joined the tide of people. I turned back to see if Hal was still there, but he was gone. I looked at Kate's car as she finally broke free of the crowd and noticed the Cape Cod bumper sticker on the back bumper.

"Hold on," I said. "Isn't that Gus's car?"

"Belongs to Knight, Smythe, and Brown, technically. They both drive it. Since they both live in the city—"

"Okay, I have to ask. Do they live together?"

"No, not together. But the company owns the car, and they share it. They keep it in the garage underneath their offices."

"If Gus called me from a tunnel the other day, and he was following up on something, was he driving the company car? If he was, how did it get back to the office?"

"All good questions," Emma said. "Should we ask her?"

"Yes, we should," I said. I looked to my left and saw Toni Vestri walking toward me. I slowed down to chat with her.

"Who just drove past here in Gus's car?" she asked when she got close enough that only I could hear her.

"Kate Smythe. His business partner."

"I know Kate. I take it Gus wasn't here?"

"No, just his car, which she was driving," I said. "One thing Emma and I were just remarking on. Remember when Gus called me to tell me to meet him at Cambridge One? I could barely hear him because he said there was construction. He also mentioned a tunnel. I assumed he was driving somewhere, but maybe he wasn't? Maybe was walking somewhere?"

"Where's there a tunnel?" Emma asked.

"I'll deny I told you two this, but we pinged Gus's call, the one he made to you, Sully. Closest we could pinpoint, he was down by Fort Point. Heading toward Congress Street there's sort of a tunnel along the river walk."

"A couple of them," I said. "Maybe he's—"

"We're already on it, Sully," Toni said. "We haven't found him or his cell. Not even sure why he was down there."

"Maybe I know," I said. "When we were married we had a storage facility down there. We kept old papers there, seasonal clothes, Christmas decorations, that sort of thing. I think he kept it after the divorce. I remember I had to call him and have the billing changed to his credit card number."

"That's helpful, we'll check it out. *We* will check it out, Sully. Not you. Leave it to the cops. This is getting more and more complicated and I want you to stay out of it. Do you hear me?"

"I just want to find Gus," I said.

"We all do," Toni said. "But there's no love lost between you and John Engel. Seeing you, he got all riled up again. Stay out of his path, Sully. For your own sake."

She turned and walked back up to where John was parked. He gave me a salute, and as soon as she closed the door he did a U-turn and drove away.

"She's a charmer, isn't she?" Emma said.

"She's a good cop. She was a good friend. Still is, to Gus. I guarantee you she's looking for him, and not because she thinks he's guilty."

"What do we do now?" Emma asked.

"Let's go back to the apartment, see what Eric's been up to while we've been gone."

∞

I'd turned off my cell phone ringer while I was at the service. I went to turn it back on and noticed I got a text from Cassandra.

Call Holly. Payroll time. She's drowning.

Emma was crawling her way into traffic. I called Holly. She picked up on the first ring. "Hi, Sully, I was just thinking about you."

"I'm calling to check in. I just went to Mimi Cunningham's funeral."

"Obviously, I wasn't there. I actually thought about it, as a gesture to Jerry, but it's been a little nuts here at the theater."

"Nuts? What do you mean?"

"First of all, I had to put in payroll. It took me half the day to find Babs's passwords so I could sign in and pretend I was her. I'm not authorized to call it in, but people needed to get paid. Don't tell anyone."

"I won't. Tell you what, tomorrow I'll try and figure out how to get you authorized. We may need to get your treasurer to sign something, but we'll figure it out. What else is going on?"

"We had a production meeting about the next show. Everyone asked me about their budgets, and I didn't know what to tell them. I don't think Babs finished it. All I could find were budgets from last year's shows, and the year before. But nothing for this next one. People want numbers, and I couldn't figure it out." Holly sounded like she was going to cry. I knew the frustration, having had to wade through my predecessors' files when I first started my job.

"What's the next show?"

"It's a new play. We always do a new play in that slot."

"Well, can you look at last year's budget for last year's new play, make the changes?"

"Yes, but this year's show has six people, last year's had two. And scenic tells me that they need double the budget this year—"

"Scenic always wants double the budget. Would it help if I came in?"

"I guess…I was thinking about trying to leave a little bit early today to have dinner with my boyfriend. Get away from here for a bit. But I can stay—"

"No, no. We can do it tomorrow."

"I have a meeting tomorrow at ten o'clock. I don't suppose…"

"What?"

"If I give you Babs's login, would you look at the files on her computer? They should all be there. We've started to work from the cloud so that we can all work from wherever."

"It's probably not a good idea, Holly," I said. "There could be some confidential information in those files—"

"Not on these files, not on the cloud files. Anything confidential is kept on laptops. I don't know where Babs's laptop is. She must have it with her. But the cloud has files we all share, like budgets, things like that. I'd give you my password, but Babs's password will let you go in and copy things, and edit them. My password only lets you look at the files. I've been using Babs's passwords since she left."

"What's the meeting tomorrow morning at ten?" I asked.

"Another production meeting. I put them off today, but I think if I put them off any longer they can smell blood. Not that they'd do anything wrong—"

"But you need to stay in control. I get it. Send me the password; once I get home I'll look around. See if I can pull something together for you to work with. I don't suppose you know the overall budget, do you?" Holly gave me a number. "Good. Send me that too. Otherwise I may forget. I'll try to figure out how Babs worked, but I can also pull from my own files. Do me one more favor; send me a synopsis of the play. Number of characters, number of sets, you know the drill. That'll help with the number as well."

"Thank you so much, Sully. I'll send an email right now, brain dump everything I know about the show. I might have been able to pull this off myself, but not right away. And probably not correctly. You're saving me. Don't hesitate to text me any questions. Thank you again."

"So tell me, are you on the Bay Rep payroll these days?" Emma asked as I hit the end-call button.

"Sorry. I realize you probably heard most of that. Poor kid, she's in way over her head."

"How much work will it be to do this budget?"

"Hopefully not much. It doesn't sound like a huge show, and I can use Babs's old files to help make some of the decisions. First budgets are just a working document, something for everyone to discuss."

"You realize, don't you, that you've got Babs's password now, right?"

"Just to her cloud files. Business, not personal."

"Well, chances are good that her password is the same for other things as well. Or we can use it as a way to see what other files she has. If you're right, and Babs's leaving town now is an odd thing, maybe some of her files will give us clues. Technically, we won't be looking for Gus. But we can both still feel like we're doing something. Why does that seem untoward?"

"It does seem like I've been rubbing off on you, Emma, and not in a good way."

∞

I texted Cassandra back. *Thanks for the heads up. Just called Holly. Hopefully we're back on track.* I'd barely hit send when my phone rang. Cassandra.

"Sorry about this," I said to Emma.

"Put it on speakerphone this time," she said. "Last time it was hard to hear everything."

"Hi, Cassandra. How goes it?"

"Can you talk?"

"Yes I can. Are you all right?"

"I'm fine, I just don't have a lot of time. No rest for the wicked. Now that I've got the money to do the work, I've got to do the work. I know you're worried about Babs, and there's a lot going on. I was talking to somebody in the costume shop, a friend of Babs. She's worried too. Really worried. Afraid that Babs is going to do something drastic."

"Drastic? What you mean?"

"I'm still pulling the story together, but here's what I've got so far. Years ago, we're talking years ago, Babs fell in love with somebody. Apparently she never got over it, but she stayed married to Hal. Made it work. Anyway, this old love had Babs worried."

"About someone finding out?"

"No, that wasn't it. This is the part I'm confused about, but maybe it makes sense to you. Last year some guy disappeared—"

"Disappeared? Was his name Martin?"

"I didn't get names. Don't interrupt. I only have a minute more before I should get back into the shop. Anyway, this guy disappears. Her guy is involved somehow. Maybe he's the one who disappeared. I can't get a straight story. Anyway, Babs hires a PI to look for him. She had a meeting with the PI Tuesday afternoon."

"Tuesday? That must have been where she was going when I saw her at the theater?"

"Probably? This woman in the shop, she heard from Babs later that afternoon. She'd been drinking. She wasn't making much sense, just kept saying she had to make it right, that it was partly her fault. That she was going to clear the air that night, no matter what the consequences. That's all Stella told me, but I thought you should know. Not sure if that helps you find Babs or not, but I sure hope you do. Gotta go." Cassandra disconnected the line.

"Whoa," Emma said. "What do you think that meant? Babs had an affair with Martin? Or with Jerry? You think Hal knew?"

"I don't know answers to any of those questions," I said. My hands itched for my notebook but I couldn't find it. Instead, I sent myself an email with the notes from my calls. "Good thing we're almost home. I need to write this stuff down before I forget the details. I don't have any more answers to add to our 'find Gus' board, but I've got some really interesting new questions to ask."

"We should pick up some food on the way. I'm starving," Emma said. "Am I terrible? All I think about is food."

"Breakfast was a long time ago," I agreed. "I hate to make this recommendation, but how about pizza? I was sorry I didn't get to try the other two we brought home."

“Since we’re living in a frat house, sounds good to me,” Emma said. She hit the button on her steering wheel and told the car to dial the pizza place. We were connected to them right away.

“Emma, my friend, what can I get for you tonight?”

“Same as last night, Jeff. We’ll be there in about twenty minutes.”

· Fourteen ·

Emma and I came in through the alley just in case someone, anyone, like say a reporter, was staking out the building. She went upstairs to her place to grab some more wine and get changed into more comfortable clothes.

"Hello!" I said as I came in the side door of my apartment. "Hello? I could use some help here."

"Hey, Sully, sorry." Eric came around the corner and grabbed the pizza boxes for me. "I was just finishing up a conference call when you came in. Trying to find out some more information about that Newbury Street project we were talking about—"

"What's going on? You look worried," I said, taking my knapsack off and putting it by the back door. "Did the files help you figure something out?"

"Where's Emma? She should hear this too."

"She's upstairs getting changed. Get some plates out, and some glasses. I'm going to go put on pants with an elastic waistband and I'll be right out. If she comes down before I'm back, don't start without me."

"Well, if you have more index cards, bring them out. This is getting pretty complicated."

I got dressed as quickly as I could and checked my phone for the hundredth time that day hoping for a text, an email, anything from Gus. Nothing. I tried him again and got a "voicemail full" message. I hoped my text got through, but I didn't receive the "is delivered" response. Oh Gus, where are you? What are you in the middle of? I couldn't help but wish we'd stayed in touch these past couple of months. Maybe he would've confided in me, and I would've known more about what he was working on. There were so many story threads to focus on—Mimi's death, this Newbury Street project, Martin's disappearance last year, Babs taking off, Kate's odd behavior at the memorial service, Hal's desperation to get the investment back on track, Jerry's plans to leave town—which one had Gus grabbed? I sat on the edge of the bed and made a list of all those items in my notebook.

I looked down at my notes. Perhaps I'd been thinking about this the wrong way. Maybe they weren't separate threads after all, but rather loose strands of the same fabric. If I shifted my perception and thought like that, did the picture look different? I grabbed another pack of index cards from my roaming office supply bag and went back into the kitchen area. Emma was there, opening a bottle of red wine and filling Eric in on the memorial service.

I tossed the pack of index cards on the table and opened up my laptop. I noticed that Emma had brought hers down too, and Eric's had several tabs open.

"It looks like this is going to be a working dinner," I said. Emma handed me a glass of wine and I took a sip.

"Thanks for the cards. Let me pull some notes together before I tell you what I've found," Eric said. "I'll eat while I work."

"A bad habit, one I don't normally approve of. But these are not ordinary times," Emma said. She opened up the salad and put it on the bar. "Did Holly send you an email? The one with Babs's passwords?"

"Someone else's passwords? Does this have anything to do with Gus's disappearance?" Eric asked, looking up.

"I'm beginning to think everything has something to do with everything," I said. I checked my email. Sure enough, Holly had sent me the synopsis of the play, Babs's passwords, and a direct link to the budget folder from the theater. Lots to look at. I had to focus so I didn't get too distracted. I took an index card, made a note that I needed to work on the budget for Holly, and taped it to the corner of my computer. I knew from past experience that once I started working on one thing, I often forgot about everything else. That habit made me good at my job but probably had cost me my marriage.

I hit the link to the folder Holly had sent me and was asked for Babs's password. I put it in, and looked at what I had access to. I went up a couple of levels and was pleased to see that Babs was an extraordinarily organized person. The file structure seemed simple: folders were broken up into seasons, shows, categories of production, personnel, board minutes—all aspects of running a company. A quick perusal also showed that Babs seemed good at separating her personal life from her professional life. No one folder indicated that it had anything to do with Babs the person. They all had everything to do with Babs the managing director. Nonetheless, surely there were some clues.

"Earth to Sully. Here, eat some pizza. Let's let Eric tell us what he found and you can explain your cryptic *it's all tied together* comment before you dive too deeply into your project for Holly," Emma said, sliding a piece toward me. Barbecue chicken pizza. Yum. I took a bite, and then another.

"Having those two groups of files was really interesting," Eric said, wiping his mouth. "I copied them both into new directories on my computer, so that the originals wouldn't be changed. Then

I made a copy of those, in case somebody went in and changed the originals—"

"Isn't that a little paranoid?" Emma asked.

"I've been hanging around Sully too long," Eric said. "I've developed a healthy paranoia about not having multiple copies of everything. I'm glad I took the extra steps. On the copy of the copy on my laptop—hope you're following this—I ran a comparison of documents and made a list. Most of them were duplicates. A lot just showed differences in drafts. Both Gus and Hal were good about keeping all drafts of all documents. But there were a few, a dozen or so, where the final document on Gus's file did not match the final document on Hal's file."

"How did that happen? Weren't they PDFs? Were there dates that helped?" Emma asked.

"The dates didn't help as much as I hoped. It's hard to know when the changes were made, since the drafts went back and forth in Word form. It was easy enough to make the changes and then re-save the document."

"But," I said, swallowing some pizza, "someone had the original documents. Or they were signed in one of those services that certified the document itself. If Hal—and for the sake of this conversation, let's assume it was Hal who made the changes, though it was likely someone else more directly involved—"

"Like Mimi or Jerry, or Kate, or—" Emma began.

"Or someone who worked for Mimi or Jerry. Though in my experience, folks who do things like this? They work with a small group of people who know the entire picture of what is going on. Secrets are best kept by only a few people."

"Given the way our company works," Eric said, "I see that. Not that we try to pull one over on anyone, but we keep the decision-making to three people. Emma, Gus, and me."

"Anyway," Emma said, moving past the fact that Gus was the only person working on both the Whitehall Company and the Century Project's legal documents. Gus and maybe Kate. "I'm going to assume that for whoever made the changes, some of this would've started to catch up with them, wouldn't it have?"

"The changes were really tiny, but significant," Eric said. He stood up and went over to the sink, filling three glasses with water and bringing them back to the table. "That chorizo has a kick to it. Anyway, the changes were things like preferred vendors, deadlines, escrow amounts, that sort of thing. Gus's document had a deadline of May 15th, for example. Hal's had one of May 1st. If someone hit an earlier deadline, it wouldn't have triggered any concern for Gus. But in two cases, there was a late charge on services that didn't meet the deadline. Those late charges became part of the cost of doing business, and they started to add up."

"Who paid the late charges? Give me an example," Emma said. I noticed she'd stopped eating and was staring at Eric.

"Well, we paid some of them. Remember that project in Salem, the one last spring? There were several additional costs on that project that Terry explained away at the time. But now I think they were part of the scheme. The fees all went into a separate account, one which the Whitehall Company had no access to."

"Do you think Terry knew what was going on?" Emma said. "Did he sign off on any of this?"

"I have no idea. Tomorrow I'm going to call in a forensic accountant. I waited, wanting to talk to the two of you before I took that step. Once I pull that trigger, I think a lot of things are going to start happening. At least on the Century Project front. I've also got to admit, some of this doesn't look good for Gus, since it could be argued that he may have missed the deadlines on purpose. Hold on, hold on, I know. I know Gus. He'd never do anything. But it feels like, it seems like, maybe he was set up a bit."

"By Hal?"

"I'm actually thinking by somebody who worked more closely with Gus."

"Kate?" I asked. Eric nodded. "That sort of makes sense, doesn't it? Kate would have access to the documents, to Gus's work—"

"I called her earlier, asked if we could meet tonight or tomorrow morning," Eric said.

"Did you tell her why you wanted to meet?" Emma asked.

"No, just asked if she was going to be at the meeting with Jerry tomorrow, told her we should talk beforehand."

"We should talk indeed," Emma said. I looked at her carefully. She was angry. In true Yankee style, her anger was controlled, but I could see it seething near the surface. Eric could too. He took another piece of pizza and put it on Emma's plate.

"Em, you should eat. We'll figure this all out. No one is better at untangling a mess than you are."

"Actually, I think Sully's got me beat on that one," she said. She pushed her pizza around on her plate but didn't take a bite. "Your turn, Sully. What are you thinking?"

"While I was getting dressed I started thinking about all these different roads we're going down, all the stories folks are telling us," I said. "I'm starting to wonder if they're all connected in some way. I was hoping Babs's files might give us more of an insight, but so far all I see is work product. See this here—if you open this up, you'll see that she was deep in the weeds planning next season."

"Isn't it a little early?" Eric asked.

"No, not at all. She'd need to get the rights to shows before she makes the season public. She's probably planning on making the announcement in March, April at the latest. Without an artistic director, in must've been hard, but it sounds like the company worked together on this process. At least that's what Dimitri's told me. An interesting model for running a company. A model that does depend on Babs at the helm, steering the ship." I turned my computer and was showing Eric and Emma Babs's files.

"Hello," I said, having opened the file that said *prospective projects*. "Here's an interesting choice for next season. I've read it. A new play about Bernie Madoff."

"Well, a play about one of the biggest Ponzi schemes in history would be interesting. So many people in New England were affected by him. It makes sense," Emma said.

"It's the note she made on the show memo that's interesting. See here? You can see the comment field. I doubt anyone else could, without her password. She only wrote one line. 'Change the name to Jerry Cunningham.'"

"When did she write that memo?" Emma asked.

"Hard to tell now that I've got it open, but it looks like the file folder was created last week."

"That isn't proof of anything," Eric said. "But it does make me feel that the forensic accountant is crucial. We should probably postpone the meeting with Jerry tomorrow."

"Don't postpone it yet. If you do, he might leave tonight. What time is it set for?" I asked.

"Four o'clock," Eric said.

"Okay, let me work on Holly's budget for a few minutes and I'll look around the files, see what else I can find. Eric, show Emma more of what you've found. Then we can figure out next steps. How does that sound?"

"Sounds good," Emma said, taking a bite of pizza.

I went back to my computer and looked at Babs's files, including the budgets for past years. I wasn't surprised that the bottom line didn't vary much from year to year. I started to cut and paste into a new spreadsheet. I made comments so that Holly could answer questions about the production. Was the playwright coming in? Were the actors local? From her answers, she would be able to get a sense of the budget and where there might be movement to give scenic more money. I sent it to her in an email and suggested she keep some money aside for unexpected expenses. While I worked, Eric and Emma did as well. Their computers were next to one another, and they were looking at both screens.

"Budget done," I said. "If anyone cares."

"What? Oh great. That was fast. We've been looking at files," Emma said. "I've got to admit, this whole exercise is making me lose my faith in my fellow human beings. Deals are cut all over the place. Money is being skimmed—"

"By whom, can you tell?" I asked.

"Hard to say," Eric said. "Looks like Knight, Smythe, and Brown were working both sides of the street."

"Gus? I can't believe that—"

"Kate uses the same files," Emma said. We looked at each other.

"Listen, I want to loop Toni into this conversation, even peripherally."

"Who's Toni?" Eric asked.

"Toni is Sully's ex-partner. A cop."

"She's investigating Mimi Cunningham's death. I believe all of this has something to do with that."

"We don't even know what this is," Eric said. "It's going to take weeks, maybe months to figure it all out. By the by, chances are good this may not end up being good for the Whitehall name, or business."

"Eric, I have complete faith that you and Emma will get the shine back on the Whitehall family name," I said. "But this can't be about saving face or protecting your dad's legacy. This has to be about justice. Justice is messy, but it's the only thing that really matters."

"You know, Sully," Emma said, finally picking up her piece of pizza and nibbling the corner, "a year ago I would've thought you weren't for real. But now I know that your life mission is justice for all. It must be exhausting."

"It is," I said, choosing to take Emma seriously. "It cost me my job, my career. Probably cost me my marriage. Once I start to focus on an injustice, I'm determined to fix it. Mimi Cunningham may not have been a law-abiding citizen. She and Jerry may have been running a Ponzi scheme. But still, somebody took justice into their own hands and killed her. We can't have that."

Emma sighed, then looked at me. "Let's figure this out a bit more, then we'll follow your lead, Sully. Won't we, Eric?"

"All the way, no matter where it takes us," Eric said. "Meanwhile, let me call an accountant."

∞

Emma, Eric, and I continued to eat pizza while clicking keys and searching files. I started framing the idea that this was all part of one whole rather than separate parts. I made notes on index cards, putting them in the order I expected them to be in and then shuffling them around. What if Mimi Cunningham's death had nothing to do with Gus's disappearance? Or if it did have something to do with Gus's disappearance but not in the way we all thought? What happened if Mimi Cunningham's death was the middle of the story, not the beginning?

I stood up and took my cell phone. "I'll be right back. I'm going to call Toni now and let her know what I'm thinking."

"I'm not sure we're ready to let the police know we're hiring a forensic accountant," Emma said. "Not until we know what we're looking at—"

"Em, I trust Sully to use her discretion. Let's not forget, Gus is missing. That may end up being one small piece of a very large puzzle, but that's the piece I'm most worried about right now," Eric said.

"Of course, Eric, you're right. I'm glad you're on my side. I need you as my moral compass. Sully, do what you need to do."

∞

Toni picked up on the second ring. "I assume you have something for me?" she said abruptly.

"Hello to you too," I said.

"Not the best time or place for niceties," she replied.

"John's there?"

"You could say that," she said. "I won't put you on speaker phone unless you want me to."

"Not only do I not want you to, but I'll start speaking a bit more softly so he can't overhear my booming voice on the phone," I said. "Listen, my priority is finding Gus. But I'm finding that I can't look for Gus without touching parts of your investigation. There are a couple things off the top of my head you should know about. First, something hinky is going on with the Cunningham Corporation. Don't ask me how, but we have some files of Gus's and some files of Hal Maxwell's regarding a few Century Projects. Theoretically they should be the same files, but there are small discrepancies in some of them. Things like escrow balances, deadlines, preferred vendors."

"Not the first time I've heard that," Toni said. "Tough finding folks willing to go on the record, though."

"I'm going to assume this is part of the investigation but you need some hard evidence to use as proof?" I asked. Toni didn't say anything, so I went on. "I'll ask the person working on all this to get in touch with you. Should we use your home email? Get you some notes on the case?"

"That would probably be best for now. Very helpful. And yes, about your first concern, you should put in a missing person's report for Gus. It hasn't been forty-eight hours yet, but given the nature of this case, it's good to officially let the authorities know you're looking for him. I told Kate Smythe this earlier. She probably already did it, or at least that was the plan when we spoke."

"Thanks, Toni. Of course I assume this is a little rote, since the authorities are already looking for Gus?"

"No comment."

"Fair enough," I said. "Let me get my thoughts in better order, and then I'll give you a call later?"

"Any time. You do that thing you do with making order out of chaos, and catch me up when you're ready." Toni disconnected the call and I looked down at the cell phone in my hand. *That thing I do.* Back when we were partners, Toni always talked about that thing I did. That way of taking bits and pieces of information, rearranging them, and creating a new narrative for them. That thing I did, I do, is to remain open to telling a story from a different perspective. Facts were facts, but truth depended on who was telling the story. Too often facts and truth got confused.

I went back out to the kitchen and sat down. I grabbed a pile of index cards and a red marker.

"Okay gang, new project. Anything circled in red is a fact backed up by actual knowledge, not guesses. On all of this, what are the actual facts?"

"Explain what you mean, Sully," Eric said.

"Sure," I said. "Take this card, 'got a text from Gus.' That's actually a guess, not a fact. I assumed it was from Gus because it came from his phone, but did he send it? Or did somebody spoof his number, or steal his phone and send the text? Texts aren't facts. Phone calls, when we know we spoke with somebody, are facts. It's subtle, but see the difference?"

"I do," Emma said. "Other facts include things like one document is different but we can't know who made the changes."

"Exactly," I said. "It's the assumptions we need to get rid of. They may be leading us down a path, sending us in the wrong direction. I suspect that you may not be the only people looking for a forensic accountant these days. Or maybe you are, but I can't help but wonder if Gus was thinking the same thing. My priority, the thing I'm most worried about, is looking for Gus. I know we all are. So let's separate facts from suppositions and take a close look at what we really know, and where we're making leaps of logic that may not hold up."

"I'm going to make some coffee," Emma said. "This could take a while. But we need to get it done tonight."

"No time to lose," I agreed. "In the meantime, I want to give Kate a call, see if she filed a missing person report for Gus. If she didn't, one of us should. More can be done with official channels open."

"What makes you think she filed one?" Eric said.

"Something Toni said," I said. "Besides, it would give me a chance to set up a time to talk to her. She's an interesting player in this particular drama. She intersects with too much of this puzzle."

"She does," Emma said. "However, let me call her. She's a lot more likely to pick up a call from me then she is from you. No offense."

"None taken," I said.

"Maybe we should invite her over for some pizza?" Eric said.

"Kate doesn't eat," Emma said. "We could ask her over for a drink. That's more likely to get her attention."

The front doorbell rang and we all looked at each other. Neither Eric nor Emma moved.

"I'll go," I said.

"Thanks, Sully," Eric said. "If it's the press—"

"If it's the press, I'll deal with it. This isn't my first rodeo. I'll be right back."

· Fifteen ·

I looked through the crack of the open door. I'd braced my foot on the back of the door so it would only open a few inches in case I wanted to keep somebody out. I wished I'd checked my lipstick before I'd come down, in case there were cameras, but I could live with another bad picture of me in the press. There'd been plenty six years ago when I decided to—been forced to—leave the force.

"Letter for Sully Sullivan, is that right?" An arm wearing a black jacket with a yellow neon stripe along the side shoved an envelope through the crack. I bent my head and looked at the label. It was to me, and at this address.

"That's me," I said. I took the envelope from the arm and went to close the door.

"Hold up!" the arm's owner said. "I need a signature." I carefully put the envelope down on the mail table to the right of the door.

"Do you have a sender's address on this?" I opened the door halfway, bracing my knee to keep it from opening the entire way. A sinewy man stood on the stoop. He was wearing tights with baggy shorts over them. He had a mock turtleneck on, his company jacket, fingerless gloves, and goggles on top of his bike helmet. There was reflective tape all over his body. I felt cold just looking at him. He reached into his bag and took out a clipboard.

"Law office of Knight, Smythe, and Brown," he said. "Sign here, print your name there." I did as he said and he handed me a receipt.

"Kind of old school, isn't it?" I asked. "Carbonless copies? Handwritten receipts?"

"We specialize in law firms. Lawyers love hard copies and handwritten receipts. You have a nice day now. I mean night."

"You too," I said. "Be safe out there."

"Always," he said, sliding down the railing. He swung his leg over the bike that had been resting on the front stairs. He took off, going the wrong way up the one-way street, taking on Beacon Hill as if it were a prairie plain. I envied his thigh muscles, and his nerve. I was a nervous wreck riding my bike around Trevorton. Around Boston, even at my bravest, I was never that brave. Especially on a dark February night.

"Someone sent me a letter," I said, carefully putting the envelope on the corner of the kitchen table that hadn't been overwhelmed with pizza boxes, salad, wine bottles, and glasses. I stepped back and looked at it carefully. I picked it up again and looked at the underside, trying to only use the corners. I doubted there were usable prints, but just in case—

"What are you doing?" Eric asked.

"The envelope is from Gus's office. It's addressed to me, at this address."

"You think it's from him?" Emma said. "Maybe he put a delay on the delivery for some reason?"

"Or it's from Kate." I took out my cell phone and started snapping pictures of the envelope from all angles, including the ends, the wrapping, and the printing on the label. I was, no doubt, being overly paranoid. But I couldn't help but think about three cases that I'd worked back in the day. About those poor slobs who opened boxes, not expecting it to be their last act on earth. There couldn't be a bomb in this envelope, but maybe there was something else? I thought back to my training and tried to remember if I should be looking for something that would let me know if this package was dangerous.

"Earth to Sully. What are you thinking? Should we be worried? Should we call your friend Toni?" Emma asked.

I walked over and took the rubber gloves off the dish rack. I put them on and took a paring knife out of the utensil holder. I turned the envelope over and slid the knife under the flap while I held my breath. No powder spilled out. Nevertheless, I continued to hold my breath as I opened the envelope. A 4x6 card was sitting inside. I pulled it out carefully.

The card had Gus's firm's address on the top. I didn't recognize the handwriting, but I knew the name on the signature.

Gus left me a note—told me to give you certain case files if I didn't hear from him in twenty-four hours. It's been twenty-nine hours. I wanted to talk to you after the memorial service, but I had to get out of there. Call me when you get this—I don't have your cell number. I want to arrange a time to get you this information ASAP.

~Kate 617-555-0191

"What case files?" Emma asked.

"Why wouldn't she just bring them over?" Eric asked.

"No idea on either front," I said. "Let me give her a call and ask both of those questions."

∞

I didn't get voicemail. But I also didn't get a "hello" or even a "who is this?" Instead, I got silence with some heavy breathing on the end of the line.

"Hello, Kate? This is Sully Sullivan. I just got your note."

"Hey, thanks for calling. So, Gus left a package for you. He left one for me too. Probably the same package, but he knew we'd do different things with them. Anyway, I'm wrapping up some stuff here at the office. I thought we should meet so I can hand it over to you."

"Why don't you come over to Emma's house?"

"I'm on a deadline and have a couple of other meetings this evening before I leave town."

"You're leaving town? When?"

"Don't get any ideas about calling anyone. You bring the cops, I'm going to deny we ever spoke."

"I have your note—"

"Which can be interpreted a number of ways. Listen, if I didn't care about Gus, I wouldn't even be calling you. But I still can't find him and I'm worried sick. So you come here, I'll give you the package, and then you can decide what to do."

"We can decide together—"

"I've decided what I'm going to do. I'm doing it. Get here by nine. That gives you about a half hour. I'll give you the package, and let you in on a few other facts you should know. By nine." Kate disconnected the call.

"Kate wants me to meet her at the office. By nine. Is it possible to get there in a half hour?" I asked.

Emma took out her phone and clicked on a couple of apps. "It is if we hustle," Emma said.

"You mean walk?" I said.

"I mean walk. Given construction, by the time a cab got here and ran the traffic gauntlet we'd be cutting it close. Better to walk. Gives us more control of time. I make this trek all the time."

"Emma, you don't have to go with me," I said.

"Do you want me to go too?" Eric asked.

"No, stay here and work," Emma said. "I care about Gus too. We're in this together. We'll go out the back way, just in case the fourth estate is parked outside. Put on your sensible boots, Sully. We need to get a move on."

Gus's office was on the other side of Beacon Hill in a large, very nondescript office building. Emma was right; we got there in eighteen minutes by winding our way through the hill, zigzagging a path.

Emma went in the side entrance of the building and signed in. There was a sign on the front desk: *Everyone Must Sign In. No Exceptions.*

"I bet this is challenging, getting everyone to sign in," I said to the security guard, taking the pen.

"It is, but owner's orders. Been some action around here lately, folks lending out their building IDs. Management wants to know who's where when. This is the best plan so far."

"No cameras?" I asked, flashing my best "you have a tough job, I'm sympathetic" smile.

"None that do much good," he said. "We've got them on the entrances, but none in the hallways. Those are coming. Not soon enough for some people."

"That's a huge job," I said. I looked back down at the list. I didn't see Kate's name, and the log page went back to yesterday. "We won't be long," I said.

"I'll be here," he said.

"Kate wasn't on the list," I whispered as we headed toward the elevator.

"Look at you, Miss Detective," Emma said.

"I'm trying. Maybe she isn't here yet? Or she's been here overnight?"

"Or maybe she drove in," Emma said.

"Drove in?"

"There's a garage downstairs. Gated entrance. For the residents of the building and sometimes for their guests. Gus gave us a pass, but he asked for it back so that someone else could use it. Anyway, once you're in the garage you can get up into the building using the same card pass."

"Can you get outside from the garage?"

"You can. There's a fire exit you aren't supposed to use, but everyone does if they need to get out to the coffee shop around back. Folks can use their fob to let them out. But the only way back into the garage is through the lobby, unless you have a parking permit."

"Sounds like pretty tight security," I said.

"It is. There are some heavy hitters who rent office space here. A few government offices, a couple of other lawyers. Those are just the ones I know of."

"I noticed there wasn't a building directory."

"Nope. You have to know where you're going. Which I do."

We got off on the fourth floor. Gus's office was on the right, a beige door along a beige wall. A small office sign in the holder on the side of the door let you know that you were at the offices of Knight, Smythe, and Brown. I noted that the other sign holders on the floor were empty. Emma went up and tried the door. It wasn't open.

"Maybe she's running late?" I said. "I don't suppose you have a key?"

"As a matter of fact ..." Emma started to rummage through her purse again. "Here it is. Gus gave it to me in December. We were using his office while things were settling down at home."

"Don't you have offices in Boston?"

"We were in lockdown after the murder. Gus's place was safe. Not sure if he's changed the code on the keypad or not."

"Keypad?"

"Extra security on the door. You can also set it to buzz when the door opens, to let you know if folks are coming in. Annoying, but helpful if you're in the office alone.

"All we need is to set off an alarm," I said, knocking on the door. I pulled my cell out and tried Kate's number. We heard the song "She Works Hard for the Money" waft through the door. I cut the call off and the song stopped. I knocked again, but no answer. I hung up and redialed. The song blasted out again.

"Step back," I said to Emma. I took the key from her and opened the door. The keypad had a green light. I rang Kate again and followed the sound of the phone.

I found her right away. She was face-down in the hallway behind the front desk. From the color of her skin to the tightness of the scarf around her neck, I didn't think she was alive, but I checked just to make sure.

"Don't touch anything," I said to Emma. "Walk out the same way you came in, in the same path if you can." I called Toni and she picked up right away. I was relieved. Telling her that Kate Smythe was dead wasn't a voicemail I wanted to leave.

∞

Toni, John Engel, and various cops and crime scene techs were quick to arrive. Neither Emma nor I were on the suspect list, though John did his best. The signed receipt from the messenger gave me a specific time for being at home. Emma and I alibied each other; John seemed upset when we offered Eric as another witness. Emma and I had hustled over the hill, and in that short window of time Kate had been killed. I shuddered at the thought. That meant that we'd just missed the murderer, but how? I told Toni about the garage entrance and the side door. She wrote it down and nodded her thanks.

This, of course, took a couple of hours to clarify. John wanted Emma and me to go back to the station, but Emma made some well-placed phone calls that helped convince him to let us go back to our apartments after having made statements on site. The scene would take a while to process, so Toni and John had to stay put. We both promised to remain available.

By the time we headed back to the townhouse it was past eleven. I was looking forward to writing things down, sorting through the facts that I knew, spending some time alone, and thinking through things. But then I heard the hum of male voices coming through the door.

"Rehearsal must be over," I said to Emma.

"Do you want to come upstairs and work?" she asked. She looked exhausted, and pale.

I shook my head. "My computer and notes are in there. I'll head to my bedroom when I can. Come in to say hello?"

"Just to pick up my computer," she said.

"Sully, where the hell have you been?" Dimitri boomed as we opened the door. He was reaching for one of the last two slices of pizza.

"Pour me a glass of wine, will you?" I said to him. "I'm going to wash up."

"Everything okay?" I heard Harry ask from the other room. I ran some cool water over my face and washed my hands again. It didn't help. I still felt grimy.

"What happened, Sully? You were both gone so long I assumed Kate had a lot to say," Eric asked as I came back in the room. Emma was nibbling on a cookie with a far-off look that precluded conversation. Stewart handed me a glass of wine and I took a huge gulp. It was good wine, which was a shame because I didn't intend to savor it. I took a smaller sip.

"Kate Smythe was murdered tonight. Emma and I found her," I said. That stopped all conversation.

"Who's Kate Smythe?" Stewart asked.

"My ex-husband's partner."

"Is he a suspect?" he asked.

"He would be. He might be, but he's disappeared," I said. My voice caught on the word "disappeared." I looked over at Eric, who'd put his arm around Emma.

"I assume that has something to do with all of this?" Harry said, gesturing to the index cards we'd taped all over the kitchen.

I nodded.

"I don't want you to take this the wrong way, darling, but are you sure your ex has nothing to do with this?" Dimitri asked. I glared at him. "Calm down, calm down. But you must admit, the dramatic arc of all of this points to the guy who's disappeared."

Gus might have been a suspect in Mimi's death, but he was one of several. I had to admit, he was also a suspect in Kate's death. No one had said it, but who better than the lover and business partner as the prime suspect? Were the two murders connected? Again, I could only surmise. From all accounts Mimi had been strangled. And Kate had definitely been strangled.

I thought back to her cryptic note. And to our phone call. Kate had seemed odd. But all of our conversations had been odd. She'd asked us to come in by nine. Had she set up a meeting in advance?

I closed my eyes and tried to remember the sign-in sheet. I didn't recall seeing any name I recognized.

"I truly believe that Gus didn't commit either of these murders," Emma said. "We need to find Gus to find out more."

"Do you think he's in trouble?" Harry asked. He'd gotten up and was loading the dishwasher. Stewart was putting away leftovers. We'd killed the party mood.

"I think that Gus either knows what is going on or is trying to figure it out," I said. "Yeah, I think he's in trouble."

"Well, the cops need proof that he—"

"If these two women were killed by the same person, that person is dangerous. If he thinks that Gus knows something—"

"Then Gus is in danger." Emma swallowed hard. Eric handed her a napkin to wipe her tears.

"We need to find Gus," I said.

I went into my room a half hour after we got back, when the waves of exhaustion could no longer be ignored. Emma had gone upstairs a few minutes earlier. The boys offered to help us talk it through, but I encouraged them to all focus on the show. Catch Eric up on rehearsals and the stories of the Bay Repertory Theater. A few minutes later, Dimitri knocked on my door, carrying my computer and the notepad I was using. I thanked him for both.

"Do you think Babs Allyn had anything to do with any of this?" Dimitri asked.

"She intersects, but I'm not sure. I don't know her well, but she doesn't strike me as somebody who—"

"Sully, we both know that when pushed, even the most unlikely amongst us can do extraordinary things."

"True enough," I said. "I'm not going to tell you not to worry, but I will tell you to focus on the show. If you hear anything, or see anything, or remember anything, give me a call or text me and let me know. But you do your work—"

"And let you do yours. The work you are called to do." Dimitri gave me a big hug, and I held on. When I leaned back, he gave me a kiss on the forehead and left. I plugged in my computer and sat on the bed.

∞

I was mindlessly web-surfing a few minutes later when my cell phone rang. "You have to step back from the case, Sully," Toni said. No hello, how are you, that must've been a terrible shock, are you okay. Just the warning to step back. Her words had their normal effect. They got my back up.

"What are you talking about?" I hissed. "Step back from what? The only thing, the only case I've been working on is finding Gus. I'm so worried about him—"

"Listen, I'm worried too. And doing all I can to stay on this case despite my friendship with Gus. It's not always great when the prime suspect—"

"Prime suspect? What happened to missing person?"

"One woman's missing person is another man's prime suspect. John Engel has it in his head that Gus did a business deal that went wrong, got called out by Mimi Cunningham, panicked and killed her. Then—"

"What the—"

"Stop it, Sully," Toni said. "I'm telling you what John thinks, not endorsing it. He thinks that Kate found something out that incriminated Gus, and that Gus killed Kate."

"Do you believe that?"

"Of course not," Toni said. She sounded angry. I wasn't sure if it was at me, at John, or at the entire situation. "A second death, a second strangulation? Either these cases are connected or someone is working hard to make them seem connected. In any event, the attention has been ratcheted up. A lot of folks are working on this case now. Including some feds."

"Because of the Century Projects?" I asked.

"Sully, believe me when I tell you I wish you were working this case with me. But you're not. Anything you do could interfere with us doing our job. It could get Gus killed."

"That's not what—"

"You know I'm right. You only know parts of what I know, and that's dangerous. You're going to hate this, but I'm going to ask you to leave it to the professionals. Now don't get your Irish up on that. You know six years ago you'd be saying what I'm saying."

She was right. I would have been saying the same thing. I also knew that there were pieces of evidence I did not, and would not, have access to. Pieces that might make all the difference in understanding what was going on.

"Toni, I'll step back. As long as you promise me one thing."

"If I can."

"Promise me you'll keep looking for Gus and will keep him a top priority."

"That I can promise you. Finding Gus is a top priority for a lot of folks, but for me, finding him safe is the most important. I'm going to have to ask you to trust me on that."

I paused for a moment, but only for a moment. Despite our history, I trusted Toni with my life. And Gus's.

"I promise I won't do any active investigating tomorrow."

"Just tomorrow?"

"I'm taking this one day at a time. Deal?"

"Deal," Toni said. "Tomorrow I'll check in, and renegotiate."

"Toni, did you find the package of files Gus left for me?"

"No, and trust me, we're looking for it. I wonder why Kate didn't send it over with the messenger."

"I think she was trying to buy herself some time. She said she got the same files—maybe she was going to talk to someone about them? She seemed to think I would do something different with them. She was also worried about Gus."

"Still, she could have dropped them off—"

"She said she had other meetings."

"Obviously, she had at least one. With whoever killed her. I wonder if they were there, in the office, when she called you. What am I doing, running theories by you? Promise me, no more investigating. I don't want to worry about you."

"I promise," I said.

Of course, I didn't promise that I wouldn't do any research. Plus, Eric and Emma did have that meeting with Jerry Cunningham tomorrow afternoon, and I could perhaps go along with them to that. But active investigating? I'd leave that to the professionals.

For now.

· Sixteen ·

I passed out at some point, then woke up enough to put my computer on the ground and take off my glasses. I slept, but I didn't rest. Too much going on. In my brain, in my life. At one point I had a dream I was working on a big puzzle with vertical stripes that were green, white, blue, and yellow. I'd been working for hours, putting the pieces together, making it all up in perfect lines. Gus walked up and swept his hand across the table, breaking the puzzle apart, putting me back to square one. "You're doing it the wrong way. They're squares, not stripes!" he said. I woke up and had a hard time falling back asleep. Squares, not stripes. What the hell did that mean?

Was I looking at everything the wrong way? I'd promised Toni that I would step back, and I intended to. I didn't want to get in the way of the cops. But then I thought about Gus, and rethought my strategy. I was going to step back but not out. I needed to find him.

These were the questions that plagued me throughout the night. I would fall asleep, wake up, my mind would automatically start worrying until it wore me out, and then I fell back asleep. I could never quite wake up enough to get up, wash my face, brush my teeth, and go to bed properly. So when I finally did stop fighting it and decided to get up, I felt and looked like ten miles of bad road. Worse, I had fallen asleep with my cell phone in my hand, and it lost its charge. I plugged it in and went in to take a shower. I let the warm water work its magic, renewing me for the day ahead. I washed my hair, something I only did twice a week with my thick and curly locks. I got out of the shower and wrapped my hair in one towel, my body in another. I lathered on lotion and put a little makeup on. My mother had taught me from a young age that the worse you feel, the more you try. Mascara wasn't a cure-all, but it did make me feel a little bit better. I put some product through my hair and clamped it back in a clip.

I went back into my room and checked the phone. It was only ten percent charged, but three text messages had come in, all in the last twenty minutes. I checked the time. Seven thirty. Who would text me before eight o'clock?

One text was from Emma, telling me she was on her way with some breakfast sandwiches. She asked me to put coffee on. I checked my watch. She must be here already.

The next two messages were from Holly.

Huge favor to ask. I need somebody to take a road trip down the Cape. The company won't deliver, and I think I found cloth for the set. Any chance you're free today? She'd sent that text fifteen minutes prior.

The final text had just come in. *Got a call from Dimitri. So glad you're going to go, and help us. I owe you one. Couldn't pull this off without you. Thank you thank you thank you thank you thank you.*

From Dimitri? What the—?

I finished getting dressed and walked into the kitchen area. Emma and Stewart were futzing around, pulling out plates and napkins, unloading bags of goodies. They both had spots of pink on their cheeks, indicating that they'd been outside. Together? Curiouser and curiouser.

Dimitri was lining up coffee cups. He poured coffee into three of them and then looked up, saw me, and poured a fourth.

"I hear I'm heading down to the Cape," I said, accepting the offered cup of coffee.

"You are indeed," Dimitri said, taking a seat at the table. "You told me to be nice to Holly. She sent me texts, several of them, telling me that she needed to drive down to the Cape to pick up some sailcloth for the set. I've got to hand it to her, she's industrious. She was going to go herself, but we've got three meetings set up this morning before rehearsal. One with a board member who's concerned about Babs's absence. Holly can't miss that meeting. I suggested she send you down to pick up the cloth. It doesn't have to be this morning. I understand they're open until six."

"What makes you think I don't have other things to do today?" I asked.

"Well, for one thing, I believe the police have asked you to stop investigating. They gave Emma a courtesy call requesting the same thing. Not that I expect that this alone would stop you, but I was up half the night thinking about it. It isn't safe for you, my friend. I hate to sound like your—your—"

"Friend?" Stewart said. "Sully, sit down. We got some sandwiches from the breakfast place down the street. I also got a cinnamon roll, thought we could split it. Emma's too healthy for that, so don't bother to cut her a piece."

"I didn't say I was too healthy," Emma said. "I just find it ironic that we both decided to take a run this morning, and then you ended it with a sugar bomb."

"Well, honestly, I thought my secret would be safe. Who knew there was somebody else who saw a thirty-five degree morning as an invitation to get a run in?" Stewart asked.

"Not me, that's for damn straight," I said. "Did you go together?"

"Not intentionally," Stewart said. "First of all, true confessions. It was less of a run, more of a walk. I was leaving out the front door, and took a right, thinking I'd go to the Esplanade. Emma came out on the next block. To tell you the truth, I didn't recognize her at first."

"I left out the alleyway. We ended up just walking over the Longfellow Bridge, turning around, and coming back," Emma said.

"It was icy," Stewart said. "Next time—"

"We can discuss exercise routines in a second," I said. I broke a piece off my breakfast sandwich. It was so, so good. The biscuit alone would have been perfect: light, flaky, with layers. But then fluffy scrambled eggs, perfectly crisped bacon, and unbelievably sharp cheddar. Perfect. "Back to Dimitri scheduling my day." I took another bite and looked over at Dimitri.

"More like, keeping you safe and out of harm's way," Dimitri said. "At least for the day. I know you, Sully. If you don't have something to do today you're just going to get into trouble."

"I am not going to get into trouble—"

"Please. One of the best things about you is that you don't hesitate to put yourself in harm's way to help other people. I admire that. But it seems to me, with two women killed within a week, that harm's way is a bit too close right now."

"So you want to send me on some wild goose chase picking up sailcloth?"

"Hardly a wild goose chase. We don't have rehearsal tomorrow, so the scenic crew is going to spend the day doing what they can to salvage the set. It's the last window of time we have to make changes. Without the cloth? Without the cloth we're stuck with the shiny iceberg from hell. Do it for me, Sully. Please."

Dimitri and I had a brief staring contest, but I blinked first. "Oh, all right. I'll go pick it up," I said.

Stewart slid a piece of cinnamon roll at me and gave me one of his most dazzling smiles. "Thanks, babe," he said.

"Let me drive you," Emma said, shooting Stewart a look. "I need the distraction, at least for a couple of hours. It's a nice bright day for a trip down the Cape. We can drive by my house there, make sure it's locked up tight. Last winter the plumber didn't latch the side door and it was flapping for four months. I've been meaning to drive down for a few weeks now."

"You have a house on the Cape?" I said. There are a few rules in life—one is that folks who live on the North Shore of Massachusetts are North Shore people. Folks who live on the South Shore, and the Cape is on the South Shore, are South Shore people. Emma had a house in Trevorton, on the North Shore. But she also had a house on the Cape?

"Not a big one. More of a cottage, really. Hal Maxwell told us about the house one day over lunch, that his neighbor was moving. It was Terry's idea to go look at it. A place we could go to get away from my family. Next thing I knew, Terry had put an offer down, and we owned the house. He'd been down there several times, golfing with Hal—"

"Don't you have a meeting this afternoon with Jerry?" I asked.

"If we leave in the next hour or so, we'll be back in plenty of time for the meeting. As I said, I'm getting squirrelly. Eric has made it clear he doesn't want me around for a couple of hours. I'm driving him nuts."

"Are Eric and Harry still asleep?" I asked.

"No, they went out for breakfast," Dimitri said.

"This apartment's like Grand Central Station and they wanted some alone-time," Emma said. "Serves him right. It's the nicest place for folks to gather in the entire building."

"Dimitri, did you sleep on Stewart's couch again last night?" I asked.

"I did. Honestly, that couch is a lot more comfortable than the bed I've been sleeping on. I'm half inclined to move in."

"You're more than welcome to," Stewart said. "Of course, it really isn't my place to offer, but—"

"The apartment's yours for as long as you need it," Emma said.

"Maybe they'll take you running with them tomorrow morning, Dimitri," I said. I smirked, and took another piece of cinnamon roll.

∞

We decided to take Emma's car down the Cape. Though the Mini-Cooper had less room inside then my car did, it was a more comfortable ride. Besides, I was too distracted to drive and I suspected Emma knew that.

We'd been driving for a few minutes when she looked over at me. "Hard to believe that last night was only last night. You know?"

"You mean Kate?"

"Yes. Poor Kate. She wasn't always my favorite person, but no one deserves—"

"You're right, Emma. No one deserves to die like that. We'll make sure she gets justice, I promise you that."

"What do you mean? I thought you were off the case."

"Taking a bit of a break, letting the police do their thing. Clearing my head. But I'm not convinced they're going to necessarily do right by Gus. Dimitri was right last night when he said Gus was the perfect suspect in all of this. Mind you, I don't want them to stop looking for him. But I can't help but think it would be better if we found him first."

"Are we going to look for Gus? Or are we going to pick up some sailcloth?

"Right now, we're going to pick up some sailcloth. Get some fresh air, see the ocean—"

"Let's have a nice lunch somewhere that has decent seafood and some good beer," Emma said. "Then we'll head back and meet with Jerry. Hopefully we'll have a clearer picture about questions to ask. Who knows, maybe Jerry will be down here too."

"Too?" I said.

"I keep forgetting, you don't know the area. My house is in one of the Cunninghams' first gated community projects, Century Cape. I'm not sure if you remember a few years ago, when there was a plot of land on the Cape that was rezoned for property use? On top of a landfill."

"That must have been a hard sell," I said.

"Not this kind of development. This included a nine-hole golf course, some townhouses, small cottages, a few more upscale houses. All developed around a man-made lake in the middle of the neighborhood. Ocean views for a few houses. A limited number of housing units. The golf club and course were private, for residents only. Manufactured Cape Cod charm."

"Sounds a little awful," I said.

"Doesn't it? I was skeptical. But after Terry spent several weekends down there golfing, I came down with him one weekend and saw the house. I fell in love. The entire neighborhood feels like it's been here forever, but it's less than ten years old."

"So you and Terry bought the place."

"We did. It's how we started doing business with the Cunninghams. Terry figured if they could create Shangri-La on a dump, maybe they had something. Anyway, I own a small three-bedroom cottage, Cape style. It has a great porch that oversees the ocean in the distance. The Cunninghams' house is grander, right on the water. Bigger but not ostentatious. It's a little more like those small Victorian summer cottages up in Trevorton. Two floors. Basements. Widow's walks."

"How did the town like the project?" I asked.

"The project really turned the area around. Because of the increased tax base, the town built a new elementary school. An arts center was built as part of the work the Century Foundation. I think the Century Foundation was originally created just to help that arts center get off the ground and get staffed. But then the Cunninghams' charitable work took off too."

"All this was just ten years ago?" I asked. "What did the Cunninghams do before they built things?"

"They lived in California up until they moved east a few years ago. Remember when I mentioned that Eric was starting to do some research? He's got a couple of people sending him reports, and he's passing them to me. I was up half the night reading. Seems like the Cunninghams lived out in California for about fifteen years, in different towns. Same sort of legacy, huge projects that were done with partners. Then one of them, the Elements Tower I think it was called, started running into construction issues. There were design flaws that required more investment. Everyone was surprised when their business declared bankruptcy. A lot of folks were left holding the bag. The Cunninghams blamed their partners."

"Wow," I said. "Why hasn't this story been told publicly?"

"According to everything I read, mostly last night, mind you, nobody blamed the Cunninghams per se. But it seemed as if the business environment became more hostile to them, a little less likely to give them resources or the benefit of the doubt. So they moved here."

"What do you mean by 'benefit of the doubt'?" I asked.

"What do I mean by 'benefit of the doubt'? You know, when you're just starting out you need to have money to do anything. At first, businesses really need to see that cash, or evidence of that cash, before they'll go into business with you. But then after a while, trust and reputation kick in. Folks assume that you're good for the cash. You always have been. In the trust phase you can have access to a lot of cash without any collateral."

We were making good time out of the city, whizzing down 93, heading toward Route 24. "Works the same with funders," I said. "You need money to get money. You only saw the reports last night?"

"Eric and Gus were doing research for a while. They kept me out of it, but after Kate was killed, Eric thought I should know everything. Last night he emailed me a couple of the reports that Gus sent him on Monday. According to everything Gus could find, the Cunninghams were, and are, flat broke."

"Broke?"

"Broke."

"What does broke mean in your world?" I asked. "They were down to their last million?"

"At the minimum, the Cunninghams were in over their heads," Emma said, ignoring my jab. "They could come out of it, but it would take some new partnerships, or investors with cash to add."

"What got Gus wondering about all of this?"

"He started to hear rumors that bills weren't getting paid on Century Projects, so he started checking on the finances. He was building a case—"

"Building a case was in his DA blood."

"Well, given what I was going through, he and Eric decided to leave me out of it until they had proof."

"Proof? Of what?"

"I guess to Gus's far more cynical mind, the Cunninghams were running a slow con. Gus was doing his best to untangle the Whitehall company from them, and to make sure that when and if the Cunningham Corporation went down, the Whitehall reputation didn't suffer. Well, didn't suffer any more than it already has. After last Christmas, the old family name is a bit tarnished."

"Can you forward me these reports you've been reading?" I asked.

"Once we stop. Five miles to the bridge. Whoosh. That always makes me so happy, seeing that sign. We're heading down to one of my favorite places on earth. Or it was. Terry and I were happiest here, away from my family and the business. But I think I may want to sell the house, my secret hideaway."

"Secret? What do you mean by that?"

"It's a tight-knit community. You have to sign guests in; you can't rent out your house. When Terry and I were down here, I was almost convinced we could be happy. Eric knows how I feel about this place, and how I feel about the Cunninghams. He told me Gus has been working on building this case against them for a while."

"When did he loop Eric in?"

"The last week or so. Gus wanted to be sure, I guess. But apparently the feds have caught on to the scam somehow. A friend of Eric's tipped him off to this last night. That's why Eric sent me the reports, to get me up to speed so we could legally get ahead of it." Emma's eyes were focused on the road, which was just as well. I would have hated for her to see the irritation on my face.

"Anything else you haven't told me?" I asked.

"No, that's it," she said, looking over at me. A tear rolled down her face. "I'm sorry. I should have woken you up last night, but I wanted to go through the reports on my own. Process them."

"Eric isn't trying to handle this himself, is he? The legal stuff, I mean."

"No, that's why he called his friend to get some recommendations on forensic accountants. His friend is also a lawyer. Eric's immersing himself in the numbers, and in the files we shared with him. He's going to meet with his friend tomorrow, in case we need legal advice and we don't find Gus in time to get him up to speed."

The silence hung.

"Like I said, as soon as we stop, I'll forward you the reports," Emma said. "Can you read while you're riding in the car?"

"Yes. One of the side effects of being a cop for so long."

"Then you'll know what I know. We'll go get this sailcloth, then we'll get some fresh air and a nice lunch. After that we'll head back, meet with Eric, go to our meeting with Jerry, get in touch with your friend Toni, and get back to work looking for Gus."

"Full day," I said.

∞

Turns out, enough fabric to cover a set is a lot of fabric. A lot. The two guys who were loading the sailcloth laughed really hard when they saw the Mini-Cooper.

"Do you have another car coming?" they asked.

"Nope, just the one. Don't worry, it will fit," Emma said.

She climbed into the back of the car to move some things around, lower seats, and perform other magic acts. The guys brought out bolts and bolts of fabric, but they all fit. It was like a clown car for sailcloth.

"And this is all fire retardant?" I asked. I was used to some of the rules around fabric when it's used onstage, and I'd learned it's better to be safe than sorry.

"Ay yup. Here's the certificate in case anyone has any questions."

I looked inside the envelope the man handed me and pulled out the legal certification about the fabric itself. "Terrific, thanks. You need me to sign anything?" I asked.

"Yes, if you can just initial this sheet here, that we gave you all the fabric, that would be great," he said. "What are you going to do with it?"

"I'm not exactly sure, but I think your cloth is going to save the set of *Romeo and Juliet*."

"My wife loves that play," he said. "She drags me to every production of it she hears about."

"Well, tell you what. Give me your name, and you can bring your wife to see it at Bay Rep."

"She'd love that. Much appreciated. Ed, Ed Shea," he said, shaking my hand.

"Sully Sullivan. Great to meet you."

"Sully?"

"Born Edwina," I said. "My father gave me the nickname. Ed, I hate to be a pain, but could I get a copy of the receipt I just signed?" I had no idea what Babs or Holly required for paperwork but I wanted to make sure everything was all set. Given all that was going on, the last thing they needed was to have to track down a receipt.

"Sure, come on in."

I followed Ed into the shop. He walked over to a copier and turned it on. I lagged behind to take a look at the room. The open space was both a workroom and a showroom. Pictures of beautiful boats were everywhere. Samples of wood and sailcloth were displayed on one wall. A big book of paint colors was strewn across one of the desks. There was no pretension in this room, but there was a lot of quality. Quality that likely cost a lot of money, but I admired that the room said much more about quality than show. I walked over to one of the walls and looked at a series of photos of beautiful sailboats racing in the harbor.

"You in the market?" Ed asked.

"In the market?"

"For a boat," he said. "I've been watching you look around, take it in. Even caught you running your hand along that twenty-seven footer out in the yard."

"It reminded me of a boat my dad had when I was growing up. We used to have wonderful adventures on that boat. I miss it. I miss him."

Ed nodded. "No boat of your own?" he asked gently.

"Not yet. I live up in Trevorton, and occasionally I'll lease a boat and take her out for sail. But I haven't taken the plunge myself. It's a big step. You need to have time to take care of her."

"I wish more folks thought like you," he said. "Nothing sadder than to see a boat somebody bought as a trophy sitting out in its mooring, never used. A lot of that going on these days." Ed was a true New Englander. Part cranky Yankee, part old salt, part big softy.

As I was leaving the office, I happened to look to the wall on the right. There was an architectural drawing of a dock with several boats tied up to it, and a small open bar that went over the edge of the water.

"Where's that?" I asked.

"I should take it down. That, friend, was a pipe dream of mine I honestly thought I would see become a reality. An old man's foolishness. What made me think a big operation like the Century Project would be interested in my idea? Just wish they hadn't dragged so many people into the whole thing."

"The Century Project? Jerry and Mimi Cunningham's project?"

"The same. 'Course, I don't want to speak ill of the dead, but they sure had us going for a while. Promised they'd fund my bar, expand the boatyard, and support a couple of other projects. Gave us enough money to get started, but checks started to bounce. We had to stop work two weeks ago. They're not in any rush to come down here. And now with everything that's happened back in Boston—you hear about that?"

"I've heard about it, yes," I said.

"Like I said, I'm not wanting to speak ill of the dead, but Jerry Cunningham sure won't get a lot of sympathy down here. Broke a lot of folks' hearts, he did. Including mine."

· Seventeen ·

Ed and I talked for a few more minutes, and I asked him for his card. While he was getting it, I took a picture of the architectural drawing. Was this another piece of the puzzle? I went back to the car, and Emma was already in it. All the fabric fit, though she couldn't see out the back window.

"You're not going to believe this," she said.

"What?" I didn't even want to guess.

"Jerry Cunningham sent Eric and me an email. He needs to reschedule our meeting. He's delaying his departure, and he said he'd be in touch on Monday."

"Whose idea was it to close the escrow?" I asked. "That's what this meeting was about, right?"

"Gus's idea. In fact, he was very insistent. I probably wouldn't have forced the question right away, but Gus thought it was prudent."

"Do you think Gus might've been testing the Cunninghams? Trying to see if they could come up with the cash?"

"Escrow isn't supposed to be touched. If the cash isn't there, that's a real problem. I wish Gus had talked to me more, told me what had him so worried."

I told Emma about my conversation with Ed and the unfinished Century Projects around town. "Ed made it sound like the money had just started drying up. He said he was having a tough time getting a straight answer out of the Cunninghams, but they promised that the next time they were down, they'd stop by for a conversation."

"Did Ed believe them?" Emma asked.

"I think he wanted to," I said. "But he reminded me of my dad when he was trying to think the best of somebody but knew better in his heart."

Emma put her cell phone on a cradle on the dashboard and made sure it was connected to the system in the car.

"Call Eric," she said to the phone.

"Home or mobile?" an automated woman's voice asked.

"Mobile." While the phone call was connected, Emma pulled out of the boatyard. Instead of going left, back to the highway toward Boston, she took a right. After a couple of rings, Eric picked up the phone.

"Eric, Sully and I are in the car. We just picked up the sailcloth. Sully had an interesting conversation with someone at the boatyard. Remember that dock-and-bar project?"

"Hello to you too, Emma. Hi, Sully. Yes, I remember that project. It was an exciting way to bring a little bit more business into the harbor—"

"Well, apparently it's not going to happen. Money is gone. Sully thinks money is why Jerry canceled our meeting this afternoon. Do me a favor? Can you check on the escrow account? See how much money is in the account? Also, could you send Sully the reports you sent me?"

"It's going to take me a minute, but sure. All of the money was in the account earlier in the week. Gus checked."

"I'm sure its fine," Emma said. "Call us back. We're going to take a ride."

∞

My phone buzzed. I looked down. A text from Toni.

What do you know about Martin Samuel?

She was asking me? Or was she looking for help connecting some dots. I wrote back in a series of texts.

Disappeared a year ago. Cunninghams on the boat with him.

Daughter Holly works at Bay Rep, with Babs Allyn, wife of Hal Maxwell.

Babs went to Vermont but no one's heard from her. She and Hal were on the boat too.

Holly thinks Martin is still alive. Babs is trying to find out what happened to him. The anniversary of his disappearance seems to be triggering them both.

I waited for a second, and then the text response came back. *Did Babs seem concerned the last time you saw her?*

I wished Toni were on the phone so I could trade information. But she wasn't, and I didn't want to play games with her. She needed information.

When I saw her at the theater, she was fine. Heading out to a meeting. That evening at the reception, she was a wreck. Something must have happened in between.

You have any ideas? Toni texted.

Maybe easier if we talk? I wrote. The story about Babs hiring a PI hadn't been confirmed, and couldn't be explained in a text.

In the car with John. Think of anything else, ANYTHING ELSE, text me.

"Sully, you okay?" Emma asked.

"I'm fine," I said. "Toni was texting. I think she's trying to fill in some of the details that they may have skipped."

"You mean she's catching up with us?" Emma said, smiling at me.

"She'd lose her mind to hear you say that, but yes. She's catching up with us."

"What did she—" Emma's phone started to ring. She hit a button on her steering wheel and said, "Hello Eric."

"The escrow account is empty."

Emma pulled over to the side of the road and hit the steering wheel hard. "Who—"

"The bank is scurrying to figure it out. They were only five of us with access to that account. Me. You. The Cunninghams."

"And Gus," Emma whispered.

"And Gus," Eric said. "Needless to say, I'm looking into this."

"Eric," I said. "I'm going to text you Toni's cell phone number. Don't wait too long before you update her. All of this is leading somewhere, but I have no idea where."

Emma pulled into a little sandwich shop, not the quaint seaside restaurant she'd planned on but a misplaced diner that look like it had seen better days. There was only one other car in the parking lot. It didn't seem Emma's style, but I understood her compulsion to find a place to sit and absorb.

The escrow money was gone. For me it was more of a fact, another fact to add to the unknown sordid and random lists running through my head. But for Emma? For Emma and Eric and the entire Whitehall family? Escrow was money. Real money. I didn't know much about the family finances, hadn't been brought into that loop. I doubted I would understand much of it anyway. I knew enough to know that they'd had some liquidity issues ever since December.

Was the escrow account going to help them fill some gaps? Help them bridge some more months of expenses while they tried to right the ship?

We walked into the diner and paused. "Sit wherever," a voice called out from the back. There was an open pass-through and a woman working the grill. "I'll be right out."

Emma walked to the right, to the middle booth. The Formica table was worn in parts, and the metal strapping around the edges was bent in more than one place. But the table was clean and the seat cushions on the benches were covered in bright fabrics. I looked around. The diner was likely a tourist trap in the summer, but it had its own charm. All the decorations were whales. Paintings, signs, cross-stitch samplers, place mats. Whales.

"I was just about to give up and close for the day, glad to see somebody come by. Winter's so quiet, I work half-days. I've got a cobbler that's aching to be eaten." An older woman with *Edna* embroidered on her bowling shirt came over and wiped the immaculate table top. "Hope you're hungry. You want menus? Little limited this time of year. Specialty of the house is grilled cheese sandwiches and tomato soup—"

"That sounds perfect," Emma said. "Maybe with a cup of coffee? And a glass of water? I promise I'll save room for the cobbler too."

"I'll take the same," I said. The waitress brought over our coffee and water and set them down in front of us. She reached back behind the counter and got a bowl of creamers and some sugar.

I took a sip of the coffee. It was strong and delicious. Food-wise, the day was looking up. "What time do you close?" I'd thought about getting our food to go, but all of a sudden the thought of sitting here drinking coffee for a little bit felt like a good idea.

"No worries," she said. "I got plenty to do. You folks enjoy your meal. Let me go get the sandwiches on the grill. You'll like it; the special blend of the cheese is my own. And the bread's homemade. So's the soup, of course."

As the waitress left, Emma pulled out her phone and started flipping through screens. "Will you do me a favor? Do you have access to those files Hal sent me the link for?"

I took out my phone. "Yes."

"Good. I'm going to pull up Gus's files—" Emma tapped on her phone for a few seconds. "Eric said he's going to send me some examples of discrepancies, screenshots of the accounts. I just can't believe … I mean, come on. You know how much property the Cunninghams have built down here? How much they're still building? How can they … "

"Okay, I've got the files open," I said. "Give me an example."

Emma read out the name of a file in Gus's folder. I sorted Hal's files by name, and looked. The example she'd given me wasn't there. I ran a search, went up a couple of levels, and searched there.

"I can't find it," I said. "Tell me another one."

Emma did, and I couldn't find it in Hal's folder. She texted Eric, and he sent her some more file names. The same thing happened. I looked at the number of files in Hal's folder, blinked, and refreshed it again. The number was decreasing by the second.

"Someone's deleting files," I said to Emma. I wiped my hands and started to text. I tried to call Eric, but his phone went to voicemail. I texted him, telling him to back up everything one more time, on a USB drive if possible. I also told him to disconnect his computer from the Internet.

The waitress brought over sandwiches and soup and refilled our coffee cups. "Careful," she said. "This is hot. Don't burn your mouth; you want to save your taste buds for dessert." She went back to the kitchen.

I was relieved when Eric texted back that had already made copies on two separate USB drives, and he would disconnect from the Internet as well. I texted that I'd call him in a few minutes.

The bowls of soup were generous. The bread had the misshapen look of an Italian peasant loaf. I could see melted cheese poking up through a couple of holes on the bread. It was toasted a perfect dark golden brown and I could tell just by looking at it that butter was a major ingredient of the sandwich. I pulled off a corner and blew on it gently. I popped it into my mouth and had to roll it around my tongue so it wouldn't burn. The risk was worth it. It was delicious.

"So, here's what I think," I said, purposely keeping my voice calm. "You need to eat your sandwich. I'm serious. I want to take a drive over and see these houses that the Cunninghams built, and then we can head back to Boston. You up to that?" I said.

"Sure, I guess so. But shouldn't we..."

"What? We can't do much to help Eric from down here, but there isn't much we can do back in Boston either. Time to bring in the authorities."

I texted Eric one more time. I wanted to let him know that he should give Toni one of the USB drives. I told Emma what I was going to.

"Of course, the chain of evidence may never hold up in court, but that's a lawyer's problem, not Toni's."

"I don't suppose we could hold off—"

"Nope." I took a sip of my soup. Still a little too hot, but delicious. "We need to keep her informed. Too much at stake," I said.

"Sully, what's going on? Do you think the money has anything to do with Gus's disappearance?"

I stirred my soup around and took another spoonful. The temperature was perfect. For some folks, eating during times of stress is impossible. That's never been a problem for me. In fact, during long investigations I've always gained weight.

"Gus figured something out. That's becoming clearer and clearer to me. We may not know exactly what he found out until we find him, but someone's worried and has started deleting files. That's always a sign you're getting close. Hard to tell who's deleting those files, but it sure seems like Jerry Cunningham has a lot going on. Let's stop by your Cape house, take a look around. Maybe seeing the house that Jerry built will inspire us."

· Eighteen ·

"Sully, what the hell's going on?" Toni thundered before I even had a chance to say hello. I signaled to Emma that I was going to step outside and take the call. She nodded and went back to texting between bites of food.

"Didn't Eric call you?" I asked. I stepped into the small foyer in between the front door and the diner itself. It had probably been built to keep heat in during the winter and AC in during the summer. It wasn't warm, but it did give me a sense of privacy. I leaned against the wall between both doors.

"He called, he texted, he emailed. I'm on my way over to pick up a USB drive he told me you said I had to get from him. Of course, it won't necessarily hold up—"

"Toni, you can't authenticate anything. I know that, you know that. What didn't help making these verifiable is the fact that the files were disappearing like hot dogs at a baseball game while I was looking at Hal Maxwell's file folder. What Eric's going to give you are copies of files from both Gus's computer and Hal's computer. There are several files—Eric will give you a list—that should be exact duplicates but aren't. Details are different."

"But we don't know if they're really from Gus, or Kate, or really from Hal Maxwell or Jerry Cunningham, do we?"

"You can probably verify the Gus files by doing a trace on his computer and looking at his cache. I assume you have his computer?"

"No comment."

"Which I assume means yes. He also was using cloud-based storage devices, but I'm sure you figured that out already. Ask Eric to show you the links he sent to make sure you have them. Anyway, Hal's links get to the Cunningham files too. Who knows who has access? I don't know who's erasing them or who created them. But what I do know is that Eric did some comparisons and found discrepancies in a few of them. He also did some research and there's escrow money missing. Something's going on. You probably have a bigger picture of this whole thing than I do. All I know is that there's a bunch of different parts of this that are starting to come together to form one puzzle."

"For you, maybe," Toni said. "You were always better than I was at connecting dots that don't seem to go together. It's a real gift. Seems to be wasted in your new line of business."

I didn't respond. Not being a cop was one of the great heartaches of my life, but I liked to think I'd moved on. Maybe not. Talking to Toni had a sweet sadness to it. I was glad that I was reconnecting with an old friend. But knowing she was on the case and I was just a bit player, if a player at all, made me miss my old life for the first time in a couple of years.

"Sully, you still there? Sorry about the bitchy comment. I'm having trouble figuring out what's part of this case and what isn't. How far away are you? Maybe you can meet me at Eric's place—"

"I'm actually staying with Eric, but I'm down the Cape picking up some sailcloth. It's a long story. I'm with Emma."

"Where on the Cape?" Toni asked. "Anywhere near the Cunningham community, what do they call it—"

"Century Cape? Yes, pretty close. Emma has a house down here, you know. We were thinking we'd drive by."

"I didn't know she had a house there. So did—or does—Martin Samuel, depending on which side you come down on in response to the 'is he alive or dead' question."

"What side do you come down?" I asked.

"The dead side. Been doing a little research on that story. I'm not surprised they didn't find the body, but I've never seen a living person able to leave absolutely no trace when they disappear. From what I can see, a lot of folks were looking for him. Including the authorities down there, the Coast Guard, and most recently, Babs Allyn."

"I heard Babs was looking for him from his daughter, Holly. Babs hired a PI. She went to meet him the afternoon before the party at the University club."

"I don't suppose you talked to Babs after that meeting, did you?" Toni asked.

"No, I didn't. Didn't even know where she'd gone until later. I wish I had talked to her."

"I wish you had too. The PI's being closemouthed. I hope he doesn't go off the grid, but I can't stop him. I'm waiting for some search warrants to come through, but I'm having trouble with that too. Nobody has filed a missing person on Babs, even though nobody's spoken to her."

"I was going to reach out to somebody up in Vermont, see if they could go by and see if she was there. Holly hasn't sent me her address yet—"

"I'm ahead of you on that one. No one is at their house up in Vermont."

We both let that sit for a minute. Where was Babs?

"Do they have another house?" I asked, anticipating Toni's answer before she gave it.

"In the same neighborhood as Martin Samuel's house. Hold on for a minute, Sully; I'm going to go outside to finish this call." There was a pause, but Toni didn't mute the phone. I heard John Engel bleating in the background but couldn't hear what he said. A minute later, Toni was back on the phone.

"Sorry about that. Folks are starting to gather around me. I can't talk long—John's going to find me eventually. I can't get anyone to go down to the Cape to check on Hal's house down there. Even though the last signal we have from Gus Knight's phone shows that he was over the bridge, in the Bourne area. Even though—"

"Gus was down the Cape?" I said as my throat got dry and my heart started to pound. Was Cape Cod the "CC" that Gus was referring to? Not the Cunningham Corporation?

"As far as we can tell, the last signal from his phone was a text."

"Who did he text?"

"He texted Babs Allyn. She didn't respond."

I took a deep breath, held it for five seconds, and let it go slowly. "That means something, I'm sure of it. I don't know what—"

"Neither do I. But I do want to share one more piece of information with you, off the record. Martin Samuel had two insurance policies. One left everything to his daughter, Holly. Including the house down the Cape. The other was partner insurance for the business. That left everything to Hal Maxwell and the Cunninghams."

"The Cunninghams?" I asked.

"Yup. Seems like the Cunninghams, and the Century Projects, are more than just clients. They're business partners these days.

Apparently some policies kick in on the anniversary of Martin's disappearance because of some sort of abandonment clause for the business. This leads me to the reason I wanted to get out of earshot. Houses down the Cape, Gus's phone down the Cape, you're down the Cape."

"A coincidence—"

"I don't care if it's a coincidence or if you're just further down some road that I don't even see yet. As a citizen, you can go and look around, especially if Emma's with you."

"Are you asking me to investigate?" I asked.

"I'm asking you and Emma to look around since you're down there. Would she be open to that?"

"Someone stole a lot of money from her. I'm sure she'd be more than open to that."

"Just be careful. And keep me posted. Make sure your phone is charged. Don't do anything stupid. Got that?"

"Got that," I said. She ended the call without saying goodbye.

The real question was, got what?

∞

I told Emma what Toni had said.

"Let's go look around," she said, eyes straight ahead.

If I hadn't known the area contained a Century Project, there was nothing that would have told me. We drove down a side road for a couple of miles, housing clusters on the left, a large privet hedge on the right. The hedge looked to be at least ten feet tall, perfectly groomed even in the dead of winter. There were some leaves missing, and I noticed that behind the hedges was a large fence. Enough for privacy, and probably to keep folks out. After a while, there was a break in the hedge, and a road led to a gatehouse. As Emma drove up, a guard came out.

"Ms. Whitehall, ma'am, I'm surprised to see you. I mean, I didn't expect—"

"It's nice to see you. It must be pretty quiet down here this time of year," Emma said.

"You'd be surprised," the guard replied. He looked to be in his mid-fifties, with thinning gray hair on top of his head. Ex-cop or ex-military, I'd guess. He leaned down to look into the car and gave me a once-over. I had no doubt he'd be able to describe me accurately should the need arise. "Yes, ma'am, you'd be surprised. Lots of folks enjoy the quiet of the winter."

"Plus it's so beautiful down here," Emma said. "This is my friend Sully. I thought I'd show her the house. We were down in the neighborhood running an errand for her theater."

"I believe your house is closed up. Saw to it myself."

"We weren't planning on staying, just taking a drive." Emma said.

"Well, the clubhouse is closed, it being off-season and all. But if you need to warm up or use the facilities, feel free to stop by the gatehouse on your way out."

"Thanks. We may take you up on that. Unless Jerry Cunningham is here?"

"No, I haven't seen him. Haven't seen anyone, really. 'Course I was off most of the week, down in Florida visiting my ex-wife. Our kids were down there, staying with her for school vacation week."

"Lucky you," Emma said. "I may need to go somewhere warm soon. But I'm stuck here. I mean, in Boston, for a few more weeks at least. I'll check in on my way out."

"That would be much appreciated, thank you. And, Ms. Whitehall, my sincerest condolences on your troubles. Let me know if there's anything I can do to help."

"Thank you so much. I'll do that." Emma rolled up her window and the guard went back into the gatehouse, raising the gate to let her through. I gave him a small wave as we drove by, noticing the cozy glow coming from inside the gatehouse, which looked much more like a small cottage.

"You didn't remember his name, did you?" I asked.

"Terry was always so much better at that than I was. Besides, he spent more time down here than I did. He was the South Shore guy. I'm a North Shore gal. We should have known the marriage would be troubled."

After we drove into the community, Emma drove straight ahead for quite a way. I noticed that to the right was the edge of what appeared to be a golf course. As we drove along the course, there was eventually a turn to the right, but Emma kept driving straight.

"Basically, there's a double loop going on here. The outer loop has the bigger houses and more commodities that folks are looking for, like the golf course. Half of the houses face the golf course; the other half of the loop faces the ocean. The center loop surrounds a man-made lake. The cheaper houses are not directly on the ocean, the lake, or the golf course. And cheaper, of course, is a relative term."

"How many houses in total?"

"Sixty, I think. All different sizes. A couple of townhouses near the clubhouse at the golf course. Our house is, as I said, not one of the biggest. But we're right on the lake. Upstairs, off the master bedroom, you can see the ocean in the distance. It's what my mother would've called 'a little piece of heaven.' Or it was. I honestly don't know if I can come back down here, given all that's happened. Believe it or not, it would probably make me miss Terry."

"I believe you," I said. "After my father died, I thought about keeping his house since it was closer to the ocean, closer to town.

But I just couldn't bear it. So I got my little gatehouse, settled in there."

"Any regrets?" Emma asked.

"None. But I did wait a bit before I decided. I think you should do that too. Just some unsolicited advice."

As we drove, the houses were clustered together, but there was enough space between them for a bit of privacy. I looked out both sides of the car and could see that there were only three or four different types of houses but every house had its own unique personality, likely owner-driven. We pulled into a driveway of what Emma considered a "small" house. I did not. It was a lovely two-story Gambrel Cape. We were coming in the back, and I noted the dormers on the second floor with a deck in between them. That must be the master bedroom. There was a large, wrap-around deck all along the back of the house, which continued around the side. There were several levels to the deck, and I had no doubt there would be furniture and grills filling the space during the summer.

"Nice deck," I said.

"It goes all along the front of the house too. Leads down to a small dock on the lake. We can walk around if you'd like—"

"How about if you drive me around first, show me the Cunninghams' house, let me get a lay of the land. If it's still light by the time we're done, we can take a walk. It looks like nobody's been walking around here for a while." I surveyed the ground, the mounds of frozen snow that showed no signs of footprints.

"Sure, we can take a drive."

"Can you also show me Hal's house?" I asked. "Maybe Babs is there."

"Hopefully she's down here. I'll also show you Martin's house."

While Emma backed out into the quiet street, I pulled my notebook out of my bag and started taking some notes. I drew a rough sketch of the community and tried to mark out whose house was whose. "Let's see if any of these houses look like they've had visitors."

"Hal's house is right over here," Emma said.

I forced myself to exhale the breath I hadn't realized I'd been holding.

∞

From the outside, Hal's house looked as if there had been a bit of activity. We both got out of the car and stood in the half-shoveled driveway. It had been a cold and snowy winter, and the Cape had much more snow than Boston did, so there was a nice layer of ice over the snow that helped indicate what might have gone on. Though there were a few broken places on the snow that indicated a footprint, they led up to the front door, which had a huge mound of snow on the front stoop. Just to make sure, I stepped into the footprints and tried to open the screen door on the front of the house. It was blocked: frozen shut. I did a quick look around and didn't see any other steps indicating someone had been there.

"Emma, is there a back entrance?" I noted that there was a gate in the fence that surrounded the property. It too was mounded over with snow, and I couldn't imagine how it could be opened.

"There is a back way," Emma said. We both climbed into her small car, which she'd left running to keep warm. "As you can see, Hal's house backs up onto the golf course. We could try and get in from over there—"

"Let's go to the Cunninghams' first," I said. I looked around and dusted off my observational skills. "We're playing beat the clock with the sun. I'd rather explore in daylight as much as possible."

We drove around the loop to the Cunninghams' house. True, it wasn't the largest in the community, but it certainly was the most ideally situated. It sat up a little bit on the crest of a hill. As you faced it, to the left there was the ocean. To the right there was the golf course clubhouse. Because of the location, there were no houses abutting either side. I assumed that there were also no houses behind the Cunninghams', and I asked Emma about that.

"No," she said. "Nothing on the back side of the Cunningham house except the golf course. They do have a fence along the back, sort of an invisible netting situation that prevents stray golf balls from flying into the house or the yard as much as possible. Mimi got sick of fishing golf balls out of their pool."

"They have their own pool? Isn't there one at the clubhouse?" I said.

"Yes, a nice one. The Cunningham pool is more of a lap pool. Mimi and Jerry are both fanatics about exercise. See over there? They have a much bigger fence between them and the clubhouse proper."

"Does the clubhouse rock in the summer?"

"I don't know if 'rock' is the word, but there's certainly a party atmosphere. Not just in the summer. The clubhouse opens the first week of April, closes the day after New Year's. It's a long season down here. As you can see, a few folks live here year-round. Most people do what we do, close it down for the dead of winter. The snow just makes it too hard to get down here a lot."

"Well, it doesn't look like the Cunninghams have been here recently." Again, we'd stopped the car and gotten out. The Cunninghams' house had been shoveled out with a lot more care. But the heap of snow in front of the front door indicated that they hadn't been down since the storm the previous weekend. I walked to the right of the driveway. Like at Hal's house, there was a fence that surrounded the property, classy and understated but doing what it was intended to do and blocking the view of the back yard. This fence butted right up to the fence along the golf course.

I looked around and noticed the cameras—one on the house, one on the garage, one on the fence. Red lights on them all. I felt like waving at the gate guard. I wouldn't have been surprised if he was bundling up to find us and ask what we were doing. We both got back into the car again.

I rubbed my hands together. "Maybe we should check and see if anyone came in the back door—"

"Let's check Martin's first," Emma said. "We might as well be thorough."

"Has anyone been using his house?" I asked.

"Not regularly," Emma said. "Holly was down a few times to check on it, but she didn't sleep there. She'd stay with Hal and Babs. Here it is."

The sun was falling fast by now, and the blue-gray February sky cast Martin Samuel's house in an ominous light. Of all the houses we'd seen, Martin's was the smallest by far. While the others bumped up to what I assumed were their property boundaries, Martin's sat in the middle and was closer to the road. The man-made lake in the center of the development was his backyard view. Also, unlike the others, he didn't have a fence surrounding his property. I could see straight back to the frozen lake. The view was magnificent.

"This is stunning," I said.

"It is, isn't it?" Emma said. "The Cunninghams only offered three or four different types of house plans to choose from, but Martin did what he could to make this unique. Did you ever meet him?"

"Once or twice, but I didn't really know him."

"He had the soul of an artist," Emma said. "I know that sounds pretentious, but it's true. He wasn't particularly handsome but he was magnetic. When you spoke with him he acted as if you were speaking pearls of wisdom he'd never heard before. He was incredibly curious and read voraciously. He was also never without a sketchbook.

Down here, he carried his paints with him wherever he went. I have a couple of his paintings. We all do. He was a wonderful artist."

"A good man?"

"Not sure if he was a good man or not. I've stopped being able to tell. Thinking back to last summer, I realize now how much he was missed. How much this place just wasn't the same without him. He was a presence, a force. I still can't believe he disappeared like that. Holly kept insisting he'd come back, got most of us to believe it. She was convinced that he was just taking a sabbatical. But—"

"It's been almost a year, right? Sounds like the anniversary of his disappearance is triggering a few things. I can't help but wonder what, exactly."

"Part of the puzzle you're trying to put together?" Emma asked.

"Maybe," I said. "But I'm low of facts for this one. I think Holly mentioned hearing from him after he disappeared? I can't remember exactly what she said."

"I did hear that there were signs of life," Emma said. "We never talked about it, of course. Hard to bring up in conversations. I do know that as the summer wore down, Holly got more despondent. I think that's one reason she went to work for Babs. They're very close."

I looked at Martin's house, the condensation on the windows causing interesting ice art. "You said nobody's been down here?" I asked. "See the frost on that front window? That tells me that the heat's been on."

"He lived here full-time, so the house never gets shut down. I assumed that Holly would have closed it up, but maybe she comes down on her days off? Look, the front door doesn't have that mound of snow on the stoop," Emma said.

We both got out of the car. The sun was giving its last gasp of light and the red light danced across the frozen yard. We didn't have a lot of time to look around. I grabbed my cell phone and turned on the flashlight feature. The front walkway and stoop were clear. I walked up to the front door. The screen door was locked, presumably from the inside. I looked to my left and there were no footprints leading around that side of the house. I retrace my steps back and met Emma back in the driveway.

"See over there?" Emma said. "There's a path that's been sort of shoveled. Folks do use this as egress to the lake. Martin always let them. Maybe that's why the path is clear?"

"Maybe that's why," I said. "Let's see what's back there."

We followed the path to the back of the house. The sun was really dropping now, and the moon hadn't come out yet so we moved slowly. The setting sun glistened on the ice on top of the snow. Where people had veered from the path, and the ice was broken through, there were voids of bouncing light. Sure enough, the path led right down to the lake, which was frozen over. Probably a great place for ice skating. I walked almost to the edge of the water and looked around. Nothing by the lake. Nothing I could see.

"It's beautiful," I said to Emma, who was standing at my side.

"It's cold," Emma said.

"Sure is. I wish we could see in these windows."

"The entire back of Martin's house is glass," Emma said. "There's another path that goes right up to his back deck."

"Let's go back and see if we can see inside the house before we lose the sun completely," I said.

We turned around and headed back toward the driveway. I took my cell phone and used the flashlight to sweep both sides of the path, seeing if I'd missed anything. Closer to the house the path to the back deck had been cleared, and the deck itself was clear but icy. I held on to the railings as I walked the perimeter of the deck. The French doors in the back of the house were locked tight. I cupped my hands against the windows and looked around. The entire back of the house was an open plan, with the kitchen on the left, a dining room table in the middle, and a living room on the right. A hallway led off the kitchen, presumably to a bathroom or a front room. Maybe a bedroom. No one was there. But as I swept my eyes through the house, a faint strip of light caught my eye. I peered in closer and used my cell phone flashlight to sweep the room. The light was coming from under a door in the hallway.

"Is there a basement in this house?" I asked.

"I think so," Emma said. I walked to the right of the deck and peered over the side. Sure enough, there was one of those plastic domes that kept snow, rain, and hopefully vermin out of the basement window wells. I noticed that it was covered with snow, as were the steps down to the side of the house. I held on to the railing and lowered myself to the yard level. The snow came up over my knees, but I pushed forward, breaking the ice. I use both hands to clear the plastic bubble and noted that the glow of the light rewarded my efforts. I kept clearing until I'd cleared enough of a space to look down into the basement. My voice caught in my throat and stifled the cry that had come wrenching up from deep in my gut.

"Sully, what's wrong?"

"Call an ambulance," I screamed. "I found Gus."

· Nineteen ·

I broke one of the panels in the French door, unlocked the door, and let myself in. The house was cold but not freezing. The heat must have been on. I went down to the basement and found Gus where I'd seen him, tied to one of the lalley columns, his hands taped behind his back. He was slumped to the side, and his hands had a blue tint because of the pressure on his wrists.

"Oh please oh please oh please oh please oh please," I muttered as a mantra while I knelt down and took off my gloves. I was careful not to move Gus too much as I desperately sought for a pulse. His skin felt cold, but my hands were too. After what felt like forever, I finally found a pulse. Faint, but it was there. I looked at the vomit on the front of his jacket and the blood that had congealed around the wound on the side of his head.

I took off my coat and put it gently around him. Emma had come halfway down the stairs to let me know the ambulance was on its way. I told her to go upstairs and turn up the heat. And to bring me a blanket.

"Gus," I said quietly. No response. "Gus," I said more loudly. "Gus, it's Sully. You're safe."

∞

The gatehouse guard—it ends up his name was Ben—waited for the ambulance and accompanied them to the house. He and Emma both pulled me away from Gus to let paramedics work. Ben took off his coat and draped it around my shoulders, and Emma wrapped her arms around my waist. After they'd worked on Gus for a while, they were ready to transport him. We heard them call in *unresponsive, stable,* and *head wound.*

Emma made a call and handed the phone to one of the paramedics. "This is Courtney O'Connor—she's a doctor at Brigham and Women's. Tell her what you just said."

"Ma'am, we don't have time to—"

"Just do it," Emma said. The paramedic did as he was told and had a long conversation with Dr. O'Connor. At the end, he conferred with his partner and it was decided that Gus was going to Boston for treatment.

∞

"Wasn't that taking a chance?" Toni asked me. She'd come into the hospital waiting room a few minutes earlier with a large French roast coffee for me. She'd also brought herself one, and a bag of food.

"It may have been, because it was an extra hour's drive. But Dr. O'Connor was willing to treat him in Boston and she has a great reputation. We probably would've moved him here anyway. I don't know, Toni. I just let Emma take over."

"Where is she?" Toni asked.

"She's driving the sailcloth over to the theater."

"That couldn't have waited?"

"The show must go on," I said. I smiled slightly, but I was serious. Emma had fought me, but I wanted to make sure the crew had what they needed to fix the set tomorrow. Besides, there wasn't much she could do for Gus or for me sitting in the waiting room.

"Tell me what happened," Toni said. I noticed, and was grateful, that she didn't sugarcoat it. She knew my cop instincts had kicked in and that I could talk about what had happened this afternoon. I needed to talk about it, to help process my feelings. So I told her all about the visit to Century Cape.

"Somebody decided to use Martin's house to hide Gus," Toni said. "Didn't the guard notice it was being used?"

"He said he'd been away, and since Martin had never turned the heat completely off in his house, the assumption was that his daughter was following the same example. It's definitely worth following up with the team down the Cape. Whoever took Gus left the light on in the basement. If they hadn't, we might not have found him." My voice caught a bit.

"But they did, and you did. Don't go there. Let's figure out who did the hiding instead. My money is on Babs Allyn."

"Babs? Why Babs?"

"She hired that private investigator, Jack Megan."

"Jack Megan? Really?"

"Why, do you know him?"

"I do, and probably so do you. He's a retired cop," I said.

"I don't remember him, but that doesn't mean anything. Gus had used him a lot lately. He called him several times a week. Apparently Megan specializes in divorce cases, but I'd imagine he's doing other work for Gus."

"Jack also does research work. Typical private investigator fare. Has he told you what he was doing for Babs? Or for Gus?"

"He's a hard man to find, and we're having trouble getting a warrant to force him to talk. He's not in his office, not at home. Not answering his cell. 'Course, it probably doesn't help that it's a cop calling him."

"Maybe he's on a case?" I asked.

"Maybe," Toni said. "They found Gus's phone, by the way. In the basement. There was an unsent message to you. To tell you he was sorry about lunch. He'd taken an unexpected trip to the Cape and would you come meet him. As I told you, the last text he sent that went through was to Babs."

"Babs, huh? She does seem like a logical suspect." Toni and I looked at each other. Even though we hadn't been partners for years, I understood her as well as I had six years ago. There was more to this, a lot more that she couldn't say.

"Here's the deal, Sully. I brought you some caffeine, some food. Two old friends sitting and talking. Catching up. I have nothing to do with the case around Gus. I have nothing to do with the case around Babs Allyn. My focus is trying to figure out who killed Mimi Cunningham, and why. See if her death is connected to Kate's death. There's some evidence that links the two—no, I won't tell you what it is—but we don't understand the connection. Yet. Figuring out the 'why' has gotten a lot more complicated. Your friend Eric is helping me think that through. But I've been warned off expanding my parameters in this case. 'Stay focused, Vestri.' The John Engel mantra."

"He's a jackass," I said.

"He is that. But he's also my partner. So I'm staying focused. Visiting my friend in the hospital, checking in on my other friend, mentioning that Gus's phone had a different number for Jack Megan, and writing that down for her information. In case she wanted to let this Jack Megan guy know what happened to Gus. Her call."

Dr. O'Connor came out to update us on Gus's condition. "He's got some swelling of the brain, so we've put him in a medically induced coma. Frankly, given the extent of his injuries and the fact that he's been without treatment for, what, two days? I'm surprised he's not in worse shape. But I'm glad you brought him in here. We got some good folks taking care of him."

"Good thing he's got a wicked hard head," Toni said. She smiled and I smiled back.

"When will he be able to wake up?" I asked.

"Not till tomorrow at the earliest. I'd suggest you go home and get some rest. There's nothing you can do for him here, at least not right now. Feel free to go in and say good night, but I really do suggest you get some sleep. I promise I'll call if anything changes."

∞

Somehow Gus looked worse in the hospital than he had in the basement. Maybe it was because he was so pale next to the hospital sheets. The hospital Johnny, which he would have hated, barely moved as he breathed. There were tubes and pumps and machines surrounding his bed. The beeps reassured me that he was alive, but I would have given anything for him to talk to me.

"Get well, buddy," Toni said. She leaned over and kissed him on the forehead. She stepped back and away to give me space.

I leaned down and put my lips close to his ear. "Gus, I've got some stuff to do to try and make this right. I'll be back, I promise," I whispered. I kissed him on his cheek and then lightly on the lips. I stood up and took a deep, raggedy breath.

"Toni, would you give me a ride to my car? I've got a couple of errands to run tonight," I said.

∞

Toni gave me a ride back to the garage where my car was kept. On the way we went over the timeline of the case, or cases. Mostly I talked, she listened and asked questions. I didn't get any new information from her; not sure if she got anything from me.

"I guess Gus is off the suspect list?" I asked.

"He is for me, but he never was on mine to begin with. I've had to stay neutral, given that he's my friend. But John was going after him hard. Speaking of which, I've got to meet up with John, make sure he doesn't screw this case up."

"To be fair," I said, "there are a lot of moving parts here. Hard to know what matters, what doesn't, and what you're going to need to prove the case later. It's a little easier for us civilians to look into things on our own and let you know if we find anything worth knowing."

"You know I would never, ever, suggest that. Make sure your phone's charged, and let me know what you find out from Jack Megan."

"Will do," I said. "Thanks for the ride." I got out of the car and walked toward the garage elevator.

The problem with underground garages was that cell phone reception was lousy. The problem with Boston was that once you left the garage, it was tough to find a place to pull over and make a call. The problem with me was that I couldn't drive and talk. I plugged my phone into the charger and checked the time. Nine o'clock. It was late but I wasn't going to wait till tomorrow to make this call.

After leaving the garage, I looped around the Boston Common, then went a block over and drove past the Park Plaza before I found a space to pull over. I found the piece of paper Toni had given me with Jack Megan's other phone number. It didn't match any I had. I wondered if it was a burner phone. I called it and got a full voicemail box for my efforts. So I texted:

Jack, it's Sully Sullivan. Writing as Gus Knight's ex-wife. He's in the hospital, in a coma. I'm also friends with Babs Allyn, looking for her. I have a lot of questions and I think you may have some answers. I need to see you. Tonight.

I sat in the car for five minutes, ignoring the car that had pulled over, blinker on in hopes that the parking gods were smiling on them tonight. My phone rang. Jack preferred to call rather than to text. Made sense; easier to deny the content of the conversation.

"Sully here," I said.

"Jack Megan," he said. "What the hell happened to Gus?"

"Nice to talk to you too, Jack. Somebody hit him on the head and left him for dead in Martin Samuel's basement down the Cape."

"Down the Cape? What the hell was he doing down there?"

"I have no idea," I said.

"He going to be okay?"

"There's reason for optimism. We had him brought up here for treatment."

"Damn, didn't see that one coming," he said.

"You heard about Kate Smythe?"

"I did," he said. "They have any idea who did that?"

"Not that I know of. I think it has something to do with Mimi Cunningham's murder but I have no proof, just my gut."

"Gus and I were talking about you a couple of weeks ago," Jack said. "We both agree you have world-class instincts."

"For a theater administrator," I said. I was perversely pleased at my ex-husband's compliment. "Listen, I'd like to see you. Tonight. Catch you up with what I'm thinking, see if you can fill in some gaps for me."

"I'm lying a little low right now," he said.

"I'll meet you wherever," I said.

"Okay, but no cops. You got that? No. Cops. I know you still hang out with them on occasion."

"I'm flying solo tonight," I said. "Where should we meet?"

"There's a bar in Brighton. The Bus Station. You know it? Meet you there in twenty minutes." He ended the call, and I answered somebody's parking prayers by pulling out of the spot and heading over toward Harvard Stadium.

∞

I love bars like the Bus Station. Loud, slightly seedy bars that feature '80s rock, only use iceberg lettuce, and have no pretensions, but do have an excellent beer selection. I inhaled the wafts of burgers and fries that met me at the front door and my stomach rumbled. I scanned the room and saw an average-height, well-built black man stand up from a corner booth. I smiled despite myself. Good old Jack, scoring a prime location on a Saturday night. I wondered if he was a regular.

I walked up and we gave each other a hug. "Good to see you, Sully. Have a seat. I ordered a large plate of fries, got a beer coming from the bar. Plenty of fries to share. Want a drink?"

A beer sounded really good, but I wanted to stay focused. "Just a seltzer."

Jack called the order out to the bartender, who nodded. "You're on the job," he said. "I know that look. Tell me about Gus."

So I did. I told him what I knew, and the timeline I'd worked out. I included information about Babs in the conversation.

"I hope to hell he's going to be okay," Jack said.

I looked over at his shaved head and deep brown eyes. The news of Gus had shaken Jack up. He'd worked with Gus for a lot of years, back when he was still on the force and Gus was in the district attorney's office. Unlike a lot of folks, Jack hadn't cut ties to me when Gus and I got divorced. Our paths had crossed this December, and we'd had a couple of meals together since then.

"They think so, but he's in a medically induced coma right now. I'm glad we found him when we did."

"We?"

"I was with Emma Whitehall. Long story. We didn't set out looking for him, but one thing led to another—"

"And your gut kicked in," Jack said. "Good thing for Gus."

"Good thing for Gus," I said. "And for me. Listen, I just found out that Babs Allyn had hired you. Did Gus recommend you to her?"

"Babs who?" He asked, his eyes darting toward the bar. The bartender came over with the drinks and let us know that the fries were on their way. I waited till he was out of earshot to respond to Jack's question.

"Jack, I'm tired and I still have adrenaline flowing, but we both know I'm going to crash soon. The cops know Babs Allyn hired you. I want to know why, and what for. I'm assuming it had something to do with Martin Samuel's disappearance?"

Jack looked at me and clenched his jaw. He took a long sip of beer, and used his napkin to wipe the foam off his upper lip. I watched his face contort as he wrestled around with the question of what to do.

"I saw Babs on Tuesday," I said. "She was heading out for a meeting and never made it back to the theater. I saw her again that night, and she was a hot mess. Did she see you Tuesday afternoon?"

Jack nodded slightly.

"What did you tell her?" I asked.

"You've heard of client confidentiality—"

"I have, and I respect it. But I want to point this out. No one has seen Babs since that night. She's either on the suspect list or something's happened to her. I talked to Martin's daughter, Holly, and she mentioned that Babs was investigating Martin's disappearance. I'm assuming that's what you two met about. I don't know Babs well, but she seems like the type who would protect Holly from harsh realities, until she couldn't. From what I understand, Holly and maybe Babs thought Martin was alive for a long time. But lately they've been having doubts. Have I got this part of the story right?"

Jack took another pull on his beer and set it down. "You do," he said. "I'm worried about her too. Babs, I mean. A couple of months after Martin went missing, she got a postcard from him, from an island near where he'd disappeared. Told her he was okay, he'd be back soon. Holly got a similar postcard a couple weeks later. On both of the postcards, Martin asked them to hang tight, not to look for him. He was taking care of some business."

"Was it in his handwriting?"

"That's the problem. He sent them through this mail service they have down there, where you go online, type in a message, chose a picture, and then the company sends it out. On both postcards he used a phrase that he'd used before, and that made them feel like he'd sent the postcard. They both hung on to the hope those cards gave them. But then, when they didn't hear from him again, and it was coming up on a year, Babs decided they needed to look for him. Hal Maxwell and the Cunninghams were making noises about getting him declared dead so that his will, and some of the insurance policies, would kick in. Babs hired me to see if I could find anything out."

"Did you find anything?"

"I did some research on that mail service. Anyone could've used it, set up an account under Martin Samuel's name, so there's that. Not real proof of anything." Jack took a long pull from his beer and continued his story. "I went down there, asked a few folks about the disappearance. Seems there were a bunch of folks staying on the Cunninghams' boat, which was moored out in the harbor that night, not on the dock. The crew had taken the dinghy back to shore and were planning to come back out in the morning to make breakfast and set sail. Crew came on board in the morning and no one could find Martin. Apparently he took a lifeboat and his suitcase and left the boat in the middle of the night. Anyway, that's what everyone thought."

"Who else was on the boat?"

"Hal Maxwell. Babs Allyn. Mimi and Jerry Cunningham. Fred Ginger—"

"Who's Fred Ginger?"

"A business associate of the Cunninghams. Helps them with their offshore banking."

"Nice."

"Right? That's a can of worms I stayed away from on this job. Anyway, that was it. From what the crew said, there had been a lot of drinking that last day and into the night."

"The entire crew left?" I asked. "Was that normal?"

"When the Cunninghams were staying in port, yes," Jack said. "The crew would leave late and come back at dawn. From what I could find out, most of the time the Cunninghams and their guests were sleeping, or passed out, and missed the crew's departure."

"Did Babs remember them leaving?" I asked.

"Babs said she passed out around midnight. She didn't hear a thing. She doesn't remember what time, or if, Hal came to bed."

"She didn't remember a thing? She must be a pretty sound sleeper."

"From what I can gather, she was a pretty heavy drinker. That was the last drink she had, as a matter of fact."

"Until Tuesday night," I said.

"Really? She'd been drinking?" Jack said.

"I think so," I said, trying to remember the details of the last time I'd seen Babs. Had I seen her with a drink? Or had I assumed she'd been drinking? "At least, she seemed tipsy. She was furious. I couldn't understand what she was saying to the Cunninghams but she was disheveled, you know? Babs was never disheveled."

"She was pretty upset when she left our meeting," Jack said.

"What did you tell her at your meeting?" I asked.

"I told her I thought that Martin Samuel was dead. There was no moon that night, so the harbor was dark. Really dark. I don't see how a drunken person could've gotten on a lifeboat, made his way ashore, and no one saw him. Plus I talked to a couple of folks from the crew. The Cunninghams paid them well, very well. One of them said he'd thought maybe the boat had changed moorings the next morning, but he couldn't be sure. And since everyone seemed so upset, he didn't say anything."

"The boat had moved?" I asked.

"Maybe, but I couldn't get that verified," Jack said.

"You think the crew was paid off?" I asked.

"They may have been," Jack said.

"What did the authorities say?" I asked.

"They aren't convinced nothing happened, but they couldn't find any proof. They did a thorough search of the boat, didn't find anything. They did say it was clean, really clean. They smelled bleach, but Mimi Cunningham explained that away by saying that Babs had gotten sick on her way to bed. The police kept the boat down there for a few months in case new evidence came up or they found Martin's body, but they finally released it in October."

"Where's the boat now?" I asked.

"The Cunninghams had it sailed up from the Caribbean. It's actually at a slip in Charlestown." Jack took a napkin and wrote some numbers down on it after double-checking them on his phone.

"Did you tell Babs where the boat was?" I asked.

"I didn't have the information when she asked Tuesday. I haven't heard from her since. The news about the guy who thought the boat was moved pushed some buttons for Babs. 'They kept telling me I was crazy because I remembered something different' she kept saying. Anyway, she never called to ask where the boat was. But Gus did. So I told him. Didn't hear from him again either, but I wasn't worried till I heard about Kate Smythe's death."

"Did you go check out the boat yourself?" I asked.

"I didn't, not yet. Too many fires burning right now, but it was on my list for tomorrow. Believe it or not, I have to go stake out a client's husband tonight."

"Hi ho, the glamorous life of a private investigator," I said. One of the reasons I always gave for not becoming a private investigator after I left the force was that if I couldn't wear the badge, I didn't want to do the job. That was true. The other reason was that the work of private investigators was brutal and solitary. That said, if I didn't have other things on my mind, I might have volunteered to go on Jack's stakeout with him. See if they were as awful as I remembered.

The fries finally arrived and I picked one up off the plate. It was steaming hot, so I blew on it for a few seconds and then took a bite. It burned my tongue but it was worth it. I took another sip of the seltzer and unrolled a fork from a napkin.

"Thanks for the information." I tapped the piece of paper with the boat slip location.

"You're going to go down there now, aren't you?" Jack asked. I didn't answer but I did look away. "Dammit, Sully, how about you wait until daylight and I'll go with you?"

"I won't be able to sleep. I need to see the boat, you know? I can't help but think what happened on that boat has something to do with all of this. Maybe Babs is there? I promise I won't get into any trouble. I'm just going to look around a bit." Jack looked dubious. I picked up another fry with my fork and blew on it. "Jack, you go do your job. I'll call the cops and catch them up after I get back from the boat. I'll keep you out of it, of course."

"How about you call them first, let them check the boat out?" he asked.

"Where's the fun in that?" I asked. I took a paper napkin and put some fries in it, smiling over at him. "I'm going to go satisfy my curiosity, look at the boat, give Toni Vestri a call, go home to sleep, and start fresh in the morning."

"You be careful, you hear me? Text me if you need me. Gus will kill me if I let anything happen to you."

"Ten-four on that. Thanks for the fries." I put out my fist and Jack bumped it. I got up from the table and went back into the February freeze.

· Twenty ·

Allston and Charlestown are both in Boston, not far apart in distance, but getting from one to the other took some thoughtful maneuvering. I did some mental calculations. Were the Bruins or the Celtics playing? I didn't think so, but I couldn't be sure. Storrow Drive was the best way to go at this time of night. Like much of New England, Boston had been built on old cow paths that had been paved over. The side roads were complicated to traverse easily, but often made more sense than trying to go on major roads during prime travel hours. Of course, these days prime travel hours seem to go from six in the morning to midnight.

Charlestown had a high-priced apartment complex on the water. I knew there were some boat slips, and I'd noticed that several boats were still in the water the last time I'd taken a walk on the other side of the harbor. Someone had explained to me that the harbor didn't freeze over easily, and that the complex made sure that the water around the slips was churned during the winter.

It was a gated complex, so I parked a block away. I'd gotten my coat back from the paramedics and found my gloves in my pockets.

They were still wet from digging in the snow. Fortunately, my car was like a traveling suitcase and I went into the way back to see if I could find another pair of gloves. Bingo: gloves, a black scarf, and a black watch cap. I stuffed my curly mop into the hat. Not a fashion-first look, but it was warm. I put my wallet with my ID in my pocket and left a business card on the front seat. I pulled the charger out of my phone. Almost 57 percent. I grabbed a small flashlight from the glove box and put it in my pocket. I took a deep breath and held my hands in front of me. Steady as a rock.

Getting down to the boat slips required me to walk to the right to get to the water's edge, and then veer left to head toward the dock area. The only other way in was through the buildings onto the grounds, which would probably require IDs or keys. It was February, and strolling by the water was not a pastime, especially this time of night. I didn't see anyone. I turned on my small flashlight and kept it low to the ground, using it to make sure I wasn't going to slip on anything. If anyone asked, I was out for a walk, so using a flashlight made sense. I kept toward the water's edge, and when I was closer to the docks I looked around. I didn't see security or cameras, but I still pulled my hat down lower and shut my flashlight off.

I walked down the dock but then was blocked by a large gate that provided security to the boatyard. Probably a good idea so kids wouldn't hang out on the boats docked there, but a pain in the neck for me. I shined my flashlight in an arc. The gate didn't go too far into the water's edge. I took a deep breath and put my fingers through the chain link. I shimmied to the end of the gate and then carefully turned myself around and shimmied back to the dock. By the time my feet were back on solid footing, I was sweating and had started to shake. I put my hands on my knees and took a deep breath. One thing was for sure—I wasn't leaving the boatyard the same way I came in.

I walked down the dock again. I looked at the slip of paper Jack had given me and compared the numbers to the ones on the first column I came upon. After walking to the next pole, I turned to the right, walked farther, and looked at the number of the first slip. I understood the system. On each dock there were several slips on each side, so the boats had walkways on three sides of them. There weren't many boats in the water, but there were more than I'd thought there'd be. If I was right, three docks up was where the Cunninghams' boat was docked. I wished I knew what it looked like.

I thought about texting Toni and letting her know what I was up to, but I decided to look at the boat first, see what I could find. I took a right.

I'd expected the dock to be slippery and metal, but I was wrong on both counts. It was wooden, possibly a manufactured wood, but the traction was good. It was also quiet as I walked. There were three boats in slips on the left, two in slips on the right. I pulled out my flashlight and put my hand over the end, letting a tiny bit of light filter out. I moved forward slowly. The boat in the middle, on the left—was that a light? I inched forward. Yes, there was a faint light coming from inside the cabin. I moved closer and looked at the name on the boat. The boat's name was Mimi.

Each slip had a small gangplank separating the boats. I suspected it also provided extra security during storm surges, helping the boats not clang against each other. I looked behind me, but nobody was there. Not that it would've been easy to see in the inky night. Could I see in those portholes? What happened if someone was in there? If Jerry Cunningham was having a drink, maybe I'd join him.

I walked over to the Mimi and had to stand on my tiptoes to see inside. A blonde head was leaning over the stove, pulling a pot of boiling water off the burner and pouring it over a tea bag. Was it

Babs? A gust of wind came up and I grabbed the side of the boat to steady myself. I must've made a noise, and she looked up. I gasped.

Mimi Cunningham.

∞

I crouched down beside the boat. I hoped Mimi hadn't seen me, and was grateful for the black hat I'd found in the back of the car. I pulled out my phone and found Toni's number. I was about to hit send on the call when I heard a voice to my right.

"Hands where I can see them," the voice said. I looked over and vaguely made out a figure. I recognized the voice. Jerry Cunningham. "Who is that?" he asked.

I hit the send button and hoped for the best. I put the phone in my pocket and held both hands in front of me, toward Jerry. I had put my flashlight in my pocket when I got closer to the boat, and now I cursed that decision. If I could have flashed the light in his eyes, maybe it would have startled him. But he was blocking the gangway and I couldn't get past him without taking a flying leap to reach the dock. Flying leaps had never been my forte, especially not on a cold February night.

"I've got a gun. Who's there?" Jerry repeated. Mimi opened the door to the cabin and light flooded the dark in a wide wedge. She came up and peered at her husband.

"Jerry, what's going on?" she whispered.

"Get back down there," Jerry said. He spoke in a full voice, well aware that nobody was around to hear either one of us. "We have a visitor. We're coming down now." Jerry gestured with his gun to the side of the boat, using his flashlight to show me the way. I thought about trying to do a mule kick once he was behind me, but he must have expected it because he stayed back until I got on the deck. "Down below," he barked. I did as I was told.

Mimi Cunningham was standing back, away from me. I looked around and thought about grabbing the hot water, but then felt the gun at the back of my head. "Sit down, over there." I sat in the banquet seating, taking the bench that put my back to the deck door. My best hope was to get both of them in front of me and then take a running leap. Timing would be critical, since Jerry had the gun and I had nothing but my wits.

"Mimi, close the hatch." Jerry came around and sat on the other side of the table. "Sully? Is that you?" He had the gun trained on me. I'd misjudged the size of the cabin while I was outside. It was quite large and very comfortable, with three seating areas. I looked straight ahead and noted a few stairs by the kitchen area that led below decks. That must be where the bedrooms were.

"It's me, Jerry. Didn't realize that you had your boat up here in Charlestown until a friend told me about it a little while ago. I've been trying to find Babs Allyn, and I wondered if she was staying on the boat. I had no idea I'd be running into Mimi." I turned and faced Mimi. "Mimi, I thought you were dead."

"Good, you're supposed to," she said. She sat on a couch that was on the other side of the cabin, facing the table. She picked up her cup of tea and bobbed the tea bag vigorously. She took it out, drained it with her fingers, and then tossed it into the sink.

"Jerry did a good job," I said, "making us think you were dead. Even came up with a corpse. Or created one?"

"No, we didn't create one. What do you think we are?" Jerry said.

"I think you are, or may be, crooks," I said. Neither one of them blinked, so I went on. Was Toni listening to this, or had I gotten her voicemail? Did the call even connect? I needed to focus on the now, give her clues if she was listening, figure out how to save myself if she wasn't. "I've been hearing about some money shenanigans with the Cunningham Corporation."

"We're not murderers. Never that," Mimi said. She was sitting in very faded light, so it was hard to see her clearly. That said, her hair was tied back in a ponytail and she didn't seem to have makeup on. She was wearing yoga pants and an oversized fleece. Mimi was not looking her best. "Even we have our standards, don't we darling?" she said as she turned toward Jerry.

"Mimi, drink your tea. I need you to sober up, sweetheart. We have a lot to do." He smiled at her and she smiled back. She took a sip of tea.

"The tea needs sweetener," she said.

"Sorry, darling, you'll need to drink it black. Mimi's right, though, Sully. We'd never kill anyone." Jerry winced. The circles beneath his eyes were more pronounced. He took the hand without the gun and ran it over his chin. He needed a shave, and his eyes were sunken. He sat back on the bench and looked at me with fatigue and curiosity.

"What are you doing here?" he said.

"I met with the private investigator that Babs hired. He told me she had been looking into Martin's disappearance, and also mentioned that your boat was here."

"So you thought you'd stop by and—"

"See if Babs was here. I had no plan beyond stopping by. It's been a long day. I thought I'd look around, hope it inspired some thoughts. Now I'm wondering if I was wasting my time looking for Babs…"

"You got it in one," Mimi said. "Sully's really very clever, isn't she, sweetheart?"

"Babs was the person killed in the park?" I asked. My chest tightened but I forced myself to breath and remain calm.

"Whoever did it thought she was me," Mimi said. "Babs had taken my coat—they look alike. My ID was in the pocket, so they assumed it was me. Then they called Jerry to come down and identify the body."

"Couldn't they have done a visual identification?" I asked. "Didn't they know it wasn't you?"

"Whoever killed Babs kicked her in the face," Jerry said. A shudder ran through him. He swallowed hard and continued. "She was unrecognizable. So they thought she was Mimi. I, of course, knew she wasn't, since Mimi was beside me when I got the call. But I went down to make the identification. I knew right away it was Babs. But I told them that yes, it was Mimi."

"And they took your word for it?" I asked.

"Of course they took my word for it, Sully," Jerry said. "Surely it can't be a surprise to you that some people get more accommodations than others in their grief? Trust me, the idea of Mimi being killed did not require a great deal of acting for me to appear upset."

"And everyone thinking that Mimi was dead would offer you time, right?" I asked. "You needed to come up with some way to put off people like Gus Knight for a little while longer while you got your finances in order."

"Our finances," Mimi said, "were never going to get in order. We need to start over. Again. Challenging but not impossible. We have one more act in us, don't we darling?"

"We didn't kill Babs," Jerry said, pointedly ignoring his wife. "We simply took advantage of a situation. That's how we've made a fortune throughout the years. Several, actually. Taking advantage of situations. Staying nimble."

"Did you kill Martin Samuel?" I asked quietly.

"Martin, dear Martin," Mimi said. She got up and walked over to the kitchen area, opening the cabinet underneath the sink. She pulled out a bottle and set it down on the table by her seat. "He's the ghost that haunts us all, don't you agree, darling?"

"Please be quiet, Mimi," Jerry said. "Sully doesn't need to know everything—"

"She may as well," Mimi said. She unscrewed the top off the bottle and took a deep swig. "Sully knows the worst of what we've done, or she's guessing it, from the look on her face. I won't have poor Martin's blood on my hands. It's bad enough I see his face every time I close my eyes these days. Staying on this boat has been a nightmare."

"Darling—"

"True confession time, Sully," Mimi said, ignoring her husband. She poured a healthy shot into her tea cup. "Want some bourbon? No? Well, you're welcome to it if you change your mind. I've got nothing better to do. Jerry won't even let me go online just in case somebody's watching us—"

"Not just in case," Jerry said. "Feds are all over the place. The only safe haven we have is this boat, mostly because no one knew it was here and they didn't know to bug it."

"So paranoid, my love," Mimi said. "But probably with good reason." She took a sip of tea and added more booze.

"Sully doesn't need to—"

"We decided to go down to the islands, take a little sailing vacation, do a little business," Mimi said. "We were working on some banking paperwork with our friend Fred. We all agreed to be in the same room together, so that everyone would be complicit if anything happened."

"We all?" I asked.

"Hal, Martin, Fred, Jerry, me. Terry Holmes tried to come down but he couldn't get away. He sent us his proxy instead."

"Babs was there," I said.

"She wasn't part of the deal," Jerry said.

"So Babs didn't know what was going on?" I asked.

Jerry sighed and watched his wife as she closed her eyes to better enjoy her tea. "No, Babs didn't know," he said. "Hal wanted to keep her out of it. So did Martin, for that matter. There seemed to be a complicated relationship there, don't you agree, darling?" he asked Mimi.

"Woo boy, that's one way to put it," Mimi said.

"That night, Hal and Martin began to bicker," Jerry said. "Martin got up and took a swing at Hal—"

"Hal was surprisingly limber, don't you think? He just jumped back, out of the way," Mimi said.

"Martin lost his footing and hit his head," Jerry said.

"He hit it there, right there, on that corner of the table, right under your elbow. Probably if you look really closely you can see part of Martin's skull in the wood," Mimi said.

I lifted my arm up and hugged it close to my body.

"We cleaned it," Jerry said. "God knows, we cleaned it. Anyway, we broke mooring and motored out to deeper waters. We were afraid Babs would wake up, so at one point Mimi went down and gave her half a sleeping pill. We motored out and met a friend of Fred's, who took poor Martin, his suitcase, a pile of cash, and our lifeboat. From what I understand, the idea was to take him farther out to sea, sink the boat, and let the sharks do what sharks do. If anything was found, it would look like Martin got turned around when he left the boat."

Mimi poured some more bourbon into her cup and handed it to Jerry. He took a long swig and handed it back to her.

"We got back into the harbor," Jerry said, "but somebody else had parked at our mooring. We took another one close by."

"Martin dying a year ago—the timing couldn't have been worse," Mimi said. "We thought we convinced people he'd taken a runner, but then Babs started to stir it all up again." She made a stirring gesture, tossing tea all over the cabin. "There's nothing more pious than a reformed drinker on a crusade. She'd been causing no end of trouble lately."

"So you killed her?" I said quietly.

"No, we didn't," Jerry said. He looked me right in the eyes and didn't blink. Was he telling the truth?

"Are you going to kill me?" I asked. "Because I've got to say, Jerry, that gun is making me nervous."

Jerry looked at me again, and looked down at the gun. He blinked a couple of times. I suspected the gun was making him nervous as well. Something in me made me doubt that it was even loaded, but in this small space I wasn't about to risk finding out.

"No. What we'll do is tie you up, leave you on the boat," Mimi said.

"We'll need to move up our travel arrangements, but that's easily done," Jerry said. "Tomorrow or the next day, we'll get a message to the authorities letting them know where you are. Hopefully you'll survive the cold, though I'm sorry to say we'll have to turn off the heat on the boat. It isn't safe to leave it on while we're not here."

"Just like you did with Gus," I said. "Hopefully you won't bash me as hard on the side of the head. We're not sure he's going to recover from that."

"Like Gus? What are you talking about?" Jerry asked. He looked genuinely surprised.

I didn't have a chance to ask him another question, because at that moment the hatch opened with a bang and a hand holding a gun pushed its way down, followed quickly by a shoulder and then a police officer's head.

"Freeze, don't even think about moving," the officer barked.

Jerry dropped the gun on the table and put his hands up.

"The body was Babs Allyn?" Toni asked for the third time. I was sitting in the back seat of her car. She and John were sitting in the front seat, both twisted around to see me while I told them my story one more time. The Cunninghams were on their way downtown, but Toni and John were in no rush. They knew the Cunninghams would lawyer up quickly. Plus, all three of us knew that John and Toni would have to wait in line to be able to question them.

"It was Babs. Somebody thought it was Mimi. She'd accidently taken Mimi's coat."

"Or so they say," John said. "Maybe they gave Babs Mimi's coat on purpose?"

"Maybe?" I said. The story didn't hold together for me yet, but I wasn't sure why.

"I still don't understand how the mistake didn't get caught," Toni said. "This day and age, seems like something that would get double and triple checked."

"You'd think," I said. "But I bet the Cunninghams had ways of slowing down regular processes. You both know that rich people have a different justice system than the rest of us. Wouldn't be the first time corners got cut, or some clerk got enough money to buy a new car, seemingly out of the blue. Plus, the husband confirmed the death. Who would doubt him?"

"Heads will still roll," John said.

"I have no doubt, and I'm not making excuses. The cause of death seemed pretty cut and dry, though. And Jerry had an alibi."

"All of that is going to have to be checked again," Toni said.

"Of course," I said. "Jerry did mention that her face had been disfigured in the attack—"

"Disfigured is one word for it," John said. "Thankfully, it was post-mortem. There was a lot of anger behind that."

"What did the Cunninghams have against Babs?" Toni asked.

"They said they didn't do it," I said. I told them about the conversation we'd had, leaving nothing out.

"Do you believe them?" John asked.

"I do. I believe that they're con artists and maybe sociopaths, but I don't believe they're murderers."

"The officer who found you said that Jerry Cunningham had a gun trained on you—" Toni said.

"I doubt he was going to use it. Maybe he would've. There was desperation in the air."

"I don't suppose you asked them about Kate's death?" Toni said.

"No, I didn't." I rubbed my hands together to warm them up. "Interesting, with Mimi alive, it puts a new light on that, doesn't it? I wonder if Kate knew Mimi was alive. Would she blackmail them?" I asked.

"From what we're finding out," John said, "I wouldn't put it past her."

"Maybe they wouldn't do the deed themselves, but perhaps they'd hire someone to kill Kate?" I said.

"The same exact way Mimi, I mean Babs, was killed?" Toni added.

"Hey," John said, "she doesn't need to know—"

"Shut up, John," Toni said. "You know she's going to keep thinking. Might as well make sure she's on the right track. Both deaths caused by strangulation, garroted with a scarf. Done from behind."

"Were the scarves similar?" I asked.

"Possibly singular: *scarf*," Toni said. "The scarf that killed Mimi—sorry, Babs—appears to be the same one that was left by Kate's body. We're waiting for more tests to confirm that."

"So, same killer. Or someone trying to make us think it's the same killer and using a similar scarf. That indicates inside knowledge."

"Any luck with the sign-in log or cameras?"

"No. Turns out that Gus's office building has a lot of security gaps as far as seeing who comes in and out. It may be intentional, to give folks with offices privacy for some meetings," Toni said.

"By the way, we've kept a lid on the scarf details," John said.

"I'm sure you have," I said. "But let's not forget, Jerry Cunningham had enough juice to get folks to agree to a misidentification. The Cunninghams and their ilk have got some influence."

"That's going to be an ugly investigation," Toni said.

"I wonder, what did Kate know?" I asked. "For that matter, what did Gus know? Was Kate killed because of what she knew, or who she was threatening with what she knew?"

"From what your friend Eric is starting to uncover, Kate had her hand in the till," John said.

"Really?" I said. "It looks more and more like she was killed because she knew too much."

"About Jerry? You just said you don't think he killed Babs."

"But maybe Jerry killed Kate," I said. "Maybe Mimi killed Babs, and killing Kate was an attempt at misdirection?"

"Once Gus wakes up, we'll be able to get some more answers," Toni said. "Yeesh, this is a mess. We're going to have to go back and rethink the entire investigation."

"You stay out of it," John said, looking right at me.

"I'm out of it," I said. "From here on out I'm focusing on theater. But if the Cunninghams did do it? Makes a certain kind of sense. I just didn't get the feeling that Jerry could... oh, never mind. I'm tired. Is it okay with you if I head home?" I asked Toni.

"Stay available. Don't tell anyone about Mimi or Babs, all right?" Toni said.

"I won't, I promise," I said. "Your news to share." I knew that sharing the news would be another way Toni and John would make sense of what had happened, by measuring reactions. I didn't want to take that tool away from them.

"You up to driving or you want a ride?" Toni asked.

"What are we, a taxi service?" John said.

"I'm okay to drive. It's not that far. I'll talk to you tomorrow," I said. I looked down at my cell phone. It was just past midnight. "I mean, later today."

· Twenty-One ·

I was bone-weary but my brain was whirring. I called the hospital to check on Gus and was told that he was still in his coma. I told them I'd be by in the morning. Even if he was still in a coma, it would do him good to hear my voice. I realized someone needed to tell him about Kate when he woke up, and hoped I would be there to do it. I'd hate for it to come from John Engel.

There was a text waiting for me. *You okay?* It was from Jack Megan. I wasn't about to tell him that Babs was dead in a text. I'd let the cops tell him about his client. I'd be following up with him sooner rather than later. He deserved to hear part of the story from me at some point.

Heading home. Check in with Toni Vestri. She has news.

You can't tell me?

Cop news to tell. Need her number?

Got it. Will touch base tomorrow.

Do that, I texted back.

I drove slowly. I was exhausted. The streets were quiet, but the bars were starting to let out so there was a hum of activity. I did a loop around the neighborhood, hoping for a parking space. I lucked out and found one up the hill about a block away from the townhouse. I'd need to wake up early to move the car so I wouldn't get a ticket, but at that point, I didn't care.

I was gathering my things, and a text came in from Toni. *They lawyered up. Wondering if Babs was mistaken identity, or intended? Will leave you to ponder that tonight. Talk in the a.m. Heading home.*

Toni had a point. We'd all been assuming that Mimi Cunningham was the intended target, obviously for good reasons. I hadn't really shifted from that, but now? What if Babs was the target? The idea of Babs being strangled in the park, feet away from where I was having dinner, was horrifying. Poor Babs. If only I'd gone after her or Gus had put her in a cab. I shook myself. That thinking wouldn't do any good.

Shifting my thinking, considering that maybe Babs was the intended target, changed the whole case for me. Murder itself was terrible, and violent. But strangulation took passion and intent. It wasn't a quick or easy way to kill someone. Over the years I'd found that incredible passion could tip to violence more often than I like to think about. I didn't know if it was better to believe that Babs had been killed on purpose or by mistaken identity.

Suddenly Holly flashed through my mind. Someone needed to tell her about Babs. I texted Toni and asked her if it was public yet.

Not yet. Morning. Just heard from Jack. Told him I'd call him first thing.

I want to be around when you tell Holly, I texted back.

Will do, was the return text. There were a lot of people who are going to be affected by Babs's death. Arguably, more than had been affected by Mimi's death. Babs's life intersected many, including mine, and I had no doubt she would be missed.

The weight of her death hit me suddenly, and I sat for a minute and wept for her. I wouldn't tell anyone else what had happened until Toni gave me the okay, but it was a heavy secret to keep. I really hoped no one was home, and I could just go to bed.

I dried my eyes and rewrapped my scarf around my neck. The watch cap was still on my head. Probably for the best, since taking it off would be a static fright show of curls.

I locked the car and double-checked that I'd actually done it. I was so tired. Then the names started coming to me. Holly. Hal. The Cunninghams. Emma. Gus. Eric. I went through the mental Rolodex of my head, trying to think about who would want Babs dead, and why. I thought back to the night of the reception and how angry she'd been at everybody, including Hal. And how out of sorts Hal had been.

Hal. Hal had something to do with every aspect of the case, no matter which way you looked at it. Hal? I thought the world of Hal. Everyone did. But in the last two hours I'd found out that he'd been doing illegal business with the Cunninghams and helped to cover up Martin's death. I wondered if Babs had figured out part, or all, of that story. Did Jack Megan tell her something that triggered a memory? I couldn't imagine how Babs must have felt. Especially if she blamed Hal. Lying from your partner was a particular type of betrayal.

Hal. Whenever we were trying to figure out who was doing what, he'd never been on the list for long. But now? Now his wife was dead. And like it or not, husbands were always on the top of the suspect list. Did he deserve to be there? What about Holly? Had she snapped for some reason? Had Mimi lost it?

I walked down the hill a block and then got my bearings. I looked around. If I took a left I could get in the alley gate and go up the back way. Avoiding the granite steps seemed like a good idea. Everything was icing over and the sidewalks were slippery.

I hoped Eric was awake. I wanted to talk to someone. I could trust him with everything, including all the secrets of the night. I let myself in the back door and made my way up the back staircase. A half a flight, Amelia's apartment. Three more staircases, Eric's apartment. Max was standing on the back staircase, looking at me. The back door was slightly ajar and I was about to call out when Max head-butted my calf.

"What's up, guy?" I said softly. "You okay?" Max buried his head into my hand and then stepped aside to let me pass. I moved slowly into the room. The streetlights cast enough of a glow that I could make out a figure standing at the kitchen table sweeping everything into a bag, including my laptop. I flipped on the light switch and Hal Maxwell looked up, startled.

"What are you doing?" I was so surprised to see him I was frozen in place. Hal was too. I moved into the room, but Hal reacted more quickly than I did. He grabbed the bag and started running toward the front hall.

I started to run after him. I moved toward the kitchen table but saw a body lying on the floor. Eric. Oh no. Not Eric. I knelt beside him and checked his pulse. He groaned softly and moved. He was alive. I forced myself to stand up. I needed to get Hal.

"Stop!" I screamed. "Somebody, stop Hal!" Maybe Stewart was up. Where was Emma? I ran out the front door and hustled down the stairs. My knees were killing me, but I kept pushing. I couldn't let him get out. I was three steps from the bottom landing and he was fumbling with the locks on the front door. I was just about to leap the distance between us when the door swung open. Hal stepped aside just in time to avoid being clipped by it. Emma stepped into the foyer. Hal grabbed the back of her coat and pulled her to him. He grabbed her neck in a chokehold. The front door slammed shut in the tussle.

"Nobody moves," Hal said. "I'll kill her, I swear I will."

"Nobody's moving, Hal. Please don't hurt Emma," I said.

"I never meant to hurt anyone—" he began.

"Of course you didn't," I said. "I know how much you loved Babs."

"Babs? Babs is in Vermont. I told you that already. You believed me, right?" Hal's eyes were wide, and his arm tightened around Emma's throat. She started to make noises that didn't sound good. I lowered my voice, and spoke gently.

"Hal, I found Mimi Cunningham tonight."

"You found Mimi Cunningham?" He loosened his grip a bit. "Where was she? I've been looking everywhere for her."

"You should have asked Jerry," I said. "She was hiding out on their boat. You know it's up in Boston again, right?" Hal shook his head. "It's in a slip in Charlestown. Nice boat, but Mimi seemed a little stir-crazy. She was surprised to see me."

"Jerry said he was leaving tonight but I didn't think he'd be leaving by sea. Bastard."

"She and Jerry are down at the police station," I said. "It's unraveling, Hal. But people don't think you did it, not yet. Let Emma go, don't make it worse." I took a step down. One more step to go and then I'd be on the same level as him.

"Make it worse? How could it be worse?" Hal said. "If only Babs hadn't pushed it that night. If only she had trusted me, like I asked her to. But no, she wanted to reopen the case of Martin's disappearance. That would've ruined everything—"

"Hal, let go of Emma—"

"She was going to leave me, you know that, Sully? Of course you do, everyone does. But you know what she told me that night? She told me that she and Martin had been having an affair, for years. That it was him she really loved. Him."

"You had no idea?" I took the final step down, careful to keep my face in a neutral, sympathetic pose. I didn't look at Emma. I kept eye contact with Hal. I sensed a growing desperation in him.

"None. Not until that night. You have to believe me, I never meant—"

"I know you didn't. Hal, let Emma go. Come on, you can do it."

As if in a trance, Hal tightened his grip. Emma was turning a shade of blue. I was tired and my brain wasn't working. *Focus, Sully. Focus.* I needed to figure out what to do. I inched slowly toward Hal without looking away. He needed to trust me, and to let go. I needed to convince him of that. Rational Hal was gone. *Focus, Sully, focus.*

"Gus put it together, of course," Hal said. "Damn him and his double-checking on every little detail. The investigator in him just couldn't let it go. He made a couple of phone calls and learned about the identification Jerry did and how it wasn't up to procedure. He already mistrusted the Cunninghams, and so he started to put it all together. He called me and told me he thought Mimi was alive. I played along, suggested we take a trip down the Cape, since surely she was there? I picked him up, kept him talking so he didn't have a chance to text you, Sully. We got to the Cape in no time." Hal was looking right at me, and I forced myself to hold his gaze. "The Cunninghams had already made everyone believe it was Mimi, to buy us more time to dig out of this hole. They had no idea I—they'd never believe Hal, good old Hal, could have killed Babs. I went along with Jerry's plan. It was a good one. We could have done it too. I thought we had a chance, especially once I got Gus out of the picture. But then Kate got greedy."

"What do you mean?"

"Kate was more than happy to take money from every pot available. She was part of it from the beginning. All of it. I don't feel bad about Kate. I should, but I don't. She was a terrible person."

"What did she do?" I asked. I noticed when Hal kept talking he loosened his grip. Until I got close enough to tackle him, I needed to keep him talking.

"She actually tried to blackmail me. Can you believe it?"

"She knew what you'd done to Babs?" I asked. I thought better of my question right away, hoping it wouldn't push a button, but Hal was too far gone for that.

"No, she had no idea about Babs. She knew about the money, the laundering. She threatened to tell Gus unless we met her terms. Of course, it ends up that if you look at some of the accounts, she was scraping a little bit off the top the whole time. Bitch. I hate to speak ill of the dead, but really, what did she think would happen? She called me because she thought I was the safe choice, that Jerry was dangerous. Little did she know. I had nothing to lose, not anymore." Hal leaned up against the wall beside the front door. He loosened his grip on Emma but not enough for her to fight him off. Having him leaning made it tougher to topple him over. Emma was still struggling for breath, but Hal was oblivious to her.

"I called Jerry about the files, told him I'd go to the authorities unless he stayed in town and helped me clean things up," Hal continued. "Jerry called me a loose cannon earlier today. Damn right I'm a loose cannon. They needed to help me get away. But then they deleted all the files. That's why I came over here, to get proof. To get something that would keep Jerry Cunningham off my back, make him help me get away. I need to get away."

I heard the voices of Stewart and Harry out on the stoop. They were laughing and sounded a bit drunk. Hal looked over his shoulder at the front door and stepped forward while they were fumbling with the lock. The door swung open hard, catching Hal on the shoulder. He pushed Emma away. I rushed forward and caught her before she fell.

"Don't let him go," I said to the boys as Hal try to rush out the door in between them. They both stepped in to block him and pushed him backward. He fell back against the staircase. I heard the breath knock out of him as he slumped down. He was still awake but wasn't moving. Yet.

"Harry, go upstairs. Eric's hurt. Stewart, call 911. Tell them to call Toni Vestri. And whatever you do, don't let Hal leave. He's murdered two people and just tried to kill Emma."

∞

The police were at the townhouse until four o'clock in the morning, asking questions and taking prints. Harry went to the hospital with Eric, who was released around the same time the police left. Toni told me she'd be in touch and let us know when our statements were ready to be signed. For now, Hal was talking. A lot. At one point I reminded him to call a lawyer. I didn't want the case to fall apart on a technicality.

I went into bed shortly after the police left. I was surprised that I fell asleep right away. And slept straight through. When I woke up at nine I put on a sweatshirt and walked out into the kitchen area. Everyone, including Max, was gone. There was a note on the table instructing me to go upstairs to Emma's apartment. I went up the back stairs and let myself in. Max was happily sitting on Eric's lap. Eric was leaning back and looked very pale.

"How you doing?" I asked. I leaned over and gave him a kiss on his temple. "Shouldn't you be resting?"

"I am resting. I have a wicked headache, but coffee will help that. As long as Harry makes it, not Emma."

"That's enough out of you," Emma said. "I'm trying to host a brunch here. I tried with the coffee, I really did."

"Making good coffee is a skill Harry excels at," I said. I sniffed the air but only smelled coffee. "Did you say something about brunch?"

"On its way," Emma replied. "I ordered locks, bagels, blintzes, pastries, and a bunch of other stuff from a deli over in Kendall

Square. Should be here any minute. Stewart drove your car over to get it—"

"My car isn't in the garage—"

"You told us where it was last night, don't you remember?"

"No, I don't remember much."

"Well, Harry's making fresh coffee. I'm going to sit."

She took a seat at the table. I sat down next to Eric on the bench and patted my lap. Max gave me a look and closed his eyes again. "I could never make coffee as well as Gus could," I said. "I sometimes wish I'd made him show me how before I signed the divorce papers. Speaking of which—"

"He's fine," Emma said. "I called the hospital and checked on him a few minutes ago. Sully, you want some of my bad coffee or to wait for Harry's good coffee?"

"I'll start with the bad. Caffeine is caffeine. Have you all been up for a long time?"

"About a half hour or so," Emma said. "I texted Harry and told him to come up here for breakfast. Your place is kind of a mess. You think the police will need to come back again?"

"I doubt it, but I'll call Toni later to double check. Emma how are you feeling? I wish you'd gone to the doctors last night."

"Just bruised, I feel fine." Her voice sounded a little raspy, and there were some bruises around her throat. But I understood her wanting to stay close to her little brother, especially after all they've been through these last few months.

"So, Eric, what happened last night? You up to talking about it?" I said.

"Sure. I spent the day looking at the numbers, texting back and forth with Emma, making copies of things, answering Toni's questions when she emailed them. It was close to midnight and someone knocked on the front door. I assumed it was Stewart or Dimitri, maybe they'd forgotten their key. Harry had already texted me that he was going out for a drink. Asked me if I wanted to come, but I'd said no. Anyway, Hal was at the front door. He started telling me about needing a backup sent to him. He wasn't making much sense. I told him I needed to text Toni, make sure that was okay. My phone was back up in the apartment, so Hal followed me upstairs. The next I knew, Harry was leaning over me."

"Finding you like that scared me to death," I said, patting his knee. "I was so relieved when you moved."

"I'm fine. It's only a bump on the head."

"There's a lot of that going around," I said. "Gus wasn't so lucky."

Eric reached over and squeezed my hand. He held on, and I was grateful for the comfort.

"So, Sully, spill," Emma said. "Start with finding Mimi Cunningham—"

"Oh no, no, no," Eric said. "Start with finding Gus—"

"You're both wrong," Harry said, bringing in a fresh pot of coffee. He topped mine off and the aroma hit my nostrils. Heaven. "You've got to start from this whole money thing that Eric's been trying to explain to me. Last I remember, we sent you and Emma down to the Cape on a quick trip to pick up sailcloth. Next thing we know, you've solved two murders, prevented another one, and broke open a con game the likes of which we haven't seen around here for a long time."

"You may as well make another pot of coffee, Harry," I said. "This is going to be a long story."

· Twenty-Two ·

"It was really all right?" Dimitri asked for the fourth time.

It was opening night of *Romeo and Juliet* and we were slowly making our way out of the theater. Dimitri had stopped in the aisle and was waiting intently for my answer.

"Dimitri, it was more than all right. It was terrific. I mean it. Even if I didn't know all you'd gone through to get here, I would have been impressed. But considering what you had to deal with? Amazing."

"Not as good as our *Romeo and Juliet* at the Cliffside?" he asked. We moved toward the lobby, where the opening night party was being held.

I hesitated before answering, but then decided the truth needed to win out on this one. "No, not as good. But honestly? I don't think I'll ever see a *Romeo and Juliet* as good as that one. That was something. But this one was great. You gave it a different lens, different perspective. You didn't do your *Romeo and Juliet* again—you rediscovered it in a new way."

"It *is* quite a company. It was an honor to work with these actors. Bringing Stewart Tracy in was a stroke of genius, of course. Harry's a wonderful Romeo. Cassandra did brilliant things with the costumes, and the set was saved. I think what really brought it together, though, was the tragedy of Babs's death. Everyone knew this was part of her legacy, the last show she worked on."

I looked over at Holly Samuel. She was wearing all black, less for dramatic effect and more because she was in deep mourning. She was so young, and had borne so much tragedy already. But she seemed to be holding up. The board was planning on keeping her in place, and had her on the search committee for the new managing director of the theater. They had offered me the job, and I told them I would think about it. But I never even considered taking it. I didn't want to move back to Boston. Trevorton was my home.

"Is that your ex-husband? With Emma?" Dimitri asked. A waiter came by and Dimitri took two glasses of champagne, handing one to me.

"Yes it is. I'm glad he was able to make it. He's only been out of the hospital for a few days."

"That must have been tough, losing his girlfriend in that terrible way. Tragic. I hope the play didn't resonate too much for him."

"Well," I said, trying my best to take any snarky tone out of my voice, "it turns out that she was hardly a Juliet. More of a Lady Macbeth. She'd been playing both sides against the middle for a while, cutting side deals, skimming off the top. She also wasn't immune to a little blackmail, which was her undoing. Of course, no one deserves to be murdered. But there's no doubt she was deeply complicit with the con that the Cunninghams were pulling."

"But Gus wasn't?" Dimitri asked. "That's hard to believe. Sorry, Sully, you know what I mean."

"It is, unless you know Gus. Gus and the Whitehalls were definitely not in this loop. It's going to take them all a while to sort this out, but I've no doubt that they will."

"It does seem like they've had more than their share of a hard time lately, doesn't it?" Dimitri asked. "So tell me, are you going to take the job?"

"What job?"

"Managing director. The board chair told me that they offered it to you right after they offered me the job as artistic director."

"Are you taking the job?"

"No, I'm happy at the Cliffside. We're growing, finally becoming what I wanted it to be. Of course, if you move on, I'd rather work with you—"

"Dimitri, that's the nicest thing you've ever said to me. No, I'm a Cliffside gal. At least for a while. I did tell them I would help them with their search and advise on operations while they were looking for staff."

"As did I," Dimitri said. "They have next season sketched out, and I made a couple of suggestions. Some new work. That play of Pat Gabridge's that we did last summer—"

"Great idea. It deserves a Boston premiere. So, we'll both help them get on their feet. Meanwhile, we plan the Cliffside summer season. Which, I'm happy to say, thanks to the Whitehalls tapping a few donors will for sure include building our new production center. Not as fancy as it will be eventually, but the shell of the building will be up and operational this summer."

Dimitri reached down, lifted me up in his arms, and gave me a hug of pure joy, twirling me around once before putting me down on my feet again. Champagne went flying, but he didn't care.

"That's wonderful!" he said. "Having the production center up and running will make it much easier to refill the wave machine every night, and make sure it's operational."

"Wave machine?"

"My dear Sully, we're doing *HMS Pinafore*. Surely you understood that we must create the sea for the audience. There must be waves."

"Of course, waves with water," I said. Tonight was not the time to discuss this in depth. I took a deep breath. "May the waves only be on the stage," I said, lifting my glass to him in a toast.

"Ha! Not unless our luck changes," Dimitri replied, clinking my glass back.

Acknowledgments

You write alone, but getting published takes a community. And what a community I have.

This series dovetails with my life as an arts administrator and teacher. I am so grateful to the New England arts community for their inspiration, creativity, dedication, and commitment. Being part of this community has been one of the great blessings of my life.

I'm especially grateful to StageSource, the service organization for the theater community. StageSource bookended a phase of my arts management career and is the support of so many artists and organizations.

Thank you to Marcia Bartusiak for bidding on naming a character at the Lyric Stage Company's benefit auction.

Thank you to Terri Bischoff, Sandy Sullivan, Kevin Brown, and the rest of the Midnight Ink team. This series has a place in my heart and I will be forever grateful to all of you for publishing it.

I blog on The Wicked Authors with five amazing women—Jessie Crocket, Edith Maxwell, Sherry Harris, Barbara Ross, and Liz Mugavero. They are talented writers, tremendous cheerleaders, and wonderful friends. Thank you all. Thank you to my agent, John Talbot. We're on this journey together, and his support and guidance are invaluable. Thank you to Sisters in Crime and Mystery Writers of America for providing ongoing support of my writing career.

And thank you to my friends and family for their love and support. My parents, Paul and Cindy Hennrikus; my sisters, Kristen Spence and Caroline Lentz; my brothers-in-law, Bryan Spence and Glenn Lentz; my nieces and nephews, Emma, Evan, Chase, Mallory, Becca, Tori, Harrison, and Alex; and my theater friends who cheer me on this writing path with such joy. A special thanks to Jason Allen-Forrest and Courtney O'Connor for being great sounding boards. This list could be longer than the book itself. I am a very lucky woman.

© Meg Manion

About the Author

J. A. Hennrikus writes the Theater Cop series for Midnight Ink. As Julia Henry, she writes the Garden Squad series for Kensington. She also wrote the Agatha-nominated Clock Shop mystery series for Berkley Prime Crime. Julie blogs with The Wicked Authors (WickedAuthors.com) and is a member of Sisters in Crime and Mystery Writers of America. She is an arts administrator and teacher who runs Your Ladders (Your Ladders.com), an online business school for performing artists.

Instagram: @JHAuthors
Twitter: @JHAuthors
Facebook: JHAuthors
www.JHAuthors.com